ONCE BURNED

ANCHOR POINT

L.A. WITT

RIPTIDE
PUBLISHING

Riptide Publishing
PO Box 1537
Burnsville, NC 28714
www.riptidepublishing.com

Once Burned

Cover art: L.C. Chase, lcchase.com/design.htm
Editor: Chris Muldoon
Layout: L.C. Chase, lcchase.com/design.htm

ISBN: 978-1-62649-749-8

First edition
April, 2018

Also available in ebook:
ISBN: 978-1-62649-748-1

ONCE BURNED

ANCHOR POINT

L.A. WITT

RIPTIDE
PUBLISHING

To those who served, fought, and were sent away.

TABLE OF CONTENTS

CHAPTER 1
MARK

I'm done.

I looked around the living room of my rental house.

I'm . . . unpacked. Moved in. Done.

Boxes? Gone. Furniture? Arranged. Pictures? Hung. Electronics? Connected.

There was even a sad little bachelor Christmas tree in the corner. It was barely November, but I'd thought the tree might make things less depressing. Now I wasn't so sure. It was staying, though. At least until the thought of making *one more fucking change* to this house didn't make me want to burn the whole place to the ground.

For tonight, everything was done. I was settled in.

Exhaling, I dropped onto the La-Z-Boy recliner. I pressed my elbow into the armrest and stared out the bay window that overlooked the Pacific. The sun was going down, and the ocean sparkled under the changing colors of the sky. The view had been one of the selling points of the house. Very nearly one of the deal breakers too—I had an unobstructed view of the ocean through the bay window, but if I went out on the deck and looked north, I could see more.

NAS Adams was on the other end of town, but since my house was up on a hill, I could see the base from here. The ships, anyway. There was another hill obscuring most of the buildings. The bridges of the largest ships were visible where they were moored to the piers in the man-made harbor. At night, if it was clear enough, I could even see the hull numbers glowing in the distance.

Including the blinding white *9*. The USS *Fort Stevens*. My ship.

That view had almost been enough to make me pass on the house. This was supposed to be my oasis from work, not a place where it lurked right outside. Who the hell wants to look out the window and see their job?

As long as I stayed inside, though, I could watch the sunset and not have to think about all the gunmetal gray in the distance.

I wasn't even supposed to be here. Not in Oregon. Not on that ship. Not in this house. I was *supposed* to be on the downhill slide to retirement. Less than three months ago, I'd been getting ready to drop the paperwork to start the year-long retirement process. Come July, after twenty years—twenty-four if you counted my time in ROTC—I would have been done.

Then I'd unexpectedly been promoted to captain, and a call had come in telling me that if I wanted them, there were orders for an executive officer position. If I did want them, I had to agree to them right then and there, and I'd need to report in eight weeks.

Any other time in my career, I might've at least hesitated. I'd taken some slam orders before, and they were a headache and a half. Moving across the country on eight weeks' notice was enough to make anyone go gray.

But the promotion and the call had come within days of my wife serving me divorce papers, so why the hell not? I'd said yes, the orders had gone through, and now I was the XO of the *Fort Stevens*, an amphib ship that home-ported at NAS Adams. I was moved in to my two-story rental house south of Anchor Point, fully three thousand miles away from everything that had been home for the last ten years. Everything I still owned was unboxed except the gold band I'd worn for almost nineteen years. That tiny box, currently shoved in the back of my sock drawer, would stay sealed for a while.

I was here. I was settled. I was . . .

Restless. What now? I'd forgotten what downtime was.

The last few months had been a blur of upheaval, and now that things were starting to quiet down, I wasn't sure what to do with myself. Since early September, every waking hour—and quite a few of the sleeping ones—had been occupied with the divorce and my new orders. And now that was all more or less finished. The divorce was in the works. My ex-wife was handling the sale of our house in Norfolk. I'd finished checking in aboard the ship a week ago. There really wasn't much left for me to actually *do* except show up and do my job. It was all back to business as usual. Same shit, different ship.

So ... now what?

I drummed my fingers on the armrest of the La-Z-Boy, the tap of fingertips on leather seeming to echo in my otherwise silent living room. Maybe I needed to get *out* of this house and away from all the things I'd just finished painstakingly arranging. According to the clock on the end table, it was only 1845. Still early yet, and it was a Friday night, so it wasn't like I had to work tomorrow.

I picked up my phone and googled *Anchor Point*. A TripAdvisor page came up. That seemed like a decent place to start.

Restaurants. The pier. Some shops. Hotels. A maritime museum. A military museum. Typical tiny touristy town with—

I did a double take.

The High-&-Tight Gay Nightclub.

Oh, now that was an interesting possibility. The clientele would obviously be military, which was risky, but it also seemed to be the only game in town. Admittedly, I was tempted. How many years had it been since I'd touched a man? Not that I'd touched anyone in recent memory, but a man? *Long* time. I'd been thinking about it since I'd arrived in Oregon too. I had condoms and lube waiting by the bed and everything. Just had to actually connect with someone who'd be interested in using them with me.

Still, I couldn't help wondering if it was too soon.

Except *no*. No, it was definitely not too soon. Long overdue if nothing else. The ink was technically still wet on my divorce papers, but Angie and I both agreed our marriage had been over since well before she'd made it official. And now that I thought about it, going to a gay bar and maybe hooking up with a man sounded like the perfect way to break up this sudden monotony.

I saved the address in my phone, then went upstairs to get ready to go.

And I couldn't help grinning as I undressed to shower.

Because if I played my cards right, I just might get laid tonight.

I had second thoughts when I realized just how close the High-&-Tight was to NAS Adams. I'd known it catered to military, and I'd known it was near the base because of the map, but now that I was in the parking lot and could see the chain-link-and-razor-wire fence without squinting . . . Shit. It was *really* close.

Still in my idling car, gripping the wheel for dear life, I debated bailing. It was risky, going into a place like that. I hadn't been stationed here long enough to recognize faces, and accidentally hooking up with a junior enlisted guy who turned out to be under my command would be a career ender. I even had to be careful about dancing or flirting. One photo of me with my hand on the wrong man's ass, and I'd be having an awkward conversation with an admiral.

I released a long breath and let my hands slide off the steering wheel and into my lap. After a moment, I killed the engine. There was no reason to worry about getting nailed for an indiscretion unless I committed one, and I knew how to be discreet. As long as I made sure any guy I planned to hook up with was legal and—if military—not of a rank that would get me in trouble, I was fine. And for that matter, I hadn't been on the ship long enough for anyone to recognize me, let alone care if they got an incriminating picture of me. If I was going to do this, now was as good a time as any.

So, I went inside.

First things first, I needed a drink, so I moved through the thin crowd to the bar. Most guys were at or around the dance floor, or they were hanging out at tables and booths. A few hovered by the bar, some obviously intending to stay there while others left as soon as they had their drinks. I found a gap and leaned on the bar to wait my turn.

The bartender had his back turned, and he was leaning down to get something from a small fridge, and *oh, hello.*

Nice ass.

I felt myself blush and had no idea why. Two other guys were being conspicuous as fuck about checking out the bartender's tight, jean-clad ass, so why should I be embarrassed about doing the same?

Before I could think too deeply about it, the bartender stood and turned around, a couple of longnecks between his fingers, and holy *crap*, he was hot. Like *whoa.*

While he took care of the men who'd reached the bar ahead of me, I stared at him.

He had . . . not dark skin, but not pasty white like mine. It was November on the Oregon Coast, which had been stubbornly dark and overcast since I'd arrived, and he still looked sun-kissed. I suspected he was one of those guys who only had to step outside on a sunny day and he'd instantly tan to a rich, mouthwatering bronze.

His artfully messy dark hair was just long enough for a few strands to fall over his near-black eyes, and a thin beard lined his sharp jaw and framed his full lips. Not like a flawlessly manicured hipster beard, either. More like several days in a row of "meh, maybe I'll shave tomorrow." Why that made my spine tingle, I had no idea, but I didn't argue with it.

He had a short but deep scar dangerously close to his left eye, the silvery line standing out against his tanned skin, and another that nearly disappeared into his hair at the temple. There had to be a story there, and I decided immediately that I wanted to hear it. Not because I wanted to pry into things that weren't my business—there was just this sudden intense curiosity about him. He had my full and undivided attention, and I wanted him to do something with it.

He picked that moment to turn to me, stunning dark eyes fixed right on mine. He opened his mouth to speak, but then paused, and if I wasn't mistaken, gave me a conspicuous once-over. When our eyes met again, he asked, "What can I get you?" He had an accent I thought was . . . Mexican? Something that made his simple question sound lyrical and—

And he was still waiting for me to *answer* that question.

I cleared my throat. "Uh. Corona. Thanks."

He shot me a quick, friendly smile—did he blush, or was that my imagination?—and reached under the bar. I busied myself getting out my wallet and finding some cash so I didn't stare at his long fingers while he popped off the bottle cap. I found the money and glanced up just in time to see him thumb a lime wedge into the mouth of the bottle, and I had no idea why he looked right at me when he did it or why the whole picture made me hot all over.

I paid him and took my drink, and just like that, he was moving on to another customer, and I was standing there with a cold beer and a thumping heart.

I pressed the lime all the way down, then took a deep swallow to cool myself off. The zing of the citrus met my palate, and my mind's eye showed me the bartender sliding the lime wedge in, and it didn't matter if something like that should've been sexy or not. One look, and I'd gone completely stupid over him. At this rate, if I saw him do something normal, like wiping down the bar or ringing up a tab, I'd probably come in my pants.

Whoa, fuck. I really need to get laid tonight, don't I?

That was it. Of course it was. I was in a dry spell that had to be measured in months, and recently I'd been too busy with a cross-country move to take advantage of being single, and now my libido was *going* to get some attention.

I turned my back to the bar and faced the dance floor. That didn't help. All those gorgeous men in skintight clothes—and in a few cases, without shirts—moving to the beat of an up-tempo pop song I didn't recognize? Fuck. All they did was make me think of the hot bartender behind me and how much I wanted to see *him* dance like that.

Without thinking about it, I looked back at him, and . . . yeah. I wanted to see him dance. I wanted to see him naked.

What the hell?

I eyed the Corona in my hand. I was two swigs in and already zeroing in on someone. Damn, I'd expected to come in here and maybe proposition a stranger, but not *this* fast. Had he spiked my drink with something? Shifting my gaze back to him, I decided that, no, he hadn't spiked the Corona. He didn't need to.

Because *fuck.*

I'd come here hoping to find someone reasonably attractive for a roll in the hay. I was surrounded by hot men—I was vaguely aware of a few sexy bodies and gorgeous faces still registering in my peripheral vision—but I was laser focused on him. I'd never experienced that kind of attraction before. I'd done double takes. I'd ogled strangers. I'd moved pretty fast from first sight to first contact. But this? Standing here with just enough self-awareness to keep my mouth from falling open? This was new.

While he put a glass under the tap and filled it with beer, he glanced at me, and the subtle, knowing smirk told me *I* wasn't being subtle. I probably should have been embarrassed, getting busted shamelessly checking him out again, but I wasn't. In fact, the uptick of my pulse had nothing to do with embarrassment. More like an adrenaline rush because he was onto me, he knew I was into him, and he wasn't giving me a red or yellow light.

Game on, my speeding heart said.

I took another drink of Corona. It didn't do much to cool me down, but it was something to do.

The bartender continued working, and all the while, he kept stealing glances at me. Whenever he did, an asymmetrical little grin played at his lips and screwed with my equilibrium. I couldn't put my finger on exactly what it was that made him so different from the rest of the crowd or everyone I'd ever checked out before. I even tried scanning the room to see if my sex-deprived brain would zero in on someone else. Now and then, it did, but one glance back at the gorgeous bartender and I'd forget all about them. I decided it didn't matter why he stood out. He did, and I wanted him. End of story.

He effortlessly kept up with orders being shouted over the music. One after another, he handed over glasses filled with beer or colorful liquors. He took one order while he made change for the one before it, and craned his neck to hear the next one being shouted while he mixed what I thought was another Long Island Iced Tea.

At one point, he paused to brush some sweat off his forehead with the back of his wrist, but otherwise, he made it all look so easy.

He reached under the bar for some Budweiser bottles, and as he popped off the caps, he tossed his head to get a few damp strands of dark hair out of his face. God, that was sexy. Wasn't it? Or was I just that wrapped up in him? Fuck if I knew. But I hoped he'd do it again. Or maybe not. I didn't need to explain to Medical that I'd had a heart attack in a bar because this guy had tossed his hair one too many times.

The crowd waiting for drinks thinned. I hadn't realized how lightning fast his movements had been until the rush died down and he started mixing and pouring at a more normal pace.

And then, just like that, he was wiping his hands on a towel and coming straight toward me.

Oh shit. Am I supposed to say something? What do I—

"Another round?" He nodded toward the Corona in my hand.

"Um." I glanced down at the bottle. When had I emptied it? "Sure. Yeah."

He flashed another one of those knowing grins, then took a Corona from the fridge. Neither of us spoke while he uncapped it and slid a lime wedge into the top. He pushed the bottle toward me, and I paid him, and then . . .

He didn't move. He glanced to either side, probably making sure no one else was waiting, before looking at me again. "Your first time in here?"

I nodded. "Why? Am I that out of place?"

He laughed. I couldn't hear it over the music, but I could see the humor play out on his lips and the crinkling corners of his eyes, and it was enough to throw off my balance. Now that we were up close, I could see he wasn't some twentysomething kid. Not with those subtle lines on his face and flecks of silver in his stubble.

Like he isn't hot enough already.

Still grinning, he leaned his hands on the bar. "No, you don't seem out of place. I just haven't seen you before." He gestured at the crowd. "Work in a gay bar in a small town, you start recognizing regulars pretty fast."

"I guess you would." I chewed the inside of my cheek, heart thumping as I debated how ballsy I should be. Finally—fuck it. I pressed an elbow against the bar. "So if I told you I was new in town, you think you could give me some recommendations about stuff to do?"

He laughed again, still so softly I couldn't hear it over the music. His dark eyes sparkled as he leaned closer. "That your slick way of keeping me here to talk to you until you can convince me to go home with you?"

Damn, he was good.

"Maybe not as slick as I thought." I chuckled. "How about a different approach—any way I can talk you into a cup of coffee after you're off work?" My heart immediately sped up. Shit. I'd been out of the game for so long, I hadn't expected to be smooth at all, but now I was worried I'd committed some faux pas.

But he smiled, turning my insides to liquid. His voice was almost a purr as he said over the music, "Maybe you can, but you have to answer me something first."

I mirrored him, leaning in more so I could hear him. So I could almost imagine what his skin smelled like. What it tasted like. Oh God. Trying not to choke on my nerves, breath, spit, ghosts, or whatever else could come along and make me sound like an idiot, I said, "Yeah?"

He slowly ran his tongue along the inside of his bottom lip. "You active duty or retired?"

I blinked. "What makes you think I'm military at all?"

He rolled his eyes, but his tone and his smile were playful. "You think I can't tell who's military the second they walk through the front door?"

Well, I couldn't argue with that. I could spot service members at a glance from a hundred paces. Heart thumping, I said, "Active."

And I instantly regretted the answer, and even the truth behind it. Irrationally, I regretted my entire profession as the bartender sighed with palpable disappointment.

He shook his head and drew back a bit. "I don't do military."

"Not . . . You . . . Really?"

He shrugged apologetically. "Sorry." He opened his mouth like he was about to speak, but stopped as he glanced to his left. When he turned back to me with an even more apologetic look on his face, he said, "I need to help them."

Some guys had clustered near the bar and were watching him expectantly, so I stepped back to get out of their way. And to give that hot bartender some space. As much as I wanted to be persistent, what was the point? I knew a rejection when I heard it. He'd said no. Message received. I despised pushiness and wasn't about to be that way to him.

So while he poured drinks in between throwing a few more glances my way, I headed for the dance floor to search the crowd for someone who might say yes.

But I hoped the bartender would change his mind.

CHAPTER 2
DIEGO

As the guy moved toward the dance floor, he paused for a drink from the Corona bottle. For fuck's sake. I was here five nights a week watching guys drink from bottles and straws, and I'd seen so many guys sucking face on the dance floor or sucking dick in the bathroom that I barely even noticed anymore. Why the hell was my heart beating faster over his lips around the mouth of that Corona bottle?

And why the fuck did he pick that moment to lick his lips like that?

I jerked my gaze away and focused on my job. Enough ice? Enough clean glasses? Enough garnishes? The bottles in my well—did any of them need refilling? Would any of them look as hot in his mouth as—

What the fuck, Diego?

I shook myself and kept working. On autopilot, I mixed cocktails for some guys who'd obviously been pregaming. They were using the bar to stay upright, laughing at nothing, and could hardly enunciate their drink orders. They weren't quite to the point where I had to cut them off, but I doubted it would take more than two or three shots to get them there.

They were well on their way to shit-faced, and that worked to my advantage right then because my mind was only half-focused on the . . . whatever it was they'd ordered. Screwdrivers. Right. I reached into the well for the bottle of vodka and, while I did, stole a glance at the guy who'd been chatting me up a second ago.

And caught him watching me.

He quickly returned his attention to the dance floor, and I fought back a smile.

You think you're so smooth, but I saw you.

Men hit on bartenders all the time. It was nothing new. What better way to get a free drink than to flatter the shit out of the guy pouring it? Except I couldn't remember the last time someone had looked at me like that. Usually, if a customer was staring at me, I immediately started worrying he was with ICE or something. Not that anyone had ever come in here and asked to see my green card, but that didn't stop me from being paranoid.

This guy hadn't pinged me as an ICE agent or anything like that. He'd just . . . looked at me. Like there was no one else in the room.

There were other guys in the room, though, and I could pick out half a dozen who were watching him like he was watching me. The younger customers *loved* older guys. If a silver fox wandered in here, we'd pretty much start taking bets on how quickly some twentysomething would be tugging him toward the men's room. All he'd have to do was make eye contact, exchange a few flirty comments, and nod toward the back, and he'd have his dick down someone's throat in no time.

An image flashed through my mind of that man on his knees with *my* dick down *his* throat, and I shivered. And even though I knew it wouldn't help me focus, I cut my eyes toward him again.

He was a tall white guy, probably my age or maybe a little older. Most of the High-&-Tight's clientele was midtwenties or so. If I had to guess, I'd have said he was at *least* in his late thirties. Early forties, actually. Was that why he had my attention? Because he wasn't a kid like half the guys who came in here?

As he watched the other men dancing, I watched him. He didn't dress to show off or stand out. An open blue shirt over a snug white T-shirt. Jeans that weren't tight enough to give away if he dressed to the right or the left. He looked more like a guy who was here to unwind with a drink than someone who wanted some dick before the end of the night.

"Two whiskey sours," someone called over the music.

I shook myself and turned toward a guy with a military haircut and two swallows tattooed across his bare pecs. Instantly my mood darkened. Always did when I saw someone sporting that familiar ink.

"Two whiskey sours," I repeated through my teeth, and went to work.

A whiskey sour was easy. I could make it in my sleep.

Well, as long as I didn't have someone distracting me.

Come on. Focus. Get a fucking grip. Every time I worked here, I was surrounded by good-looking men. I was even hit on by them sometimes. So why the hell was this one screwing with my head enough to make me almost botch a whiskey goddamned sour?

I managed to make the drinks, though, and handed them over. The shirtless man with the swallow tattoos left, and before I moved on to the next customer, I let my gaze drift toward the dance floor again.

There he was. Right where I'd left him.

He picked just that moment to shift his weight, pulling my focus to the way his jeans sat perfectly on his ass. And to the way he stood—straight, shoulders back, but not like he had a stick up his ass. And how hot it would be to bend him over something.

Fuck. It hadn't even been that long since I'd been laid. Long enough I'd been browsing Grindr before I'd come to work today, but it wasn't like I hadn't seen another man's dick recently. I wasn't hard up for sex. So why the hell did I want him so bad?

Because I can't have him. Or at least shouldn't *have him.*

I bit my lip as I watched him. I'd turned him down, but I wasn't going to lie—the guy was tempting. Couple of inches taller than me. Shoulders a man could definitely grab on to for leverage. I was kind of afraid to talk to him because he might let it slip that he was a bottom, and then my self-control would be gone.

I tore my gaze away from him and tried—again—to focus on the next order.

Yeah, he was tempting, but no way. I was not giving in to that temptation. He was military, and I didn't do military. Which sort of limited my options in a military *town*, but oh well. It was a deal breaker and that was the end of it.

I let myself steal yet another glance. He had to be an officer. Probably a high-ranking one too. He was old enough he'd been in at least fifteen or twenty years, and the way he carried himself screamed someone with authority. I knew that look. The kind of guy who walked around like he *knew* he owned the place, so he didn't *have* to puff out his chest and strut to make sure everyone else knew it. He had that quiet confidence that made my mouth water.

Why did he have to be military?

Okay, so almost everybody who came in here was. It was a military-themed gay bar outside the fucking base gates in a tiny, isolated town. Who did I expect to show up? The Chicago Bulls?

Plus, if I was honest with myself, the military guys hadn't *always* been off-limits. For a while, I'd been fine with them for a one-night stand or the odd semi-regular fuck buddy. I just wouldn't date them. But after I'd let myself get too close to one, and wound up hurting over him? No more military dudes. And I stuck with that. Usually. My first instinct was always *Yeah no, not gonna happen*, but once in a while, if he was hot enough . . .

This guy *was* hot enough, so why the fuck was I hesitating with him? He was sexy. He was obviously interested. So what if he was Navy?

Between drink orders, I watched him getting cozy with another guy on the dance floor, and why the fuck was I jealous? *I'd* turned *him* down.

But the way he moved his hips when he danced . . . and that look in his eyes when he was flirting . . . and that flash of pink when he licked his lips . . .

Why was I so obsessed with this man's mouth?

Because he had full, dick-sucking lips. Because my gut said he knew how to kiss. Because I wanted to know how those straight, almost-perfect teeth felt on my shoulder.

Because I'd slept alone for the last three weeks and I was starting to get stir-crazy and he was fucking sexy so why the hell not?

I sighed. There was another military man who'd made my breath catch like this one had. Somehow I'd kept my shit together and pretended to be a consummate professional instead of a drooling idiot, but two times in my life, I'd met a man's eyes and nearly stumbled. This guy and my friend Dalton. I'd known immediately they were military, and I'd known immediately that I wanted them.

Dalton and I had barely lasted through the end of my shift before we were blowing each other in the back seat of his car. This hot officer . . . where would we have wound up tonight if I hadn't been such a coward?

I chewed the inside of my cheek as I watched him dance.

Everything I'd ever had with Dalton—the sex back then and the friendship now—had been worth breaking my rule. Ending our relationship, though? Backing away when I'd realized my heart was in deeper than it should have been?

That was the memory that had me refusing military men. It was why I was resisting the hell out of this new guy.

Except it was also the *same* memory that had me second-guessing that resistance. For the last few months, I'd been debating where I'd gone wrong with Dalton—by hooking up with him in the first place or by jumping ship when things had started looking serious. Since we'd broken up, I'd been twice as reluctant to get into bed with Navy guys, and twice as likely to regret not getting their phone number the next morning.

I searched the crowd for that hot officer, and found him in a matter of seconds. He'd sidled close to another guy, and they were leaning in to hear each other over the music. Grinning. Laughing. Holding eye contact for way too long.

I gritted my teeth. Jealous. I was fucking *jealous* because someone was flirting—and getting somewhere—with a man I'd turned down.

The fact that he was military was becoming less and less relevant. He was hot, he was here, and he'd been interested when he was at the bar. Now he was letting his shoulder brush against some jackass who needed to get the fuck out of my club.

I kept an eye on them just because I could. I kept working too, though, because I didn't want to add "too busy perving on customers" to the list of reasons for Hank to cut me loose. In between mixing drinks and ogling him, I looked over my station to make sure I had everything I needed. Turned out I was running low on ice, so I went into the back. Before I picked up the bucket, though, I stopped to rub the ache out of my knee. Or at least rub out some of the ache. It never stopped hurting completely, and it was always worse in the winter. Being on my feet for hours didn't help, so it was going to be sore as hell by the end of my shift. Fridays and Saturdays meant the best tips and the worst pain. Always did.

Carrying a bucket of ice didn't help. I had to grit my teeth the whole way back to my station. Didn't dare limp either. Soon as I started favoring the bad knee, the good one—well, the less bad one— would start hurting too. I'd ice them both when I got home tonight.

See? He wouldn't want you anyway.

I shoved that thought aside. It was a stupid habit I'd never shaken since I'd gotten hurt. The scars, the gimp knee—how attractive, right?

In reality, even the younger guys almost never had a problem making do when my shitty knee acted up. They'd just put me on my back and ride me. Would *this* guy put me on my back and ride me?

I shivered and almost dropped the bucket of ice. I was losing it tonight, wasn't I?

And I'd lose my job if I didn't pull my shit together.

At my station, I dumped the ice into the bin and got back to work.

A dozen or so drinks later, just when I'd started getting my head together, the hot guy appeared at my station again, a grin on his lips and an empty Corona in his hand. With a playful upward flick of his eyebrows, he held up the bottle. "Any chance I can bug you for another one?"

"Not bugging me." I reached under the bar. "It's my job."

As he looked through his wallet, I noticed there was a distinctive tan line on his left ring finger.

Well that changed the rules a bit.

Either he was married, in which case he was off-limits even if he was a civilian without a gag reflex, or he was divorced. Recently divorced. On the rebound.

I didn't do rebound relationships, but rebound sex? *Me gusta.*

Except—

Oh, fuck the military. I wanted him. I wanted to know what sounds he made when I had his bottom lip between my teeth, and I wanted to know if nails up his back at just the right moment would make him come, and . . . and if I kept going with that train of thought, I was going to have a very uncomfortable hard-on.

Screw it. I needed to un-reject him. I'd deal with him being military later. Right now, I just wanted him.

Except there was that tan line on his finger, and I needed to know how often he covered it up before this went *any* further. While

I popped the cap off his drink, I nodded at his hand. "Where's your ring?"

He looked down, then back at me. "In a drawer in my dresser." He inclined his head a little. "I just got divorced, if that's what you're asking."

I fought a grin. *Jackpot.* "Sorry to hear it." I handed him the drink. When he pushed a ten across the bar, I waved it away. "This one's on the house."

He blinked. "Really?"

"Well, on one condition." I winked and grabbed a pen from under the bar. I quickly scrawled my number on a napkin, then put that beside his Corona. "The beer's free as long as you take this."

"What is—" He picked it up. "Is this your number?"

"Only one way to find out." I grinned and hoped my nerves weren't showing.

He blinked. "I thought you weren't into military men."

I was as conspicuous as possible about looking him up and down. When our eyes met again, I said, "I feel like breaking that rule tonight."

His lips parted, and I thought he shivered. "Oh yeah?"

"Uh-huh."

He glanced at the number, then back at me. "So, if I put this in my phone, what name should I put it under?"

"Diego."

He took out his phone, entered my name and number, then slipped both the phone and napkin into his pocket. He was grinning when he looked at me again. "Got it." Extending his hand across the bar, he added, "I'm Mark, by the way."

"Mark," I said as I shook his hand, like I needed to commit his name to memory. "So, Mark . . . I'm not off until after closing, but if you want to hang around . . ." I fought the urge to gulp nervously. As long as one of us thought I was calm and cool, we were good. "The after-party might be worth the wait."

His eyes lit up. Dios *mío*, he was pretty. Way too pretty for me to be getting anywhere near since he was a military guy, but I'd already asked, and he was already saying, "Yeah. Sure."

"You won't get bored hanging out here?"

He smiled, and his gaze slid up and down my body. "No. I don't think getting bored will be a problem."

CHAPTER 3
MARK

Diego and I couldn't make much conversation after that. The club was too loud and he was too busy. So, we kept it to flirtatious glances and suggestive comments. That was fine by me. I knew everything I needed to know—he was either gay or bi, he was into me, and he was game to hook up after closing.

At last call, we exchanged one last sultry look—holy fuck, those eyes—and I left. He'd asked me to wait for him at a diner around the corner, and it only took a minute to find the place. The night was getting seriously fucking cold, and I wanted us to be able to make a quick escape when he caught up with me, but I'd also had a few drinks in pretty rapid succession, so I walked the block or so to the diner.

A handwritten sign on the diner's door confirmed they were open twenty-four hours, so I went inside. Sleigh bells jingled so loud they could probably be heard from the base, and a waitress with dark circles under her eyes smiled sleepily.

"Just one?" she asked.

"Uh, no. Two. I'm waiting for someone." Right then, I noticed the sign that said they wouldn't seat people until the whole party had arrived. "Oh. I can wait if—"

"It's okay. We ain't all that busy this time of night." She pulled two ragged laminated menus from the pocket beside the register and nodded sharply for me to follow her.

I didn't know if we even needed menus. From the way Diego and I had been looking at each other, dinner or coffee or dessert didn't seem like necessary steps. That or I was just itching to get him into my bed.

This was his idea, though, and that was after he'd turned me down once. God knew what had changed his mind or how long we'd end up staying here. I wasn't looking a gift horse in the mouth.

I skimmed over the menu and ordered a Mountain Dew. A little caffeine for the road wouldn't hurt. I also ordered a piece of cake I didn't really want just so I'd have something to soak up the alcohol. I was mostly sober by now, but if I was going to drive, I couldn't be too careful.

While I sipped my soda and nibbled the slab of carrot cake, I looked around the diner. It was a charming little place. That seemed to be the MO of Anchor Point—the "seaside small town" charm was everywhere. This restaurant in particular had a sailboat theme, and I had to give them credit for not being over the top about it. There were some framed paintings on the walls along with some shadowboxes containing various knots. The single cash register was behind an old brass helm someone must polish regularly since I couldn't see a hint of tarnish.

Maybe it was too soon to decide, but . . . I liked this place. Not just the diner either. I liked Anchor Pont. Time would tell if the small-town charm wore off and got annoying, but for tonight, I liked it. If there was a place in this world where I could make a fresh start after my divorce, this was it. The town was tiny, quiet, and on the opposite coast from Norfolk. Perfect.

Anchor Point even seemed cleaner, though it was entirely possible I just hadn't focused long enough to see the dirt. Sort of like how a cheap motel could seem perfectly immaculate and respectable, but once the sex was over and the smoke started clearing, it was hard to miss how the wallpaper was curling at the seams and yellowing along the uneven molding. The peeling laminate of the nightstand would let the particle board show through, and the uneven shadows on the ceiling would give away the dust that had been building in the light fixtures for God knew how long. And suddenly I'd realize I was lying in a seedy room with someone I never should have fucked.

Well shit. That train of thought had derailed in a hurry.

I shook myself and took another bite of the carrot cake. Yeah, this town was a good place for the new start I desperately needed.

Sighing, I stared out the window at the neat row of buildings across the street. A couple of shops and a dry cleaner, maybe. The signs were hard to read now that the whole town had rolled up its streets and gone dark for the night.

I'd made a lot of mistakes in my past life, and I'd make more in my new one. At least adultery wouldn't be one of them this time. I glanced down at my hand and wondered when I'd started thumbing the groove my wedding band had left. Then I looked out the window again.

Even if Anchor Point eventually showed its yellowing edges and dusty fixtures, it was a new start. A chance to get the future right after doing such a number on my past.

My ex-wife had fucked up too, and in a lot of the same ways, and we'd forgiven each other. I wondered if she'd forgiven herself. Next time I talked to her, maybe I'd ask. And if she said yes, maybe she'd tell me how.

Clanging sleigh bells jarred me out of my thoughts, and I looked up just in time to see Diego stride through the front door. He gave me a quick grin, then paused to say something to the waitress. Ordering a Coke, I thought.

While he did that, I looked him up and down. Overhead fluorescents never did anyone any favors, but they were hardly detracting from the hot man I'd met under the bar's dim lights.

He'd changed into a skintight black T-shirt and was huddled in a deep-brown leather jacket that had obviously seen better days. The hint of pink in his cheeks could have been from the cold outside or some lingering flush from a hot shower. Since his hair was damp and more carefully arranged than before, I assumed it was the latter.

Now he was heading this way, and I was so caught up in ogling him, he was halfway across the restaurant before I noticed he was walking with a limp.

Alarm made me sit up straighter. "You all right?"

He waved a hand, some more color blooming in his cheeks as he slid in across from me. His shoulder moved as he—I assumed—rubbed his knee under the table. "Sore. Been standing too long."

Oh, that made sense. The thought of standing behind a bar for hours on end made my whole body ache with sympathy.

"Sorry I took so long." He smiled, and it was sheepish, but somehow still wolfish at the same time. "I wanted to grab a shower."

"There's a shower at the bar?"

"Oh yeah." He waved his hand like that was a perfectly normal thing. "I thought it was weird too until the first time someone puked on me."

I almost gagged just thinking about it. "Lovely."

"Part of the job," he said with a shrug.

Well, if bartending had ever been on my list of potential postretirement jobs, it wasn't anymore.

Pushing that thought out of my mind, I played with my straw as I watched him from across the shining white table. "So, are we eating something? Or . . .?"

Diego's grin made me weak. "No. I just didn't think you'd want to wait outside in the cold while I finished up at work. Besides"—he gestured at my plate—"looks like you beat me to it."

I shrugged, pushing the crumb-covered plate aside. "Just trying to sober up."

"You didn't seem that drunk."

"No, but I like to have every advantage I can if I'm going to take someone to bed."

His eyebrows flicked up, but I couldn't imagine he was more surprised than I was by what I'd said. Or by the fact that we were even here, especially after how things had started tonight.

After the waitress had come by with a soda for him, and we were alone again, I cleared my throat. "So can I ask something personal?"

He nodded.

I hesitated, not sure if I should remind him why he'd rejected me at first tonight, but the curiosity really was getting to me. "What's the deal with the military?"

He didn't seem surprised by the question. As he spoke, he closed his hands around his glass. "The Navy fucked me. I've been known to hook up with military guys, but very, very rarely." He laughed bitterly. "I sure as shit don't date military, and it'll be a cold day in hell before I'm someone's dependent." He spat the last word.

I raised my eyebrows. "Oh." I wasn't sure what to say.

Diego shifted in his seat, staring into his soda. "To be honest, I usually won't even hook up with someone who isn't a civilian, but tonight . . ." A cautious smile tugged at his full lips. "What can I say? No matter how many times I told myself to keep my hands off because you're military, I just don't want to."

I gulped. "So, you're not interested in dating me because I'm military, but you're interested in sleeping with me?"

His smile made my skin tingle. "Nothing personal." The tip of his tongue darted across his lower lip. "As soon as I said no, I was kicking myself. So when I got another chance, I decided I didn't want you to get away."

I studied him for a moment before I laughed softly and shook my head. "I almost feel like I should be offended, but I'm not exactly diving headlong into dating myself. If the only thing we're going to do is fuck"—I gave him what I hoped came across as an appreciative look—"you won't hear me bitching."

Diego's smile broadened. "So we're on the same page, yeah?"

"If that page ends with us naked?" I nodded. "Definitely."

"Then maybe we should get the hell out of here."

Oh fuck yes.

I nodded with more enthusiasm than I probably should have, but I was beyond trying to play it cool.

Without another word, we got up. I paid at the register, and we headed outside in silence.

This was hands down the weirdest path I'd ever taken from meeting to sleeping together, but at this point, I wasn't going to argue. He could've pitched a November skinny dip in the Pacific, and I'd have gone along with it as long as—once our balls came back down—we wound up in bed.

As we walked through the diner's mostly empty parking lot, the wind off the Pacific made the night even colder. Now we definitely needed to get someplace else.

"So." I tried not to let my teeth chatter. "Your place or mine?"

"Yours is probably much nicer than mine. Unless you live on base?"

I shook my head. "No. I've done my time in base housing."

"Perfect." Diego halted, so I did too. His eyes narrowed in a way that nearly canceled out the cold. "But before we do, maybe we should make sure we're . . . compatible?"

I gulped, suddenly having visions of Anchor Point PD explaining to base security and my CO what they'd caught me doing in the diner's parking lot. "What do you have in mind?"

He didn't say a word. He closed the space between us to a sliver, and his hand slid over my hip, the contact making my pulse surge. Before I'd even adjusted to the presence of his hand, it had snaked around to the small of my back, and that sliver between us was gone, and—

Diego kissed me.

I'd expected something fierce and demanding, messy and suggestive, but he was soft and gentle. Not passive or uncertain, but gentle. Almost sweet.

Everything around us had gone quiet. Much quieter than a small town at three in the morning. Like it was all just . . . gone. I couldn't even feel the cold wind at all anymore; one touch of his mouth, and I was instantly hot all over, my whole body responding to his languid kiss.

I moaned against his lips as I wrapped my arms around him. Good thing, too, because he started teasing my lips apart with his tongue, and as he deepened the kiss, my knees liquefied. If I hadn't been holding him this close, God knew if I'd have been able to stay standing at all.

It had been longer than I could remember since someone had kissed me like they wanted me, and I didn't think my foundation had ever been rattled this hard by a simple kiss. It wasn't that I was instantly in love with him or anything insane like that. Maybe I was just thrown off because I hadn't realized how badly I needed to be touched, or because he'd seemed like someone I didn't have a chance with, or he was really just that talented with his lips and tongue. I didn't know. I just knew I liked it. A lot.

His long fingers carded through my hair as his body radiated heat through our clothes. I thought my heart might go right through my ribs.

So this is what chemistry tastes like.

Diego broke the kiss as gently as he'd started it, and when our eyes met in the lazy light of the all-night diner, his were on fire. He'd been so controlled from the start, but now he was out of breath, gazing at me with wide, gleaming eyes. "Should we get out of here?"

"Yes, we should."

CHAPTER 4
DIEGO

Mark pulled out of the bar's parking lot, and I followed his silver Lexus out onto the main drag through town. The piece-of-shit muffler on my piece-of-shit truck was extra loud tonight, and I hoped he didn't notice. I didn't usually, but when Anchor Point was this still and quiet, it was hard to ignore.

In my rumbling truck, I followed him to his place, and I knew after the first turn that he hadn't been lying about living off-base. His house wasn't just off-base—it was on the opposite end of Anchor Point.

Fine by me.

Fifteen minutes after we'd left, he led me up a short, curved driveway. He parked in the garage. I parked in the driveway. As we got out of our cars, I squinted up at the house, which was mostly visible in the glow of the floodlights. It was a little two-story house, gray with a white trim, and close enough to the coast it must've had a gorgeous view of—

Whatever. It was a house. And there was a bed inside where I needed to get Mark naked and sweaty.

The whole way up the walk, I prayed he didn't offer to give me the grand tour. He paused long enough to unlock the door, then waved me inside, and before he'd even shut the door behind us, he wrapped an arm around my waist and kissed me. So much for the grand tour.

I grabbed his ass in both hands as I kissed him right back, and he moaned softly against my lips. The kiss outside the diner had been a taste. Something restrained and calm.

Fuck restraint.

Fuck calm.

I forced his lips apart with my tongue, and I swore to God he pulled the air right out of me. We moved—kind of staggered—and Mark suddenly broke the kiss and went for my neck. His lips touched my skin, and I swore. I couldn't help it. He had me so hard it hurt, and he was turning my insides to liquid with those kisses that were somehow both soft and needy. There was nothing tentative about his touch—every kiss felt like it was exactly as much as he wanted to give me in that instant. And every one of them almost turned me inside out at the same time it made me want to beg for more.

He growled against my throat and kissed my skin so hard I thought he might sink his teeth in. I tilted my head and hoped he *would* bite me.

His hands were in my back pockets. Mine were in his hair. God knew when they'd gotten there, but now I kneaded his scalp as he groped my ass and mouthed all over my neck. Oh yeah, breaking my own rule tonight had been a damn good idea.

"Should be some condoms in the bedroom," he breathed. "Maybe . . . maybe we should get closer to those."

I groaned softly, imagining being balls-deep in him. "Yeah. Good idea."

We stumbled a few steps closer to the stairs, but there was too much kissing and groping going on to get much further. Fuck, his hands were strong, and I wanted them all over me. And I wanted to see if his knuckles turned white while he was holding the edge of the mattress and I pounded his—

"To the bedroom?" My words tumbled out.

Mark didn't say anything. He took my hand and led me up the stairs.

We got as far as kicking off our shoes before we fell into bed together. Jesus, I felt like a teenager—too horny to think. God, this was hot.

"Clothes . . ." He tugged at my shirt. "Get this off."

I nudged his leg so he'd let me sit up. Once I was upright, I started to pull off my shirt, but hesitated. I always hated this part. Especially when I'd been too caught up in groping him to shut off the light on the way to the bed.

Mark slid his hands over my hips. "What's wrong?"

"I, um . . ." I swallowed as I combed my fingers through my hair. "I've got some scars. Just . . . just so you know."

"Do any of them hurt?"

I blinked. "What?"

He ran his palms down my clothed thighs. "If any of them are touchy and you want me to avoid them, just say so."

"I . . . No, none of them hurt anymore. I just meant they don't, um, look so great."

"Okay, then." He shrugged, grinning up at me. "I just don't want to hurt you. I don't mind scars."

Yeah, we'll see about that.

Heart thumping, I peeled off my shirt and tossed it off the side of his bed. Before he had a chance to look at me, though, I leaned down and kissed him again.

Mark didn't miss a beat. Instantly, his arms were around me, and he was kissing me just as desperately as he had a minute ago. His hands roamed all over my back and arms, so there was no way he didn't feel the worst of the scars, but he didn't flinch away from them. And it wasn't like they weren't noticeable. My whole left shoulder was like leather to the touch. If he minded, I couldn't tell.

Ever since I'd recovered from the burns and surgeries, I'd hated being naked with someone for the first time. The sense of exposure was intense now that my skin was anything but flawless.

With Mark, I was aware of the exposure and of how self-conscious I was supposed to be, but I was too turned on to *feel* anything except cool air and white hot need.

I pushed myself up onto my arms. Damn, he looked good like this, flat on his back between my planted hands. "How attached are you to this bed?"

He glanced at it, then up at me, eyebrows quirked. "Is that a trick question?"

"No." I licked my lips. "But if it's some priceless antique you inherited from your grandma, I don't want to break it."

Mark shivered. "Uh. No. It's . . . just something I got off craigslist."

"Good. Let's break it."

The grin that spread across his lips made my heart go insane. "Yeah. Good excuse as any to replace it."

I laughed, and he took advantage of the moment to flip me onto my back. I was startled for all of two seconds, and then I grabbed him, dragged him down to me, and hooked a leg over his, pulling our hips together. Mark didn't resist at all. If anything, he melted against me, and he kissed me like his life depended on it.

In between making out and shucking off most of our clothes, we changed position a few times. I was on top. Then he was. Then we were on our sides. Then I was on top again, straddling him with our cocks rubbing through our boxers until he rolled me onto my back and started on my neck.

Fuck. He loved kissing my neck, and I couldn't get enough of it. He spent ages doing it. Up and down. One side. Then the other. Along my jaw. Up to my ear. Down to my collarbone. All along my shoulder, like he didn't even notice the old burns. And the whole time, his cock pressed against mine, rubbing subtly through our underwear every time one of us moved. Much more of this and he was going to get me off before we'd gotten a hand below the waist.

I started to push him back so I could get on top, but he didn't move. "Stay on your back."

"Bossy, hmm?"

"Not bossy," he said between kisses on my collarbone, "but it's a lot easier to suck your dick if you're on your back."

I shivered. "Well, shit. When you put it like that . . ."

He started moving down. For a second, I was way too aware of how exposed my scars were, but even as his lips got close to the damaged skin that started just below my collarbone, I couldn't concentrate on being nervous. He'd seen the scars. He'd felt them. If he was going to be disgusted by them, he would've been by now. But even when his lips brushed the thicker skin, he didn't act grossed out or turned off.

I stroked his hair as he continued kissing his way down. He looked up at me for a second, grinned, and kept going.

"You, uh . . ." Fuck, I could barely talk. "You don't mind guys who aren't cut, do you?"

His eyes flicked up again, and he shrugged. "No. Why would I?"

Before I could say *some guys are weird about it*, he drew a circle on my skin with the tip of his tongue, and all I managed was a moan.

He laughed so softly, the only reason I knew about it was the rush of warm breath across damp skin.

"Damn clothes." He tugged at my waistband. "Let's get rid of these."

I was covered in goose bumps as I lifted my hips so he could slide my boxers out of the way. I couldn't even find anything witty or dirty to say; I was too turned on by the thought of his mouth on my cock.

He bit my hip bone, and I couldn't stop myself from letting go of a low, strangled sound.

And then . . . oh God. He ran his tongue around the head of my cock and, a second later, closed his lips around it, and there wasn't a damn thing I wouldn't have done as long as he kept working that slick, hot magic.

Some American guys didn't know what to do with a man who was uncut, and they'd either freak out or not realize they couldn't be quite so rough, but Mark must've done this before. That or he was uncut too; I hadn't gotten that far yet.

Either way, at least he knew not to go straight to jerking me off like he might a guy who was cut. He was even gentle with his lips and tongue, licking and teasing the head just right to make my whole body hot. When he started stroking, he knew to use my foreskin, sliding it up and down the shaft until I was about to lose my mind. I didn't care how or why he'd learned to handle a cock like mine as long as he didn't stop.

Except . . . I did want him to stop. I didn't want him to make me come. I wanted to . . . God, just thinking about it almost got me off.

"I want to fuck you," I moaned. "N-now." Thank fuck my knee was just aching bearably; I was so not in the mood for pain to interfere with everything I wanted to do with this man.

"Mmm." He sat up and met my gaze. Dios mío, the lust in his eyes was burning as hot as my own.

"*Now*," I repeated.

"Yeah," he panted. "Let me . . ." He gestured toward the side of the bed. "Condom." He reached for the nightstand, stretching his lean torso and making my mouth water even more. Oh, yes, I was glad I'd bent my rules tonight. His body was amazing. As he sat over me again, condom and lube in hand, I couldn't resist running my palms up his smooth abs and thinly haired chest. This was someone who didn't just squeak by on his Physical Readiness Test. He probably still blew the 18-25 guidelines out of the water even though he had to be in his forties.

As he rolled the condom onto my cock, he looked up at me. "Go easy, okay? You're, um, not exactly lacking here, and it's been a while since I've done this."

"How long is 'a while'?"

Mark's lips quirked, and he shrugged. "Couple of years at least."

I nodded. "Okay. I'll go slow."

I sat up, and he moved onto his hands and knees. I took my time fingering him, stretching him, making sure he was ready for me. It was also the perfect opportunity to calm myself down so I didn't go off the second I was in him. And to make sure my knee really was up for the challenge. So far, so good.

As soon as he was ready and I wasn't about to lose it, I knelt behind him. Mark swore even before I'd touched his hole with my dick, and when I did, he moaned. As I pushed into him, *I* moaned.

"This all right?" I asked as I carefully worked myself deeper.

"Uh-huh." His head fell forward, and I watched a shiver run up his spine. "So good. Jesus . . ."

Yeah, it was. Holy fuck. He was tight as hell, and he rocked back and forth, driving me deeper even while I was trying to be careful. I picked up speed, and he moaned louder, and, oh yeah, it was perfect.

My knee protested, and it promised to ache like a motherfucker later, but it would hold for now. It damn well better.

I leaned down and wrapped an arm around Mark, grunting as I thrust into him. I nipped the back of his shoulder before I slurred, "You're gonna make me come. Fuuuck."

"Oh Jesus, that's hot," he moaned. "Keep—" I bit his shoulder again. "Oh *God*."

I pounded him, thrusting deeper, and murmured how hot he was, how I wanted to make him come so hard he cried. Was I speaking in Spanish? Maybe. It didn't matter if he could understand the words, though; from the way he moaned and shook under me, he understood enough.

"Yeah . . . just like that. Oh my God." He shuddered, and I gritted my teeth and gave him everything I had, and then he let go of a helpless cry as he came. I got lost in the sound of Mark losing his mind, and suddenly I was coming too, pushing deep inside him as he clenched and squeezed every last drop out of me.

Everything slowed down and finally stopped, except my pounding heart. Shaky and dizzy, I pulled out, and then I flopped onto my back next to him so I could catch my breath and wait for the room to stop spinning. Mark turned over and dropped down beside me too, probably right in the wet spot, but he didn't seem to care.

Still panting, skin gleaming with sweat, he slurred, "I am *really* glad I checked out that club tonight."

"Yeah." I licked my lips. "Me too."

CHAPTER 5
MARK

Forty-two years old, and I'd never woken up beside a man before. I'd had sex with men in my bachelor days, and I'd broken my wedding vows with as many men as I had with women, so it wasn't like I was new to hooking up with guys.

Every one of those encounters had been discreet for obvious reasons, though, and we'd never stayed in bed once we'd caught our breath. That was assuming we even got near a bed. It was usually men's rooms, back alleys, and the occasional hard-to-find nook on a ship, and once on a deserted stretch of beach on Guam. When it was over, we'd go our separate ways and hope no one had seen us.

So to say the least, it was novel as hell to wake up in my own bed with the morning sun pouring in through the windows and spilling over Diego's naked sleeping form. That along with all the twinges and aches in my tired body proved without a doubt that last night hadn't been a long, vivid, incredibly pornographic dream.

I squirmed under the covers as goose bumps sprang up all over my skin.

He was completely still, his chest rising and falling with the slow breathing of deep, peaceful sleep. And since he *was* asleep, I didn't have to worry about him being self-conscious while I drank in the sight of him.

I'd noticed the scars by his eye and his temple at the bar, but now that the light was better, I could see more of them on the side of his face. A lot more. He had some heavy five-o'clock shadow, and the smaller scars stood out like flecks of white hair in his dark beard. Thin, silvery lines, none more than three-quarters of an inch long, were scattered along the left side of his face. Some disappeared into his hair.

There was a second one near his eye, cutting a dramatic slash through his eyebrow. Some were razor-straight. Others had the distinct scalloping of a cut that had been stitched, including the two most prominent ones next to his eye.

There were more sprinkled down the side of his neck and toward his collarbone, and that was where the more dramatic damage started. A broad scar that had to be from a serious burn covered his left shoulder and upper arm and down to almost halfway across his pec. Most of it had a texture like a fine net had been put over it, and I was pretty sure that was the telltale mark of a skin graft.

On his pec, the scar had partially consumed a tattoo. Most of the ink was badly distorted, but the remaining curves made up a profile I'd seen plenty of times in my career—a swallow. The traditional tattoo of a Sailor who'd logged five thousand miles at sea.

I chewed my lip as I watched him sleep. If not for the swallow and his hackles going up over the Navy, I might've thought he'd been in a car crash or something, but no. He was definitely a combat veteran. One who wanted nothing to do with the military that had, according to his comment last night, fucked him.

I traced my gaze over the smaller scars on his face and neck, and the pattern made more sense now. Shrapnel. Like he'd been lucky and far enough away from a blast to survive, but close enough to be fragged and burned.

Tilting my head a bit, I looked at the underside of his forearm. Sure enough—more scars. A smaller burn on his elbow. More thin white lines all the way up to his wrist. I thought there was even a gouge in the heel of his hand, but I couldn't see for sure.

In my mind, I could see him throwing up his arm to protect his face, catching some of the pieces but not all of them. A chill prickled through me as I pushed away an image of him bloody, burned, in pain, and afraid. Instead, I gazed at the man he was now.

There was no way I could tell him the scars didn't make him less attractive. It would just sound patronizing, but it was true. If anything, they made me curious about him. I'd immediately wondered what the story was behind the two scars I'd noticed on his face, and that curiosity ran far deeper now. Where had he been? What had happened between his five thousandth mile at sea and now?

Was *that* why he didn't date military men? Or was there something else? He was old enough to have been kicked out when DADT had still been in effect. And I'd met plenty of people who swore off active-duty partners because there was too much separation and too much chance of a flag-draped casket.

Any one of those sounded like a perfectly valid reason to me. That was part of the reason I hadn't tried to push him when he'd said my active-duty status was a deal breaker.

But damn, after spending the night with him? While I understood if he wouldn't or couldn't date me, he was going to be a tough act to follow.

Still asleep, but grumbling like he might be coming around, Diego rolled onto his stomach and burrowed into my pillow, disheveling his hair even more. I smiled to myself. He was fucking adorable when he slept.

I couldn't resist, and leaned in to kiss the side of his neck. He tensed like I'd startled him, and I almost drew back, but then he arched against me and gave a soft, sleepy moan. So, I did it again. I kept nibbling on his neck, and as he squirmed, I ran my hand down his side and under the covers. When I snaked it toward his belly, he pressed back against me. His cock was almost fully hard. A couple of gentle strokes, and it was all the way there, rock-solid in my hand as he rubbed his ass against my own erection.

"*Fuck*," he moaned.

"Roll onto your back," I whispered in his ear.

He did, and before he'd even settled, I was kissing his neck again. He still smelled faintly of the soap we'd both used in the shower a few hours ago, and that made me even hotter. It was almost like I'd marked him with my scent, and it tickled some primal, territorial side of me. Like I wanted to claim him somehow. It was ridiculous, but so was any thought that ever crossed my mind before I'd had coffee.

Under the covers, I stroked him with one hand, using his foreskin the way he seemed to enjoy. His groans said I was doing it right, so I kept going.

Then I started kissing my way down. He arched and squirmed as I trailed kisses along his chest and his belly, and when I licked around the head of his cock, he rewarded me with a throaty moan.

Before last night, it had been ages since I'd given a blowjob, and the ones I'd given in the last twenty years had always been hurried, hidden, and guilty. A quickie that was overshadowed by the fear of getting caught and, later, the shame when I'd gotten away with it. I'd gone down on him last night to wind him up, but this? This was the main attraction, and this . . . this . . . Oh God.

My body was still heavy with sleep after I'd spent the whole night beside him, and he was sprawled in the middle of my bed with the late-morning sun sliding over his planes and contours. There was no hurry to get him to an orgasm—just slowly, lazily sucking his dick and enjoying the salt of his skin and the sting of his fingers tugging at my hair.

And I was pretty sure it was the hottest thing I'd ever experienced.

While I stroked him and sucked him, he was murmuring in Spanish, gripping my hair in both hands as his hips rocked just enough to push his dick into my mouth. He didn't seem to be in any hurry either, but after a while, his breaths started getting faster and sharper. He held my hair tighter, and some more Spanish tumbled off his lips before, "I'm gonna come. Fuck . . ."

I groaned around his cock, he shuddered hard, and his hips jerked just as he came, filling my mouth with cum and the air with curses in two languages.

As I returned to the pillows, he wiped a hand over his face and exhaled. "If I'd known this is how you start the day," he murmured, his accent thicker than usual, "I wouldn't have said no the first time."

"If I tell you I do this every day, will that convince you to come back?"

Diego laughed. "If you promise another night like last night, you definitely won't have to twist my arm to get me to come back."

I chuckled. "Guess I better stock up on condoms."

"Mm-hmm." The featherlight brush of his fingertips down my side made me gasp. "I work nights, but as long as you don't mind me showing up in the middle of the night . . ."

"Not at all." I laughed again. "Hell, we could christen every room in my house. Then I won't have to worry about having a housewarming party."

Diego trailed a fingertip along the edge of my jaw as his lips pulled into a sleepy, sexy grin. "Well, if you want me to come back and help you defile your house tonight, I'm off at two thirty."

"You better believe I do. Any chance I can talk you into staying long enough to have breakfast?"

"Breakfast?" His eyebrows quirked. "Aren't you forgetting something?"

"Forgetting—"

Diego pressed me back with a hand in the middle of my chest. With a grin, he started downward toward my cock.

Well, I wasn't forgetting it now.

Neither was he.

CHAPTER 6
DIEGO

On Sunday morning, I woke up first. Mark was still snoring softly beside me, and the sun coming through the bedroom window was like déjà vu. I was here again? How the fuck had that happened?

Last night was a little bit of a blur. We'd exchanged some texts while I was at work, and those had ramped up from flirting to telling each other what we'd do if we were alone right then. As soon as the High-&-Tight closed, I was back where I'd been twenty-four hours before—pulling into Mark's driveway.

Because hey, I was a red-blooded gay man. I wasn't going to say no to more of the kind of sex we'd had on Friday night.

What part of one-night stand *did you not understand?*

I sighed. The part where the sex with Mark was really good and I wanted to keep coming back for more, apparently.

Wait, keep *coming back?*

It was two nights. Wasn't like we were eloping or anything.

Yeah, and what will you say if he suggests hooking up again?

I squeezed my eyes shut. Oh, I knew what I'd say. I could still feel everything we'd done the last couple of nights, and yeah, if he suggested hooking up again, I'd be on board. When the sex was this good, it just didn't matter what kind of uniforms were hanging in his closet.

Keep telling yourself that.

Mark rolled over and, after he'd blinked a few times, looked at me. "Morning."

I smiled. "Morning."

"Sleep all right?" he asked.

Surprisingly, yes. I nodded. "Yeah. Just woke up a few minutes ago. You?"

"Mm-hmm." He mumbled something as he stretched. "I'm going to be feeling this for days."

"Damn right you are." I trailed a finger down his arm. "You won't be sitting down this week without thinking of me."

He shivered, closing his eyes as he grinned. "Like the sound of that."

I laughed. I shifted a little, and a twinge bit at my knee. I managed to not wince, but I was going to be limping unless I did something to help it. A shower. That would help. We'd showered after we'd fucked, but hot water would help my knee more than anything. Anything aside from asking for an ice pack, anyway, and I wasn't ready to let Mark think I needed ice the morning after I got laid. "You mind if I grab a shower?"

"Not at all."

While I showered, the aches and pains in the rest of my body made themselves known. My legs didn't feel like they were connected to my body. My hips felt every thrust I'd taken last night, but I managed to not fall on my ass. Even if it took some wincing, I made it down the stairs. I grinned as I got closer to the bottom step where I'd almost bent Mark over, before he'd panted something about the bed being more comfortable. It had definitely been more comfortable. Still would've been hot, grabbing him and doing him right there on the stairs.

Maybe another time. When my knee wasn't acting up. Which was basically never, but a boy could fantasize.

Mark was in the kitchen, which was open to his living room. As he fussed with the coffeepot, I leaned against the kitchen island and took in my surroundings. Yesterday, we'd spent most of the morning in bed, then ducked out for coffee before I'd headed home, so I hadn't really noticed much about the house outside the bedroom.

He'd mentioned something about being recently divorced, and that made sense as I looked around his house. It wasn't cheap bachelor pad shit like a footlocker for a coffee table or a milk crate end table covered in beer cans. He had sleek taste—simple black furniture, black-and-white framed prints on the walls in black frames, not much in the way of knickknacks. He didn't bother with decorative pillows, but there was a red, black, and white Navajo-style blanket draped over the back of the sofa.

And in the corner, sitting on top of an old TV stand, was a three-foot-high Christmas tree. It had a single strand of lights around it—they weren't on—and some small ornaments. A lot of blue and gold, which wasn't a surprise, and from where I was standing I couldn't decide if the gray ornament near the top was a Navy ship or something out of Star Trek.

"Coffee?" he asked.

I turned around. "Yes, please."

He poured a couple of mugs and handed me one.

"Thanks." I gestured at the tree with the cup. "A Christmas tree? Already?"

Mark glanced at the pathetic little thing, and he shrugged. "Thought it would give the place . . . I don't know, some life?"

I looked the tree up and down. "It's cute."

"If you're into Charlie Brown Christmas trees, maybe."

"Oh come on." I laughed. "It's small, but it's nice. How does it look with the lights turned on?"

Mark nodded toward the tree as if to say *Go ahead*.

Hell, why not? I crossed the room and paused to look at the gray ornament near the top. Turned out it was two ornaments next to each other—the starship *Enterprise* from Star Trek, and the USS *Enterprise* aircraft carrier. Cute.

I turned to Mark. "You were stationed on the *Enterprise*?"

"Briefly," he said as he joined me beside the tree. "Really early on."

I faced the tree again and flipped the switch on the green cord sticking out from the stand. Instantly, dozens of tiny white lights came to life.

"There. See?" I smiled. "It's cute. A little early, but cute."

Mark smirked. "So it's cute and small, and it's early. I hope we're still talking about the tree and not my dick."

I choked on my coffee and almost spat it all over the glittery tree. When I'd recovered, I set my cup down and wrapped an arm around Mark's waist. "We're definitely still talking about the tree."

He reeled me in closer. "Good. Because I don't think Christmas lights could save me from any shortcomings there."

I snorted and rolled my eyes.

Mark laughed. Then he gestured toward the kitchen with his thumb. "You want some breakfast? I'm not God's gift to cooking, but I make some decent French toast."

Whoa. A home-cooked breakfast? One that I didn't have to sweat bullets over budgeting? Fuck. That sounded amazing. I didn't want to take advantage of him or use him as a meal ticket, but damn if the prospect of French toast wasn't seriously tempting.

"Sure. Yeah. Can I help with anything?"

Mark shook his head. "No, I've got it. Have a seat."

I couldn't remember the last time someone besides my mother had cooked for me, so I didn't argue. Coffee in hand, I took a seat on one of the barstools at the kitchen island.

Mark made breakfast, and then we moved to the table.

"Wow," I said after a couple of bites. "This is really good."

"Thanks." He actually blushed. Fuck, he was cute. "It's probably one of a dozen things I know how to make without giving anyone food poisoning."

I laughed. "You're better at it than me. I've tried to make it a couple of times, and it always comes out either soggy or leathery." I made a face before skewering another piece of syrup-drenched bread.

"Eh, we all have our weak spots in the kitchen. Whatever you do, don't ask me to make my mother's meatloaf."

"Yeah? Why's that?"

"Just . . . trust me." He grimaced as he sliced off a piece with his fork. "My ex-wife tried it once and made me swear on my life I'd never commit that crime against food again."

"That bad, huh?"

"Worse. But then my mom gave us all salmonella one Fourth of July, so . . ." He shrugged.

"Salmonella?" I sputtered. "Seriously?"

Mark rolled his eyes as he nodded. "Yeah. That was not a pleasant weekend for any of us."

I almost mentioned the time the mess decks on my last ship gave about two hundred people food poisoning, but I didn't want to talk about my old career, so I let it go. "What else can you cook?"

He thought for a second while he took a sip of coffee. "I can make a decent steak. Pretty good at a few different kinds of pasta."

He paused. "I learned how to make this really amazing stroganoff, but I almost always fuck something up. If I tried to make it now, I'd probably have to call my ex-wife and have her walk me through it."

"Ever tried writing down the recipe?"

"I did," he muttered. "But I still manage to screw it up, and thank God she's a wizard at unfucking culinary disasters. That's why I keep her on speed dial."

I laughed. "Your own personal cooking lifeline. Nice."

"Trust me. I need it." He sipped his coffee. "Do you cook?"

"I try to." I played with the handle on my coffee cup. "I'm pretty good at making bocoles. They're little round cakes made out of corn dough. You can put pretty much anything on them, and my mother makes them all the time." I paused. "She does a lot of Huasteca cooking."

"Huasteca?"

I nodded. "The natives that used to live in San Luis Potosi. Or, well, they still do. Just not as many."

"Are you Huas . . . How do you say it again?"

I smiled. "Huasteca."

"Huasteca." It sounded a bit clumsy, but he was trying.

"I have some Huastec blood, yes. My ancestors were mostly Spanish, except my grandfather was Italian, and my great-grandmother on my mom's side was Huastec. She passed down a lot of the recipes." I laughed self-consciously. "My abuela and my mother are much better at it than I am. The bocoles are pretty easy, so I can't fuck them up." I paused. "There's this one dish—Zacahuil. It's . . . like a three-foot-long tamale."

Mark blinked. "That's not a meal for one, is it?"

I laughed, shaking my head. "No, that's for when the whole family comes over."

"Can you make that?"

"I've . . ." I grimaced. "Yeah, I can make it. Sort of. But it's been a long time since I've even eaten it, so I'd need my abuela looking over my shoulder if I tried to make it."

Mark chuckled.

We kept on talking. Mostly about kitchen disasters and things our mothers had made while we were growing up. That turned into who'd had the most traumatic childhood meal (his grandma's atrocity of a stuffed-pepper recipe won that one), whose school had had the worst food (my junior high's shoe leather mystery meat patties), and the weirdest thing either of us had ever eaten (possibly a tie between the live baby octopus he'd tried in Korea and my neighbor's famous frog legs).

It wasn't until I went to refill my coffee for the third time that I realized I'd been sitting long enough for my knee to get stiff. Damn, how long had we been here?

According to the clock on the microwave, it was almost one thirty in the afternoon.

"Shit," I said. "I didn't mean to stay quite so late."

"Quite so—" He did a double take at the clock. "Whoa. Well hell. Do you want to go grab something for lunch?"

I hesitated. Joining him for lunch after we'd spent the whole morning talking, and after our one-night stand had turned into two, had implications. Or at least, left the door open for implications.

It was also really tempting. I was getting hungry again, and who was I kidding? I liked Mark. Spending a little more time together wouldn't kill us. Might kill my *I'm not dating a military man* argument, because it was creeping into actually dating, but . . . to hell with it.

I smiled. "Sure. There's a place not far from here that's really good." I gave the clock another glance. "The church crowd is probably clearing out by now too."

"Sounds perfect. I'll get my wallet."

CHAPTER 7
MARK

After a weekend that had consisted of more sex than sleep, I was going to be such a wreck at work today. Hell, tired as I was, I would've gotten lost on my way from my car to the boat if it weren't for the fact that a giant flattop ship was kind of hard to miss.

Dazed, I made my way down the long pier. A few civilian contractors passed by me without a second look. Some enlisted Sailors and junior officers stopped, saluted me sharply, and said, "Good morning, sir." I returned each salute and greeting, thankful that habit and muscle memory had made those responses automatic enough to still happen even while I was in a haze.

Habit and muscle memory saved me from making an ass of myself, but I needed to be sharp. As the new XO, I couldn't be shuffling aboard in the morning like some kid who'd been partying all weekend.

Not that I was out to impress anyone or get command of a ship; my ambition had run pretty dry in recent years. Still, I had a job to do, and I did take my role seriously. I was the enforcer of the rules the commanding officer made. The CO and I would be in deep shit if the crew didn't respect us, and the upper chain of command on this particular boat wasn't held in terribly high regard these days. Not after the last two COs, the XO, and several others had been relieved for various offenses over the course of a year.

That wasn't to say other ships didn't have their fair share of bullshit in the upper ranks. When I'd been stationed on an aircraft carrier back when I had been a lieutenant commander, the CO had been so close to retiring that he'd just stopped giving a fuck. The XO had been the opposite—a hard-ass who'd throw the book at someone for the most minor infraction. The CO's apathy hadn't mattered when the XO had kept us all in line.

Then the XO had been busted with his dick in a petty officer. Adultery. Fraternization. Conduct unbecoming a gentleman. Overnight, the five-thousand-strong crew had turned almost mutinous. If the CO didn't care and the rules didn't apply to the XO, then why should any of *us* bother?

The *Fort Stevens* had roughly the same level of respect and morale right now. The junior personnel regarded the senior ranks with open contempt, and those who were senior to them but junior to me and Captain Hawthorne pretty much shrugged and wished us the best of luck.

And, of course, the ship was scheduled to go to sea for six months in the spring. Couldn't *wait* to see what happened when a crew on the verge of mutiny was tired and sex deprived with no land in sight. Especially once we deployed and brought aboard almost two thousand Marines on top of the thousand-plus existing crew, making the boat three times as crowded. Fantastic.

Once I was on board, I followed the maze of passageways to my office. The space was cramped, but that was to be expected. Everything on a ship was cramped. Well, unless you'd spent time on a submarine. I never had—aside from a tour once or twice—but some friends had, and they thought a carrier or an amphib ship were the damn Four Seasons after those claustrophobic confines.

I shuddered. There was a reason I'd never volunteered for sub duty.

I settled into my office to get some work done. I had several Sailors and a couple of officers coming in today for Executive Officer Inquiries. XOI was a step below Captain's Mast, which was a step below court-martial. These were serious offenses, which meant I needed to be focused.

That didn't mean I *was* focused, though. The minute I sat my aching ass down, my mind wandered right back to the man who'd spent most of the weekend in my bed.

He'd left Saturday to go to work, and then he'd come back yesterday for a rematch after closing. We'd gone to a café he'd recommended for lunch, and what a surprise—found our way back into my bed last night. This morning, we'd both been bleary-eyed as hell when I'd had to get up and head to the boat . . . but not bleary-eyed enough for him to refuse that blowjob in the shower.

I shivered in my desk chair. Goddamn, he was hot. And addictive. One look at him on Friday night had given me a hard-on, but I'd had no idea what was in store once I got him into my bed. Now I was suddenly desperate for him to lay me out and ride my ass again. It was as if I'd never felt anything like that before, and now I needed as much as I could get.

Except I *had* been fucked before. There were a couple of guys in my past, and my ex-wife had been very enthusiastic with that strap-on. So I was no stranger to giving or receiving anal.

Holy fuck, though. *Diego.* That man had ridden me hard until I couldn't take anymore, and when I'd begged him for more anyway, he'd given it to me. His cock was addictive. *He* was addictive.

And the way he'd talked dirty in my ear? That was . . . oh God. I couldn't even say he'd *been* talking dirty. When he'd slipped into Spanish, I'd had no idea what he was actually saying. He could've been complimenting my car or insulting my mother or reciting the Lord's Prayer. All I knew was his tone had been so utterly filthy, he'd talked me right over the edge into the hardest orgasm I'd had in years.

I shivered again, goose bumps breaking out under my uniform. Christ, that man was sexy. It was impossible not to come away from a weekend like that in anything but a good mood, even if that good mood wasn't going to last long. Which it wouldn't—not when I had a day packed with Executive Officer Inquiries. Because disciplinary hearings were *so* much fun.

I managed to concentrate enough to get through the first couple of XOIs without making an ass of myself. A distracted XO during a disciplinary hearing would really help with that ship-wide morale and discipline problem the CO and I were fighting. The minute I had my office to myself, though, I was back to spacing out and thinking about Diego. Hadn't he said something this morning about getting together again?

I sat up. He *had.* Somewhere in the middle of making out and blowing him, there'd been a *we should do this again* and an *I want more of what we did last night.* The only thing left was to figure out when or where. Or whether he was just enthusiastic about another rematch because he'd had his dick in my mouth a minute before.

So, during lunch, I slipped down to the pier to find a decent signal and texted him.

Busy tonight?

Nope. Off today. ;)

Oh, now that made things more interesting. A midweek work night wasn't the time to be starting something at one in the morning, but earlier? Oh yeah, I could do that.

Want to grab dinner & then go to my place?

Can do. When/where?

We texted back and forth for a few minutes. By the time I went aboard again, we'd made plans to meet at the café we'd gone to yesterday, since it was close to the house.

And now, with my evening plans sorted out and my libido tugging even harder at my focus, I returned to my office for the first XOI of the afternoon.

When I got home, I stripped out of my uniform, showered, pulled on a Cardinals T-shirt and jeans, and drove to the café to meet Diego.

He was there when I arrived, and he smiled as I came up the sidewalk. Then his eyes drifted down, and he suddenly looked horrified. "What the fuck is that?" He gestured at my shirt.

"What?" I glanced at myself.

"You're a *Cardinals* fan?" He clicked his tongue and scowled. "And here I was thinking you were almost perfect."

Aside from being on active duty?

I didn't ask that out loud, though. As curious as I was about his almost-allergic aversion to the military, the conversation was light and I wanted to keep it that way. "Don't tell me you're a Patriots fan?"

He made a disgusted noise. "Please. Eagles, all the way."

I scoffed, shaking my head. "Oh God. Well, enjoy watching the Cardinals stomp them on Sunday."

Diego paused like he was thinking. "They are playing this weekend, aren't they?"

"I think so, yeah." I took out my phone and pulled up the schedule. "No, wait. Two weeks from Sunday."

Diego's eyes lost focus for a second, but then his face lit up. "All the bartenders get a weekend off every month, and that's mine. Perfect!"

I grinned. "So you want to watch the game with me?"

"Hell yeah." He narrowed his eyes. "I'm always down for being there while a Cardinals fan watches his guys get stomped."

I laughed. "Uh-huh. We'll see about that."

"We will. Two weeks from Sunday."

"My place?"

He nodded. "Your place."

This was going to be fun.

We went into the café and, after we'd been seated, opened the menus. We talked while we perused the menu, meandering from topic to topic. We were still getting to know each other, after all.

After I told him one of my wild tales of being overseas, he laughed and almost choked on his drink.

"And none of you were arrested?" he asked, eyebrows up.

"None. Which was surprising—the Japanese police don't really have a high tolerance for stupid drunken Americans. Not in towns with bases, anyway."

"I'll bet they don't." He chuckled, and he didn't seem to mind that we were brushing up against the subject of me being in the military. "Why do you think they let you go?"

"We had someone in the group who was fluent in Japanese. If you've got someone who speaks the language, it can go a *long* way when you're dealing with foreign police."

Diego nodded. "I believe that. As long as a cop speaks Spanish or English, I'm good."

"Well, you're doing better than me. If the cop doesn't speak English, I'm fucked."

"They didn't make you take a foreign language in school?"

"Eh, I took French in high school and college, but I've never had much need for it, so I've forgotten most of it."

He nodded. "Yeah, that happens. To be honest, my Spanish would probably get rusty if I didn't talk to my family as often as I do."

"You talk to them often?"

"As much as I can. Calling Mexico isn't cheap, so . . ." He waved his hand.

"I can imagine."

He cleared his throat. "You close to your family?"

I pressed my lips together. "Not as close to my sister as I'd like to be, but . . ." I sighed. "That's a long story. My parents moved to Florida a few years ago, and I talk to them as often as I can. Visit too. They used to come see me, but it's hard for them to travel now."

Diego studied me. "Do they know about . . . uh . . ." He gestured at each of us.

"That I'm bi?"

"Yeah."

I nodded. "They knew I dated a couple of guys in college. They don't necessarily like it, and probably thought it was a moot point after I got married, but yes, they know. What about yours?"

"My father never knew." His expression darkened, but only for a second before he shook himself and met my gaze again. "My mother thinks he would have been all right with it, even if it took him some time to get there, but I guess we'll never know."

"How does she feel about it?"

"When I told her the first time, she cried." He closed his eyes, shaking his head. "That was . . . hard."

"I'll bet," I said, almost whispering. We held each other's gazes. The topic of our families felt loaded for some reason. Like ground we didn't need to be walking on right now.

Before I could change the subject, he said, "So your parents moved to Florida? From where?"

"Phoenix."

"That explains the Cardinals thing." He sighed dramatically. "I guess I can let it slide."

"Uh-huh. Yeah, I was born and raised there, and I've been trying to avoid the desert ever since."

"Don't like the heat?"

"Not really. And I'm pretty sure the desert was actively trying to kill me."

Diego laughed. God, I loved the way he laughed. "Trying to kill you? How?"

"Snakes and scorpions, mostly. A rattler bit me when I was ten, but it was the scorpion sting that almost killed me."

Diego blinked a few times like he was struggling to take in everything I'd just said. "Okay, now you have to tell me both of those stories."

I chuckled. "Well, the rattler was under my friend's front porch. We were supposed to tell our parents if we saw a snake so they could call one of the removal specialists, but we were dumb kids and thought teasing it would be more fun."

Diego pinched the bridge of his nose. "You're not serious."

"I totally am." I shook my head, laughing at the memory. "I got too close, it got pissed off, and . . ." I gestured at my forearm. "It got me."

His eyes widened. "It really bit you."

"Uh-huh. No scar, though. I mean, there were a couple of puncture wounds, but then I wiped out on a bike when I was a teenager, and the road rash took out the scar."

"I thought rattlesnake bites did more damage than that."

"They do, but I got lucky—it was a dry bite. Scared me more than anything, which was probably the idea. I still had to go to the hospital, and it hurt like a son of a bitch for a while, but it wasn't nearly as bad as it could have been."

"You *did* get lucky," he said. "And the scorpion?"

"That was when I was twelve. My friend—same friend—and I found a bark scorpion. Those are the really dangerous ones, so obviously we were playing with it."

Diego inclined his head. "I'm seeing a pattern here."

"I have no idea what you're talking about."

"Uh-huh. So you were teasing it like you teased the snake, and it stung you?"

"Basically. And I was so afraid of getting in trouble for playing with it, I didn't want to tell my mom. When I started wheezing and puking a couple of hours later, she took me to the ER."

"Were you in trouble after that?"

I shuddered as I picked up my drink. "*So* much trouble."

He burst out laughing. "Sounds like you deserved it."

"Hmm, probably." I arched an eyebrow. "Don't tell me you were the perfect kid."

"Me?" He put a hand to his chest. "I was an angel."

"Uh-huh."

"Well, aside from the time my brother and I took our dad's car out joyriding."

"Oh really?" I folded my arms on the edge of the table and leaned closer. "How did that turn out?"

"It went fine until we ran out of gas. *Then* we were fucked." He sipped his drink. "This tow truck driver pulled over to see if we were all right, and it turned out to be one of my dad's friends." Diego grimaced. "You want trouble? *That* was trouble."

I snorted. "So much for a perfect angel, right?"

He shrugged, grinning mischievously. "I didn't say I was a *perfect* angel. But at least I wasn't getting bitten by poisonous things I was teasing."

"Hey, don't judge me."

We both laughed, and just like we had over coffee in my kitchen and at this same café yesterday, we lost ourselves in conversation. It wasn't until long after we'd eaten and a waitress came up to the table that I realized how long we'd actually been here.

"Can I get you gentlemen anything else?" There was a subtle note of impatience in the question. Some thinly veiled encouragement to *not* ask for anything else.

I checked my phone. "Holy shit. It's almost midnight?"

"No way." Diego looked at his phone too, and his eyes widened. "Oh. It is."

We apologized profusely for overstaying and tipped her almost forty percent for having occupied a table for so long. She locked the door behind us and flipped the cheery *Open* sign over to *Sorry We're Closed*.

Diego looked back at the sign and grimaced. "Poor lady. She probably wanted to go home an hour ago."

"I know. We'll have to keep better track of time if we do this again."

He met my gaze. "Are we doing this again?"

I moistened my lips. "You tell me."

"We could. It's fun, right?"

"Yeah, it is." *Especially the part that usually comes after.*

"So, sure." He used my belt to tug me closer. "And there's also the game coming up."

"There is. But do you really want to watch that with me?" I smirked. "Because I *will* rub it in when the Eagles lose."

Diego returned the smirk. He leaned in like he was going to kiss me, but he snapped his teeth instead, making me jump. "Haven't you learned not to tease wild animals?"

"If a rattlesnake and a scorpion didn't teach me, what makes you think you will?" I couldn't resist a long kiss. He didn't object. As the kiss went on, I held him tighter against me. God, he was addictive. "Shame we stayed here so late." I held him firmly against me. "I was looking forward to taking you home."

He smiled, sliding his hands up my chest. "Just means you'll want me that much more when you do get me into bed."

"Fuck yeah, I will," I growled as I moved in for a kiss. His lips were still curved into that smile, but they quickly relaxed against mine, and the conversation seemed like it had happened ages ago. I cupped the back of his neck, and we stood there for the longest time, just letting the kiss be its own thing. Not foreplay. Not a promise of more. Not a tease. Just lips and tongues and two men getting completely lost in a long, sexy moment.

When we broke the kiss, his eyelids were heavy, and his smile was adorable with his slightly swollen lips.

"You know, since I've got that off weekend coming up . . ." He actually sounded a little shy as he asked, "Maybe we could do something. Go down to Flatstick and dance at a club where I don't have to work."

The thought of him out on a dance floor made my head spin.

I quirked my lips, pretending to give it some thought. "That could be fun."

He grinned, sliding his hands into my back pockets. "Uh-huh. Dance a bit. Fool around. Not have to worry about coworkers."

"Mmm, I like that idea. Maybe we could get a room too."

Instantly, Diego went rigid. He shook his head. "No."

"What? Why not?"

"I . . ." His cheeks colored. "It's . . . Payday is still a ways off, you know?"

I waved a hand. "I'll cover it. I want—"

"No," he said sharply. "If we're going to do this, we're splitting it. I am not mooching off you."

"Mooching?" I shook my head. "No, no. It's—"

"We split it." His tone didn't offer any room for debate.

"Okay. Okay. I'm fine with that. I just want us to be able to relax that night without worrying about getting all the way back to Anchor Point."

Diego's jaw tightened. "That shit can get expensive, you know? And I mean, even this . . ." He gestured at the café and avoided my eyes. "I can't do it very often. I, uh, really shouldn't even be doing it this much. Twice in one week."

I touched his chin and lifted it so he was looking in my eyes. "Don't worry about it. If you don't want to go, we don't have to. Or going to dinner. Any of it. I don't mind staying in."

His lips tightened, and he sighed. "I do want to go out. And I like the idea of staying in Flatstick, as long as it's one night. I just . . . don't want to mooch off you."

"You're not."

"Still." Diego swallowed. "Let's just stay someplace cheap, all right? I'll feel like an ass if it's something extravagant."

"We don't need anything fancy." I gave his ass a playful squeeze. "Just a place to sleep and fuck."

That seemed to shake some of the tension out of him, and he grinned as he leaned into me. "I love the sound of that."

"Me too. So, on your off weekend, Saturday night in Flatstick, then watch the game on Sunday?"

"Sounds perfect."

"Good. And I'm sure we can think of something to do between now and then."

"Mmm, I think we can." He kissed me again, and I let it linger because why the hell not? Yeah, when I went to work in five hours, I'd be a bleary-eyed mess, but this evening had been worth whatever penance came my way. And yeah, I'd be chugging down coffee, struggling to stay awake, and my brain would probably be all over the place, but if that was the price for a long, perfect dinner with Diego? Fine.

And in a couple of weeks, I'd have him for a night of dancing and an afternoon of football.

I could *not* wait.

CHAPTER 8
DIEGO

I t was a wonder I could function. I'd met Mark over a week ago and wound up in his bed almost every night after work. Neither of us was getting a lot of sleep, but he hadn't suggested slowing down and I wasn't bringing it up either.

It helped that I wasn't at the bar until two or three *every* morning. The High-&-Tight closed at eleven on weeknights, so I was usually out of there by midnight. Mark sometimes slept for a few hours after he got home from work so he could stay up late enough to see me. I felt kind of guilty about it—if he was half as tired as I was, getting up at six in the morning must've been killing him. Whenever he had to be on the boat early and had to get up at five? Jesus.

Thank God he didn't mind me sticking around after he'd gone to work. The first few mornings, I'd left with him, but a week into it, he'd murmured, "Just lock the door on your way out," and he'd been gone. Fine by me.

Today was a Monday morning, and after I'd rolled out of Mark's bed, showered, and poured myself some coffee in his empty kitchen, I texted Dalton.

You busy today?

Never too busy for you, baby. ;)

I laughed. We'd broken up forever ago but still jokingly flirted. Fortunately, his husband didn't mind.

I'd never been friends with an ex-boyfriend before, but Dalton? He was something else. Maybe because our relationship had never really gone anywhere, so we'd never really had a chance to piss each other off. He was military. I wanted casual sex, and he wasn't into it. So I'd told him, anyway. Truth was, I'd started falling for him, and fast, and it had spooked me. I'd said I needed to keep it casual, and he hadn't been interested. We'd just cooled it and stayed friends. Well, aside from that one hookup last New Year's Eve, which had been fucking *hot*. It hadn't made things weird, thank God, and as of *very* recently, he was happily married to Chris, who he'd been in love with even before we'd started fooling around.

Today, like a lot of days, I went over to his place to hang out until we both had to go to work. As Dalton pulled a couple of sodas out of the fridge, he said, "So, Chris and I are having a wedding reception at the end of January."

"What?" I laughed. "Eloping wasn't good enough after all?"

"Our *parents* decided it wasn't good enough." He groaned. "I mean, we explained why we did it. They get it—if we wanted to be stationed together when we got our new orders, we needed to get married sooner than later. But then we're probably going overseas, and suddenly they're freaking out like we need this giant send-off, and somehow that turned into a wedding reception." He rolled his eyes. "So, our families are flying in, and we're . . . going through the motions like we aren't already married." He paused, brow pinched. "You, uh, want to come? If you don't, it's fine, I—"

"Shut up, pendejo." I squeezed his arm. "Of course I want to come. When and where?"

"Don't know yet. We're still figuring everything out. Sometime at the end of January, that's all I know."

I nodded. "Just let me know when you've got a date so I can make sure Hank lets me off."

"I will." He smiled. "And thanks. It'll be good to have you there."

I huffed. "Like there's any question. After pulling last-second witness duty when you eloped, there better be some fucking cake in my future."

Dalton laughed and elbowed me. "Okay, fine. I guess you can have some cake."

I just chuckled. I teased him about owing me for being one of their witnesses when they'd gotten married on three days' notice, but I'd been honored to do it. And yeah, it had hurt a bit, watching another man slide a ring onto Dalton's finger.

Standing there, watching him exchange rings and vows with Chris, I'd done some serious thinking about my "no military men" policy. I hadn't been willing to make an exception for Dalton, and that said a lot. Dalton was a guy I could have fallen hard for. Hard enough that I'd been jealous as fuck when he and Chris had started dating, because I'd known without a doubt I'd missed any chance I'd ever had.

"So what's going on with you?" he asked. "You still fucking that guy? The one from the club?"

I nodded.

"Yeah?" Dalton grinned. "How are things going with him?"

"They're . . ." I swallowed. "They're going really well."

He inclined his head. "You don't sound happy about that."

"I'm, uh . . . nervous about it."

"Yeah?" Dalton held my gaze. "Why's that?"

"Besides the fact that he's a Cardinals fan?"

Dalton snorted. "Yeah. *Besides* that."

"He's military." I shook my head. "I can't fucking *do* that."

"But you *are* doing it."

I shot him a glare.

Dalton put up his hands. "Hey, I'm just saying. You've been hooking up with him for, what, a week?"

I rolled my eyes. "Yes. Hooking up. We're just fucking."

"Uh-huh." Dalton sighed. "Look, I totally get it. If the Navy had fucked me over as much as it fucked you over, I wouldn't want to be anywhere near it either. But if this guy's in the Navy and he's still got you on the hook like this?" He shrugged. "Maybe there's something there, you know? Even if it's just sex right now, there's obviously some chemistry if you keep going back for more."

Chewing my lip, I stared into my soda. He had a point. "So it probably won't help if I say we're going to Flatstick this weekend. Overnight."

He chuckled and patted my leg. "No. It doesn't help." He turned serious. "Like I said, I get why you're iffy about him. But as much as you've already lost because of the Navy, don't let this guy be another casualty. If you guys really do turn out to be a good match, and you've really got a connection with him? Especially if you're willing to bend your own rule about dating military guys?" Dalton looked me right in the eyes. "Don't be a fucking idiot about it."

"In other words, *break* my rule."

"Exactly. If he really is your type and he really does push your buttons like you say he does?" He gave my leg a gentle squeeze. "Don't be stupid."

Lowering my gaze, I nodded slowly. It actually annoyed the fuck out of me that Mark was my type. That he hit all the right buttons. I hated that the only thing I could find wrong with him was that he was in the Navy. It was a lot harder to say that was a deal breaker when everything else about the man was so close to perfect.

And I remembered all too well what had happened last time I'd bent—but refused to break—my rule. I'd let things go too far emotionally with Dalton, and we'd broken up before we got in over our heads. Except the deep, burning regret I'd had afterward told me I'd already been in over my head, and letting go of him had been a mistake.

I wasn't pining after Dalton anymore. I was glad he had Chris, and I knew they'd be happy together. Sometimes, though, I caught myself wondering if he was the one who got away. If I'd let something special slip through my fingers.

Maybe Mark was another shot at getting it right.

If I could get past all my own shit with the Navy.

I always looked forward to my one weekend off a month, but never like this. Usually I'd spend it with Dalton—and Chris if he wasn't at work—or just be lazy. If there was football on, I'd watch it at home.

Tomorrow, I'd be watching the game on Mark's impressive big-screen.

Tonight, we were going out dancing. I couldn't even remember the last time someone had wanted to go dancing. When I was in my twenties, yeah. As I crawled through my thirties, the men I'd dated hadn't really been into that scene. And I could do without it, but some nights, it was just fun to cut loose under some disco lights, especially if I was with someone who liked it too.

It wasn't that I didn't like going to clubs to meet guys. My pickup game wasn't bad, and I'd had some seriously hot hookups in men's rooms, parking lots, and strangers' beds, but the thrill of the hunt got old. Sometimes I liked dancing to relax, and it was not relaxing to be concentrating on picking up a guy. I liked going to the club with the same man I'd be going to bed with later. That way I could enjoy the dancing instead of concentrating on getting someone's attention.

At least we were staying someplace cheap tonight, and Mark hadn't pushed about why money was so tight. It had been bad enough admitting I lived paycheck to paltry paycheck, but it was less embarrassing than admitting I didn't technically *get* a paycheck. Just tips. Those details could come out later if we kept doing this.

Mark volunteered to drive too, and I didn't argue. My piece-of-shit truck ran most of the time, but whenever I took it more than fifty miles out of town, I'd spend the whole trip back praying it wouldn't crap out on the side of the road. The only thing I had to worry about this time was if I could add a few gallons of gas to what I'd already budgeted for the weekend.

Fuck it, I decided before we'd even left the Anchor Point city limits. I hadn't spent too much recently—aside from a couple of indulgent visits to the café—and I hadn't been out to have a good time in ages. As long as we didn't do this every weekend I had off, I'd be fine.

The passenger seat of his Lexus was cushy and comfortable, and there was a ton of room to stretch out my legs. Awesome. Especially since there was already a twinge in my knee letting me know I'd be limping tomorrow if I danced tonight. And I was dancing tonight.

On the way out of town, Mark asked, "So you've been to the clubs down there?"

I nodded. "I don't go very often, but yeah."

"You don't get tired of it?" He glanced at me. "After you spend hours on end at the High-&-Tight?"

"It's not really the same scene. And I'm having fun instead of working."

"True. I'm surprised working there doesn't make you turn up your nose at clubs, though." He rested his elbow on the console and his other hand on top of the wheel. "When I worked at Burger King as a kid, I couldn't go near *any* fast food chain."

"Yeah, but clubs don't smell like fry grease."

"Fair point."

I watched him for a moment. "Why can't I picture you flipping burgers?"

Mark laughed. "I did it for three years. Took me almost ten to be able to *eat* a burger again."

I grimaced and shuddered. "No, thanks."

"Yeah, it wasn't fun. But I was a teenager, so . . ." He shrugged.

We drove on in silence for a minute or two before I said, "How do you like Anchor Point so far?"

"No complaints so far. Not like I've seen very much of it yet. Just the base, the High-&-Tight, and . . . you." He glanced at me and grinned. "So like I said, no complaints."

"Hey, you have plenty of time to explore the town between when you get off work and when I do."

"Uh-huh. Except that's the time I have to use for menial things like grocery shopping, cleaning the house, and doing laundry."

I waved a hand. "Those aren't important."

"Of course they're not. Eh, I'll get out and explore it eventually. I'm probably going to be here a while."

"Yeah? How long?"

"Don't know. The boat just moved here, so it's not going anywhere. Well, besides deploying. It's not going to a new home port, I mean. And if the upper chain of command gets shuffled around again, the rear admiral will probably blow a gasket. So, I could probably stay here until I retire."

That piqued my interest even as I tried not to get twitchy over the conversation turning to the military. "When do you think you'll retire?"

"Oh hell, I have no idea. Three months ago, I was going to retire next year. Now . . ." He shook his head. "I'm still getting my bearings now, so I haven't really thought about it. But since I just made rank, there's no point in retiring until I've been in long enough to retire at captain's pay instead of commander's. And if I stick around three or four years for that, I might as well stick it out for ten and retire at thirty."

I fought to keep my disappointment from showing. Ten more years? Jesus. "And you might stay in Anchor Point that whole time?"

"Maybe."

I wasn't sure what to say. I didn't know why I bothered feeling disappointed. The man had just put on captain and uprooted his life to come here. Of course he wasn't retiring anytime soon. And staying until thirty meant three-quarter retirement pay instead of half. Sounded like a no-brainer to me.

Must be nice to have the opportunity to stay in that long.

I bit back my own bitterness. None of my situation was Mark's fault. I was happy he'd been successful in the Navy, and he deserved whatever retirement he eventually took.

It was Mark's turn to break the silence. "So, what's the plan when we get to Flatstick?"

"Check into the room, right?"

"I mean after that."

"Probably get dinner or something." I grinned. "Then we dance, we fuck like bunnies, and we go back to your place so we can watch my Eagles crush your Cardinals."

He smirked. "Uh-huh. We'll see about that." He put his hand on my thigh and ran his thumb along the outer seam of my jeans. "You have a Sunday off, and it's the Sunday our teams play each other." He glanced at me. "Kinda sounds like we're meant to watch that game together."

I laughed. "Almost like divine intervention."

"Almost, yeah." He cut his eyes toward me. "And come Sunday, you and your Eagles are gonna *need* some divine intervention."

"Oh, ha ha. Fuck you."

We exchanged glances, and I elbowed him.

Divine intervention. Pfft. We'd see about that.

We pulled into Flatstick around seven. The row of clubs was at the outer edge of town, but we didn't head there quite yet. Instead, he

drove us closer to the beach, where the tourists usually clustered. I'd made him promise to get someplace cheap, and my gut clenched every time we went near something that might be expensive.

Then he parked in front of what looked like an old house. Victorian, maybe?

Flatstick Bed & Breakfast.

"A B&B?" I asked. I could almost feel my budget going up in smoke.

"Believe it or not," Mark said as he turned off the engine, "this was the cheapest place in town." He paused. "Well, aside from the two motels that had multiple TripAdvisor reviews mentioning black mold."

I grimaced. Okay, I could accept skipping the cheapest places if they had mold problems. "But this isn't *really* expensive, is it?"

"No, not at all." He smiled. "I promise, it isn't." He nodded toward the building. "And breakfast is included, so why not?"

I looked up at the big, extravagant house, and my panic slowly receded. "Okay, fair enough."

He patted my leg. "Come on. Let's go check in."

Our room was so cutesy it made my teeth hurt. There was a giant lace doily on the table by the door with a pastel-pink vase full of pastel-pink flowers, which matched the pastel-pink walls, comforter, and picture frames. The sheer pinkness of the place probably scared off any black mold that tried to show up.

Mark put his bag on the bed. "I'm almost afraid to fuck in here."

I looked at him, eyes wide. "What? Why?"

He smirked. "Kind of feels like screwing in my grandma's house."

"What? You've never screwed in your grandma's house?"

Mark shot me a horrified look. "Have you?"

"Not in your grandma's house, no."

The longer he stared at me, the harder it was to keep a straight face. When my lip twitched, he rolled his eyes, and we both laughed.

"You're a dork," he said.

I just chuckled and dropped my overnight bag beside his on the bed. "Should we get ready to go out?"

Mark checked the time on his phone. "Want to get dinner first?"

"Good idea."

After a light dinner in town, we came back to the pink palace and started getting ready to go to the club. We didn't dare shower together or we'd never leave the room, and I wanted to get Mark spun up on the dance floor before we wound up in bed together.

I took a shower, and while he took his, I pulled on a pair of boxers. Before I got dressed, though, I took the black knee brace out of my overnight bag. I scowled at the thing. It wasn't all that comfortable, but it beat the alternative.

I wasn't fast enough. Before I'd put my jeans on, Mark stepped out of the bathroom, and his gaze went straight to the black nylon wrapped around my knee. Concern instantly creased his forehead. "Leg bothering you?"

"Not as long as I wear this, no." I smoothed a Velcro strap into place. "This and some Motrin, and I'll be good for the night." That wasn't entirely true. It was already aching, and it would be throbbing like a bitch by the time we left the club. The brace and the ibuprofen would just keep it bearable.

And then I noticed the question in his eyes. Oh shit.

"It's just an old injury," I said quickly. "Standing all the time at work aggravates it. That's all."

"You're still okay going out, though?" He searched my eyes. "If you want to take it easy tonight, we—"

I kissed him and, for good measure, squeezed his ass through the thin towel he was wearing. He whimpered softly against my lips.

"I want to go out," I purred, "and then we're going to come back here so I can fuck you." I nipped his lower lip. "My knee can handle it. Question is—can you?"

Mark shivered hard. "Oh yeah. I can handle it."

"Mm-hmm. Prove it."

"Let me finish getting ready," he murmured against my lips, "and I will."

CHAPTER 9

MARK

The club was darker than the High-&-Tight. Disco lights threw bright colors over every surface, but that was about it besides the backlit bottles glowing behind the bar.

This place was bigger and definitely more crowded too. Diego had said something about people coming from as far as Salem and Portland to dance here, which was crazy since Portland had its own thriving gay scene. On the other hand, I supposed it was a good place to go if someone wanted to dance and hook up but wasn't out in their own town. Either way, the club was crawling with people and it wasn't even nine o'clock yet.

"So." Diego turned to me, multicolored lights fluttering over his features. "Want to do a shot before we hit the dance floor?"

"Just one," I said. "Or I really will hit the floor."

He laughed as he snaked an arm around my waist. "You're not that much of a lightweight, are you?"

"Depends on what we're shooting."

"So, no tequila?"

"*No.*"

He flashed a grin, teeth lighting up under the black lights and giving him an almost demonic look. "Come on." He tugged me with him. "And I promise, no tequila."

At the bar, he shouted an order over the music. I couldn't hear him, but the bartender arranged a pair of shot glasses on the bar and started filling them with rum and a couple of colorful liqueurs I couldn't identify.

Diego paid for the shots—he'd insisted on the way here—and handed one to me. He clinked the tiny glass against mine, gave me a loaded wink, and pounded the shot. I hesitated, not because I didn't want the drink but because I was too mesmerized by him to remember what to do with it. It came to me, though, and I threw mine back, grimacing at the intense burn. There was a mix of flavors—mostly sweet with a hint of something spicy—but it went down too fast for me to catch more than the alcohol taste.

"What the fuck was that?" I asked, eyeing my empty glass.

"A Portland Pounder."

"And that is . . . ?"

Diego winked. "Booze. What more do you want?"

"Fair point."

"Should we do another? And then . . .?" He nodded toward the dance floor.

I grinned. "Let's do it."

We did one more round of shots, and then Diego led me by the hand out onto the dance floor. And just like that, we were dancing.

Okay, I was *trying* to dance. I hadn't done this in years, but that wasn't why I struggled to coordinate my body to the beat. It was this man in front of me.

He moved easily and fluidly in time with the music. There wasn't an ounce of self-consciousness in his movements or his expression, and even without the black lights making his teeth glow, his broad smile would have lit up the whole room.

I hadn't noticed until it was gone, but most of the time, Diego carried a lot of stress and worry in his face. Deep crevices. Visible tension. The tightness of his jaw. The creases in his forehead.

Right now, all that was gone. Maybe it was the music, or maybe it was that shot he'd done at the bar. Whatever it was, I didn't want it to stop. Not tonight. Not ever.

Tell me what it takes to make you smile like this, and I'll do it forever.

I didn't care that it was ridiculous to think about things like *forever* when I barely knew him and my divorce was still in the works. When I was in no position to think beyond next week. And really, I *wasn't* thinking about forever. Not the real forever. Just the kind of forever that seemed possible when I was happy and high and couldn't help wishing the night would never end. When it didn't matter that drinking, dancing, and partying weren't things that could be sustained for more than a few hours, especially after the age of forty. By the time the sun came up, I'd be passed out and sleeping like the dead, but right now, I was ten feet tall and bulletproof, and how long had it been since I'd felt like this?

Diego danced closer, gave me a wink, and then turned his back. For a few flickers of the disco lights, I was disappointed I couldn't see his face anymore, but then he was against me. Leaning into me. Moving with me. Before I knew what was happening, my hands were on his hips. Almost in his front pockets. Suddenly I had no trouble keeping time with the music. Diego was like a conduit between me and the speakers—the rhythm flowed like electricity from his body to mine, and we ground and rubbed, and my head spun as the music carried us away.

It wasn't like some pantomime of when we had sex. This was totally different. Here, in our clothes on the dance floor, orgasms were off the table. There was nothing to do but move together and absorb each other's body heat. Oh, I'd be making him come later on, but right now, it was all about how in sync we were. How our bodies just seemed to fit together and move together and—

Okay, maybe it was a *little* like when we were in bed. But different too. Unique and familiar, and hot either way. It didn't matter. It was hot, and it was addictive, and *how are you here with* me *of all people?*

Diego tilted his head back, and his lips brushed my cheek as he said over the music, "You know, I think we're the oldest guys here."

I scanned the room, and . . . yeah. I was pretty sure he was right. At least half this crowd probably still thought thirty was old.

It didn't make me self-conscious, though. So what if we didn't blend in? We'd come here to dance, and I'd all but forgotten there was anyone here at all until Diego'd said something. Hell, I didn't care if everyone here was half our age. Diego and I might have been old men a little to the right and left of forty, but we could still hold our own. We'd still be fucking like rabbits when we made it back to our hotel. The younger guys could have each other—my libido was completely focused on *him*.

A few songs later, we took a break and found a table near the edge of the room. I pretended not to notice Diego limping slightly, and he didn't seem to notice me gingerly rubbing the small of my back.

"I'll go get us some water," he panted. "Be right back."

I was about to stop him and suggest I go so he could rest his leg, but he was already gone. I watched him on his way to the bar. His limp wasn't as pronounced as I'd thought. In fact, I was pretty sure it was less out of pain and more because of the restrictive brace he was wearing under his jeans. I just hoped it was keeping the joint stable and his knee didn't ruin his evening.

At the bar, Diego had barely flagged down the bartender before a twentysomething blond sidled up to him with a grin. From the way he smiled while he talked, he was obviously flirting. Diego seemed like he was being polite even as he shook his head. The *come on, are you sure?* was unmistakable, but Diego shook his head again and nodded toward me. As he did, I swore his mouth formed the word *boyfriend.*

My heart fluttered as the blond's shoulders sank. With a sheepish smile, he bowed out and backed off, but not before throwing me an expression that said *my bad.*

I gave him a nod and pretended my pulse wasn't soaring. I knew it hadn't actually meant anything. Diego had simply used the most efficient means of fending off the blond. Still, it made me hotter than the dancing had. It tripped that same sense of possessiveness I'd had when I'd smelled my familiar soap on him. It wasn't a feeling like I'd throttle anyone who hit on him. More like a swell of pride.

Yeah, that's right. He's with me.

I suddenly needed to take him out of here. Back to the hotel. Out of his clothes.

He wanted to dance, though. He was having a good time, and anyway, I loved watching him in this light. I loved how the colors glittered in his dark eyes and across the sheen of sweat at his hairline, occasionally hitting just right to light up one of his more prominent scars. He was the sexiest man in this room by far, and who was I to tell him we were done dancing?

So after he'd come back to the table, and we'd caught our breath and cooled off with some water, I was the one who led him back out to the dance floor.

And we danced.

CHAPTER 10

DIEGO

The cab driver dropped us at the B&B, and he didn't make eye contact with me while I paid him. He'd avoided looking at us the entire ten-minute drive. I didn't care, though. Most nights, the homophobia radiating off him would've made my teeth grind, but I'd been too busy teasing Mark with a hand on his leg to get worked up over an asshole cabbie.

While the cab drove off, Mark unlocked our room. I ignored the lace and flowers and *so* much pink, and went straight to kissing and groping him. Clothes kind of started to come off, but neither of us was in a hurry. After a long night of dancing with him, I had him all to myself for the *rest* of the night—why rush?

Mark rolled on top of me, playfully pinning me down, and we kissed in between laughing like a couple of teenagers. I hadn't had that much to drink, and I'd eaten before we'd gone to the club. So why the hell did I feel this drunk?

Barely breaking the kiss, he murmured, "Think anyone noticed there were two old guys in the club?"

I snorted. "Hey. Speak for yourself."

"Oh come on. You're not that much younger than me." He lifted his head and tapped the middle of my chest. "And *you're* the one who pointed out we were the oldest guys there."

"Yeah, but just because we're older than the twenty-two-year-olds doesn't make us *old*." I grinned. "I've still got a few months before I turn forty. I'm not calling myself old until then."

Mark groaned and rolled his eyes. "Okay, that's fair. Especially since that's the day everything starts going downhill."

"Isn't that why they call it being 'over the hill'?"

"Well, yeah. They just don't bother to tell you that you wake up that morning with cataracts and gray pubes."

I laughed louder than I should have. "Come on. You don't have *that* much gray down there."

"What?" he yelped. "I really *do* have gray?"

"I don't know." I shrugged. "I usually have your dick down my throat, so it's not like I really count them or anything."

He chuckled, leaning in to kiss my neck. "If that keeps you distracted from my grays . . ."

"Are you kidding? It keeps me distracted from almost anything."

He murmured something I didn't understand, and before I could ask him to repeat it, his stubble scraped my collarbone and made me shiver hard enough to forget he'd spoken at all.

I pushed him onto his back and started to get on top, but as I did, pain shot through my knee. I gasped, glancing down like it might offer up some explanation for being a pendejo right now of all times, and the black brace seemed to glare back up at me.

Mark trailed a hand down my back. "You okay?"

"Yeah." I met his gaze. "Listen, uh, you don't mind if I leave the brace on, do you?"

He blinked. "No, of course not. I just want everything *else* off."

"This won't get in the way?"

"Not unless you were planning on having me suck your knee or something."

I burst out laughing. "No, that wasn't what I had in mind."

Mark grinned, moving in closer. "Well, I guess it won't get in the way, will it?"

And then he kissed me, and neither of us mentioned my brace again.

As drunk as I'd felt when we'd come back to the room last night, my head barely throbbed in the morning. There was some subtle thumping around my temples, but it wasn't bad. Made sense—I didn't think I'd had that much to drink.

I'd taken off the knee brace sometime between screwing Mark and joining him in the shower. It had been too sweaty and gross to put back on, but I was paying for it now. Gritting my teeth, I massaged the sore joint and muscles. If that was the worst thing from last night, though, I was happy.

Aside from the nightmares, anyway.

Damn it, I'd been doing so well. That was one of the many shitty parts of PTSD—sometimes it reared its head for no apparent reason. Nothing in particular had triggered me. Nothing had brought back the memories of being in combat. My subconscious had apparently just decided I needed to spend the night in the desert.

I shuddered, hoping Mark didn't notice. I hoped like hell he hadn't noticed last night's dreams, either. I didn't think he had. The times I'd woken up, he'd been dead asleep. Lucky bastard.

Rolling my shoulders, I shook the lingering fear and jitteriness away. At least the nightmares were relatively rare—one of the few ways I'd lucked out with this whole postcombat thing.

I got up to grab another shower and brush my teeth. Mark wasn't too far behind me, so of course we wound up tumbling back into bed together. Before long, we were sprawled on the pink bed, surrounded by rumpled pink sheets, and both grinning like idiots.

"I knew this was a good idea," he slurred.

"Uh-huh." I licked my lips. "Really good idea."

"So, would it be too soon to suggest doing it again?"

"Um." I cleared my throat. "Depends. Do you mean dancing? Or going out of town?" *And spending money . . . and getting closer to each other . . .*

He shifted onto his side, and as I mirrored him, he said, "I don't know. I'm, uh, kind of new to the dating scene, but you said you're not into military guys." With a shrug and an uneasy smile, he added, "Can't blame a man for wanting more of what we've been doing, including last night, right?"

"That's true. I guess I can't." Especially since I wanted it too. I didn't *want* to want it, but I did.

He absently played with the edge of the pink comforter like he just needed to do something with his hands. "Look, I have no idea what we're doing, but I think I should be upfront about a few things."

Something tightened in the pit of my stomach, and I didn't know if it was dread over what he was about to tell me or the fact that we were having the *where is this going?* conversation. Was this the part where he tactfully—maybe—told me he was in the closet, and that we had to be discreet when we were in town because he couldn't risk people knowing he was fucking a man? Never mind a bartender with an accent that said *I stole an American job* to people?

Wonder what he'd think if he knew I didn't have a green card.

But I tamped down that comment and all the bitterness that went with it. As neutrally as I could, I said, "Okay?"

Mark took a deep breath. "If we're just fucking, that's okay. I'm... I'm totally okay with that." He paused, and when he spoke again, he looked at me across the narrow stretch of painfully pink sheets. "But if we decide to do more than that, now's probably a good time to let you know I am terrible at relationships."

A laugh jumped out of me before I could stop it. He eyed me as if that was the last reaction he'd expected. Which was fair. And how the hell did I explain I was relieved that *that* had been his deep dark secret?

I shook my head. "I guess I thought you were going to drop some kind of bomb."

He looked almost offended. "It kind of is, isn't it?"

"Not really." When his expression didn't change, I put a hand over his. "We obviously both suck at relationships, or we wouldn't be single, right?"

His lips quirked, and he shrugged. "Okay, maybe. But I just came out of a very long and very fucked-up marriage, and I'm not feeling all that confident about whatever comes next. Sex? Got it. The rest?" He wobbled his hand in the air. "Not so much."

I fought the urge to squirm uncomfortably. There shouldn't have been anything beyond this. A couple of nights of sex, some coffee, and gone. The fact that we were still doing this—that he wanted to have this conversation, and that we were doing it in a bed and breakfast room—all that should've had klaxons blaring and me running out the door. But it didn't.

"I don't know what we're doing. Or if there's even any point in talking about it right now. I just don't want to *stop* what we're doing, you know? So I guess . . . I guess I'm saying I'm open to seeing what happens."

I chewed on the words for a minute, then nodded. "Yeah. Me too."

"Even if I'm military?"

My whole body tried to tense up, and my stomach clenched around the bitterness I really needed to learn to let go of before I lost another man to the Navy.

"It's your call," he said. "If you want to keep it to sex, then we can. If you want more, I'm game. Just tell me what you need. I'm perfectly happy with not talking about work anyway, and I won't ask you to come to any functions with me." He shrugged. "Whatever you need."

Stop being so fucking amazing.

"Okay, I can . . . That works. But I also, um . . ." My face burned. "Look, I know how the pay scales work. I know you make a fuck-load more money than I do. But I mean, I really don't have much. I'm just barely making it. So—"

"So you think it's going to bother me?"

"I think you might get tired of not doing much outside the bedroom because I can't afford it." I paused and sharply added, "And having you pay for me isn't an option."

"I'm not going to get tired of staying in." He cupped my face and kissed me tenderly, letting it go on for a few long seconds. Then he whispered, "I just want to be with you."

I chewed my lip. "Okay. I just don't want to spend your money, and I *can't* spend mine."

Mark nodded. "I'm good with that. And there's plenty we can do without spending anything." A cautious smirk tugged at one corner of his mouth. "Unless you're one of those people who doesn't like long walks on the beach."

I couldn't help laughing. "Maybe when the weather warms up."

"Deal." He kissed me again.

"When the weather warms up"? That's . . . months from now.

The thought of us still doing this a few months from now was surprisingly not panic inducing. In fact, I liked the idea. I really did. Probably a lot more than I should have.

Well, nothing ventured, nothing gained.

Nothing except a hell of a lot of heartbreak, if my past was any indication.

Taking this beyond a one-night stand to most of a weekend had been pushing it. Hooking up the second, third, twelfth times had been playing with fire, and I'd known it. Taking off for a weekend and cuddling under the covers in a room that had clearly been intended for honeymooners? Probably not smart.

But we'd done it. We were here. And I had a gut feeling that if I kept letting myself be this close to him, I'd *get* close to him. Not necessarily fall for him, but I could see myself wanting more than his dick. Hell, maybe I was just feeling echoes of the way things had been when I'd hooked up with Dalton. When we'd thrown ourselves in headfirst and let things go further than I could handle. The time I'd spent with Mark was enough to know I liked sleeping with him. In fact, I liked doing things that I wasn't supposed to want as long as he was on active duty.

Except what if I missed out on something good?

What if he was onto something, just being open to seeing what happened?

Christ. What do I do?

I knew damn well I was hesitating because calling things off with Dalton had hurt so bad. He'd been exactly the kind of guy I could have been with for the long haul, but I couldn't get over the Navy. I just couldn't. Not when I lived every day of my life with the damage it had done. At the same time, though, breaking up with him had been like handing the Navy another victory. Another piece of my life that wasn't mine anymore. I didn't want to do that again.

But *then* Dalton had nearly been killed during a patrol boat accident, and his chain of command had almost fucked him out of his career in the name of saving someone else's good name. It had been like salt in the wound, watching someone I loved getting treated that way by the same Navy that had chewed me up and spat me out. If I'd had any doubts at all about my ability to coexist with the military, they'd gone up in smoke the moment those assholes had started putting Dalton through that wringer.

After all of that, I *still* couldn't make myself pull away from Mark. Even now, I couldn't. I didn't want to.

I shouldn't have been open to it. He was military.

But as it always did, that memory surfaced of Dalton leaving for the last time.

So do I give it a shot? Or do I let the Navy win again?

I looked in Mark's eyes. He was Navy. Career fucking Navy. And I just kept on coming back.

Why can't I say no to you?

When he smiled, the warmth spreading through me was almost enough to negate the twisting in my stomach.

Fuck. I know why I can't say no to you.

Because I don't want to.

Mark trailed his fingertips down the middle of my chest. "We should go get breakfast. It's supposed to be really good here."

"Mmm, I like the sound of that." I craned my neck to look at the old alarm clock beside the bed. "We have time to eat before we go home for the game?"

"Kickoff isn't until one." He pressed his lips to the base of my neck. "We've got time."

"For breakfast *and* the drive?"

"And then some." From the way his hand was drifting lower, breakfast could wait.

I didn't protest at all. I was pretty sure we'd make it home in time for kickoff.

Barely.

CHAPTER 11
MARK

As it turned out, we made it home in plenty of time.

Diego had put on a faded Eagles jersey. I had my well-worn Cardinals jersey. As we wrangled snacks in the kitchen and waited for our pizza, we eyed each other, but we both chuckled. I had no doubt there'd be some serious trash-talking by the end of the day, especially after the Cardinals stomped all over the Eagles.

While we were getting situated in the living room, Diego pulled some ibuprofen out of his pocket and washed it down with his beer.

"Knee?" I asked.

He shrugged. "It happens. Especially after four nights in a row at the bar and one at a dance club."

I grimaced.

"I'm fine." He put his hand on my thigh and kissed me lightly. "I mean, I *am* going to be sitting on my ass for a few hours."

"Fair enough." I tugged him closer by the front of his jersey. "After your boys lose, I'll make sure you forget how much it hurts."

Leaning in for a kiss, Diego murmured, "Why do I get the feeling you'd just rub it in?"

I laughed even as I lifted my chin for that kiss. Then we exchanged grins, clinked our beer bottles together, and settled in for kickoff.

The game turned out to be one of those that tested a man's cardiovascular health. Halfway through the first quarter, we were both literally on the edge of our seats, cursing and shouting as our teams battled it out. Both sides were playing really well and really badly, with mind-blowing plays and jaw-dropping fuckups coming from all directions. By the end of the half, the score was tied and we were out of breath and sweating.

"Jesus." I flopped back against the couch as the teams dispersed for halftime. "What the fuck?"

"You know," Diego mused into his beer bottle, "if your boys hadn't fucked up that fourth down, you'd be ahead."

I shot him a glare. "Yeah? And what about that fumble right before the two-minute warning?"

He wrinkled his nose, muttered something, and took a deep swallow.

"That's what I thought."

He rolled his eyes and flipped me the bird.

Still laughing, I got up to get another bag of Doritos. On my way back to the couch, I paused to stare at Diego as he lounged, one leg propped on the coffee table and the other canted to the side. He caught me and furrowed his brow. "What?"

"Nothing." I shrugged as I continued toward him. "Just thinking how perfect you'd look like that if it weren't for . . ." I wrinkled my nose and gestured at his shirt with one of the beer bottles. "*That.*"

Diego rolled his eyes again and snatched the bag of chips from my hand.

Something must've happened in the locker room during halftime, because the Cardinals had their shit together now. By the start of the fourth quarter, my boys were up by ten.

Beside me, Diego swore into his beer bottle as the spectators roared their approval of a field goal. Shortly after that, they were well on their way to another touchdown.

"Come on! Come on!" I shouted at the screen. "Yeah, first down!"

Diego didn't say a word. Instead, he took my beer from my hand, leaned forward, and set it on the coffee table. Then he came back and started kissing my neck.

I laughed, running my palm up his back. "You're not going to distract me." Still, I tilted my head to give him more access even as I kept an eye on the screen. I wasn't made of stone, damn it.

"You sure I can't distract you?" Oh fuck—his voice was a low purr, as he dragged his fingers up my inner thigh and added, "I'll bet I can."

"We're—" I sucked in a sharp hiss as Diego's fingertips traced my straining fly. "But we're missing the game." As protests went, it didn't sound convincing at all.

"Don't think we're missing anything."

"But we're . . ." I closed my eyes as he squeezed my dick through my jeans. "Fuck . . ."

A hot breath of laughter warmed the side of my neck. "Hmm?"

"Damn it, just because your team is losing doesn't mean—"

He bit that spot where my neck met my shoulder, and my resistance crumbled.

"You are such a bastard," I moaned.

He laughed again, then flicked his tongue across the place he'd bitten. As he lifted his head, he grinned. "I'll stop if you really want—"

I shut him up with a kiss. I didn't care that I was letting him win and distract me from the game. We'd both learned real fast that it didn't take much for Diego to make me want him. We were like teenagers together—ready for sex at a moment's notice. The Cardinals would be fine without me.

Diego straddled me, and I curved my hands over his ass to pull him against me. He claimed my mouth, and we made out as he rubbed our cocks together and created the most dizzying friction.

Something happened on the screen. The commentators were talking fast and loud like they always did when things were getting exciting, and the spectators roared in the background, but I couldn't even spare a look at the TV.

"Turn it off," Diego growled. I bit back a grin and a comment about him not being able to focus while his Eagles got their asses kicked in the background. Instead, I fumbled for the remote and found the power button. One click, and the spectators and commentators were silenced. Now there was nothing to muffle the sounds of our slick jerseys brushing against each other or the wet, needy kisses in between low moans. The game was a distant memory, but my pulse raced even faster than it had during that fraught first half.

He adjusted his position a little, and I realized he was shifting his weight off his bad knee.

"This okay?" I asked between kisses. "For your leg?"

"Uh-huh. Long as I don't . . . as I don't . . ." He shivered, cursing softly. "I'm good. Trust me."

"Just say so if you want to move."

"'Kay." He kissed me again, deeper this time, and if he was even a little bit uncomfortable, he didn't show it.

What had started as a playful diversion from the game quickly turned into the main attraction. I didn't protest. We kissed and groped and fumbled with belts and zippers. By the time we had each other's cocks in hand, I was pinned to the couch, and Diego was rocking his hips, and his hand moved in perfect time with them, and it was almost like he was *riding* my dick instead of pumping it. I kept a hand on his thigh to steady myself and stroked him too. He always seemed to like it when I used his foreskin to stroke him rather than creating friction with my hand, so I did it that way, and he groaned.

"That good?" I asked, seriously out of breath.

"So good." He wasn't just rocking now—he was thrusting, forcing his cock through my fist with every motion. "Ungh…" He shuddered, letting his head fall back. "I'm gonna . . . God, Mark . . ." Whatever he said after that was either in Spanish or too mumbled for me to understand, but the breathless, desperate tone said it all. So did the way his body was steadily getting more and more tense with every thrust, until the cords were standing out on his neck and his muscles quivered under the hand I was using to grip his thigh.

I slung an arm around him and held him to me as we kissed and stroked each other. The position was frustrating the hell out of me because my body desperately wanted to move, to force myself through his tight fist, but it was also hot and perfect because Diego's hand was pumping me within an inch of my life and his body was hot and solid against mine and his kiss was . . . his mouth was . . . oh God . . .

I stroked him faster, letting his foreskin slide up and down his shaft, and he groaned as he pushed himself into my hand. I loved how he rocked his hips while I was jerking him off. I loved anything he did, especially when he was kissing me at the same time and breathing hard and trembling, and *fuck*—I couldn't hold back anymore and shot my load on both of us.

Then he shuddered, and cum streaked across my stomach and chest. In that instant, I regretted not taking off my jersey when I'd had the chance. Not because I wanted to keep it clean, but because I loved the way it felt when he came on my skin. Who was I kidding? I loved the way it felt when he came. Full stop.

Panting and unsteady, we separated, Diego flopping onto the cushion beside me, and we sprawled for a moment while we caught our breath. Then I took some napkins from beside the pizza box, and we cleaned off our hands and shirts.

"Wonder what the final score was," he slurred.

"Hmm." I picked up the remote and clicked the TV back on. The game wasn't quite over yet. The timer showed two and a half minutes remaining in the fourth, and—

I sat up, jaw falling open. "What the fuck?"

Diego howled with laughter. "Oh! Oh, look at that!" He pointed at the screen. "Who's got their shit together now?"

I blinked in disbelief. Sometime between Diego groping me into distraction and now, the Eagles had pulled it together enough for a four-point lead. They also had the ball and were well within range for a touchdown.

"What . . . the . . ." I gaped at the screen. "You can't be serious."

Diego had tears streaming down his face and could barely speak. "Oh my God. That's . . . fucking *epic*."

I tossed a pillow at him, which only made him laugh harder.

"Look on the bright side." His expression was earnest, but I could practically feel the smirk trying to come through. "Instead of witnessing your team falling apart, you were getting off."

I glared at him.

His earnestness crumbled, and he started giggling again.

I couldn't help it, and I laughed as I gathered him into my arms. "You're a real bastard, you know that?" I asked against his lips.

"Not what you were saying ten minutes ago."

I kissed him again to shut him up. He grinned into it at first, but then his lips softened, and before long . . .

Football game? What football game?

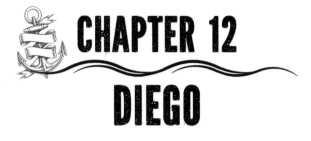

CHAPTER 12

DIEGO

Dating Mark was amazing. The sex was great, and so was just hanging out with him.

In the back of my mind, though, I'd known there was a storm coming. Not between us, but in me. I'd been pretty steady for the last few months, aside from the odd random nightmare, but as always, it was only a matter of time.

And finally, midafternoon on a Tuesday a week after Thanksgiving, the thunder came in the form of a text message from my boss.

Don't come in until I tell you.

My blood turned cold. Fuck. That was a message I'd gotten before, and I knew exactly what it meant—someone was sniffing around the bar. Maybe a health department inspector. Maybe a cop following up on a call. Someone official, though, which meant someone Hank didn't want noticing me or my accent. Neither of us needed them getting curious and asking about my mythical green card.

Cool panic skittered through me. What if they found something this time? Saw my name somewhere and asked questions? Heard someone mention me?

Shit. Oh shit. Even though I hadn't seen it firsthand, I'd heard ICE was getting more aggressive in some states. It was only a matter of time before they started cracking down here. One anonymous tip, and I was fucked.

Closing my eyes, I took slow, deep breaths. There was no point in freaking out until I knew that was what was happening. For all I knew, it was the guy from the water district coming to read the meter, and he was Mexican too, so it wasn't like he'd report my ass.

Still.

Until I knew for sure otherwise, it was possible. It was way, way too possible that my stability—if I could call it that—would get yanked out from under me. I tried everything I could think of to talk myself down and keep the panic attack from closing in. A friend had given me her leftover valium a few years ago, but that was long gone, and it would've been expired anyway.

I wasn't even sure it would have helped.

As I paced my tiny apartment, every imaginable worst-case scenario crowded into my head. I tried to remind myself that as long as I didn't show my face, no inspector or auditor would have any reason to think I worked there. There was no paper trail to let officials *know* I worked there. I only worked for tips. Everything I did was under the table. My name wasn't on the schedule or any other place in the building. I was a ghost.

Whenever some official showed up, though, or when someone breathed a word about *illegals*, I was sure Hank would finally decide I was too much trouble. He'd only brought me on board because he felt sorry for me, and because he didn't think it was right that a veteran was out on his ass like that, but he had a business to run. Sooner or later, he might realize he couldn't risk his livelihood for mine.

And there went the panicky downward spiral. Chest tightening, air refusing to move fast enough or deep enough into my lungs, I tried to will myself not to freak out, not to let it take over, not to drop to my knees and heave into the toilet until every muscle in my torso ached from the force.

This happened every fucking time, but it still caught me off guard, and it still scared the hell out of me. As soon as there was so much as a threat to my employment, I jumped like a deer who'd heard a twig snap. Except there was nowhere for me to run. I needed that job. I needed it so I could pay my rent and help my family and maybe eat once in a while. And I needed the free meals my boss gave all his employees—even me—during our shifts. If whoever was at the bar right now found something, and Hank fired me, I'd lose my income, a meal or two a day I couldn't afford even with my income, my place to live, my phone, my truck . . .

Fuck. Oh fuck. Fuck, get it together, Diego.

Except . . . why? Why *shouldn't* I panic? I was replaceable—
disposable—and I knew it. Hank only kept me out of pity, and probably
because I was saving him a shitload of money since I didn't get an
actual paycheck. Which meant, yeah, I was taking a job that could've
been filled legally by a local, but it wasn't like I could live without a
job, and it wasn't like I hadn't tried to find legal employment. But I
couldn't get a job without a green card and I couldn't get a green card
without a job, so what the fuck was I supposed to do?

Not that any of that stopped the occasional drunk asshole—or
perfectly sober asshole—from lecturing me about what "my kind" was
doing to fuck up this country.

I came here legally, I wanted to snarl at customers sometimes, *and
I fucking fought for your right to call me a job-stealing wetback, you
ignorant ass.*

I bristled and tried to shrug away the anger that was building
alongside the panic. Whatever happened, happened. I needed to get
my head together before a flashback took over. That or a panic attack.
Sometimes both. Whenever my stability started wobbling, my brain
turned to dominoes. I might lose my job . . . and my place . . . and my
truck . . . I could starve . . . I could be deported . . . and all because
of the military and all these injuries from the war that had killed my
friends and screwed up my body and left me with a head full of things
nobody should ever have to see and—

I grabbed the kitchen counter a split second before my knees
would have given out. The tunnel vision was so strong, my peripheral
vision had gone almost completely black. I took a couple of stumbling
steps and dropped into one of the kitchen chairs. I hung my head
between my knees and tried to stay conscious. Tried not to puke.
Tried not to let the panic attack take over.

I didn't know how long I sat there. Time compressed *and* bloated,
making me feel like it could've been hours or just a couple of minutes.
My shirt was damp with cold sweat. So was my hair. I'd need a shower
before I headed to work. If I headed to work. If I still had a job. If I—

My phone rang, startling me so hard I almost toppled my chair. I
fumbled with the phone, and when I recognized my boss's ringtone,
I almost collapsed into a panic again. I took a couple of deep breaths
so I wouldn't be hyperventilating when I answered.

I put the phone to my ear. "Yeah, boss?"

"It was just the health inspector following up on some bullshit." He sounded relaxed and dismissive. That was a good sign. "It's all clear for you to come on down."

I released a relieved sigh. "Okay. I'll be there as soon as I can." *After I calm the fuck down, take a shower, and calm the fuck down some more.*

"Whenever you can. It's pretty quiet right now anyway."

Yeah, but I need the hours on the clock so I can get food from the kitchen.

I didn't mention that part, though.

"I'll be there ASAP."

As I settled in for my shift, the panic refused to go away. I could function enough to work, which was good. I just couldn't relax.

This was going to be a rough night, and not just while I was at the club. I had to sleep sometime, and that terrified me. At least when I was awake, I could steer my thoughts around the shit that tried to come up. Once I was asleep, not so much.

Come on, brain. It's all good. Don't lose it. You want to get fired for freaking out?

I took some deep breaths whenever no one was looking. I still had my job. I hadn't been deported. As far as Hank or I knew, the health department inspector didn't have any reason to believe the High-&-Tight was employing an undocumented immigrant.

But the panic held on.

If anyone ever decided they cared enough to make the call to ICE, my whole world could be thrown on its ass in a heartbeat. Just having someone or something trip this fear was enough to make me physically sick. Even though there hadn't been any actual immediate danger, and it was over now anyway, I could still feel the flashbacks and nightmares that I knew were coming.

I threw myself into my job as much as I could. Focused. Focused *hard*. It was the only way I knew to keep from losing it, and even that wasn't foolproof.

I tried not to notice how much my hands were shaking while I mixed drinks and made change. I tried not to think about the churning in the pit of my stomach. I tried not to imagine how much worse the night would get after my shift was over.

But I failed.

Miserably.

Shit. Shit, shit, shit. This always happened when I felt Uncle Sam breathing down my neck. Always. It was like a cascade of stress that landed me right smack in my hellish, bloody past. It started with the hint that the jig was up and I might lose my job or get deported. Then it was like my brain went into rewind, screaming through everything that had cost me my green card and my health and my stability and my fucking *sanity*.

I was sweating and shaking and trying to claw the pieces of myself back together so I could work without feeling like I was fighting off a heart attack. Because that was exactly what it felt like when the panic took over—like I was having a heart attack. Or I was about to. Or bullets really were flying and my friends really were bleeding out and—

Breathe, Diego. Breathe.

Like that was going to help. Except it would keep me from passing out. Passing out at work meant an ambulance, which meant paperwork. Not to mention insurance I didn't have. Plus, I'd learned the hard way that passing out still meant nightmares, and the only thing that terrified my coworkers more than me collapsing was me waking up screaming. Probably part of why I'd been the first to go when layoffs had happened at my last legitimate job.

I just tried to keep my shit together. The day was hell, but tonight would be even worse. I'd spend the entire night alternating between nightmares and flashbacks—the only real difference was if I was awake or asleep—and I decided I didn't want Mark to see it.

I need to bail tonight, I typed out with shaky fingers. *Knee is acting up.*

The lie made me wince, but it was better than the truth. I knew I wouldn't be able to hide this from him forever. Eventually, he was going to find out, and he was going to see what happened when my demons caught up with me like they always did.

Just . . . not tonight.

Eventually, but not tonight.

"Hang on, Samson. They'll be here in a few minutes."

"Mom?"

"It's Ramírez. Stay with me. Look at me. Look at me, man. Hang on."

"Mom . . ."

"Come on, just hang in there, Samson. Samson?"

My eyes flew open. The cool, still silence of my dark apartment was jarring, and my ears still rang with gunfire and my own shouts. Had I actually yelled? My throat was raw, so maybe. Or that was from the hyperventilating that had left me dizzy. My landlady wasn't banging on my door or calling me, so maybe I hadn't screamed this time.

I sat up slowly. Something crawled down the side of my face, and I batted it away, but it was just a drop of sweat. One of many drops. As I settled into reality, I realized I was *drenched* in sweat.

I swore under my breath. Just what I needed. There was no point in going back to sleep for a while, especially not like this, so I peeled back the sheets and got up to grab a shower.

My legs were shaking as I stepped into the bathtub. Every scar—especially the big ones on my shoulder and my leg—itched. I didn't even know if they really itched or if I'd just convinced myself they did, but I had to fight to keep from scratching them to ribbons.

All because a fucking text from my boss had scared me. I closed my eyes as the water ran over my face. Not that I was surprised. Those texts came once in a while, and they always sent me into a tailspin. Sometimes the tailspin didn't even need a trigger. It just . . . *happened.* And it didn't even matter *why* once it started. Now the only thing that counted was how to make it stop. Which I hadn't figured out how to do. I had to just ride it out and hold myself together as much as I could until my brain unstuck itself from the past.

But this hadn't happened in a while. I'd been doing *so well.*

Now, it was all raw and burning again like fresh wounds.

If I hadn't been so exhausted, I would have stayed awake, but I couldn't. I could barely stand up. After my shower, I stripped the sweaty sheets off the bed, put some fresh ones down, and collapsed for a few more restless hours of sleep.

It didn't help. Coffee didn't either. Days like this, I missed when I could go running. I needed to run until I was too tired to think—maybe even too tired to dream. Kind of ironic I'd lost that ability around the same time I'd started *needing* an outlet.

Without those options, I'd found from experience that the best way to get a handle on things was to do as much normal, everyday shit as I could. Clean the apartment. Take care of my landlady's to-do list. Go grocery shopping.

That last option turned out to be a bad idea today. It was a Wednesday, but for some reason everyone and their mother was at the store. It was mayhem.

I needed to get a few things, though, so I knuckled through as best I could.

Someone knocked something over, and glass shattered. One of the employees shoved a shopping cart into the back of a row so it would tuck in like the others, and the metal *clang* almost sent me out of my crawling skin. An unhappy child shrieked, oblivious to the half-demolished Afghan village he was sending me back to.

That was when the shaking started—when the shrill cry hit a nerve and filled my mind with images of destruction and violence. I could taste the sand. My fingers moved back and forth on the handbasket's handle, same as they always had on my trigger guard when I'd been nervous. When we'd been walking through buildings that might or might not have been full of people who absolutely wanted us dead.

Shaking beside the bread aisle, trying to keep my breathing even, I closed my eyes and focused. *Here*, not there. *Now*, not then. Stay here. I just had to stay here, and I'd be okay. I'd—

Someone bumped into me.

I startled so bad I had to grab the bread shelf to stay upright, and I nearly knocked a couple of loaves onto the floor. A middle-aged couple eyed me in surprise but then scowled, shook their heads, and kept walking.

"Drug addict," the woman muttered.

"Fucking wetback junkie," the man grumbled. He shot me a glare over his shoulder. "Probably on food stamps and everything."

Food stamps. Fuck, I wished.

I closed my eyes. I'd heard some outrage over undocumented immigrants getting food stamps, but hell if I knew how they actually did it. I was too scared to apply for anything because . . .

Because I'd fucking get deported.

I cursed out loud, not caring who heard. It always came back to that, didn't it?

I could apply for food stamps . . . and get deported.

I could go to the VA clinic to get my knee and head checked . . . and get deported.

I could apply for a real job with a real visa . . . and get deported.

Or I could keep flying below the radar, working a job that barely made me enough to stay alive . . . and get deported.

I shook myself and pushed those thoughts away. I had the job right now, and I had enough in my wallet to pay for some groceries. I looked into the basket I was carrying. It wasn't everything I'd come for, but it would be enough to tide me over until I could handle being around people again. Or until my next shift at the bar.

Half the reason I kept my job at the High-&-Tight was the kitchen in the back. A perk of employment was one free meal per four hours on the clock. That was also why I volunteered for every extra shift I could get my hands on. My knee didn't like it, but it was one less meal I had to pay for with my rent money or the meager cash I'd scraped together to send to Mexico. Sometimes I even came in to do unpaid prep work, cleaning, and maintenance around the bar. I knew my boss was exploiting the shit out of me, but what was I going to do? Call him out on it? Report it? Fuck that. I did the work, and then I shut the fuck up and ate the free sandwich and fries. And sometimes I slipped out to my truck to stash a second one no one had noticed me or one of the sympathetic cooks making.

But I still had to keep some food around the house, and this was enough for now, so I went to the express checkout and paid.

Then I headed home, leaving all the noise and people and panic at the grocery store. I needed to pull it together. Today. Before I saw Mark again. No, *now*. Because even if I didn't go out with Mark tonight, I still had to go to work.

Work. Oh fuck. *Work.*

A sick feeling burned in the back of my throat. I wasn't out of the woods for a panic attack, but I didn't dare call in sick unless I was dying. Even then, I'd have hesitated. No tips if I didn't show up. I couldn't afford to let a panic attack or a barrage of violent flashbacks keep me from working.

Plus, while my boss was a decent enough guy, we both knew he could fire me for anything, although he'd never given me a reason to think he'd can me the second I messed up. Hell, he even let me take the same state-mandated breaks as everyone else—not to mention the free meals—and he didn't skim off my tips like the last guy I'd worked for like this. But every time he cut me slack, I was even more convinced the other shoe would drop. Like he was keeping a tally of every time he could have fired me so he'd have plenty of ammunition when he finally did.

I gripped the wheel tighter as I steered my truck toward home. I'd always known working illegally would be a blow to my pride. I'd come to the US legally, I'd worked legally, and I'd had every intention of *continuing* to work legally. When I'd had to bite the bullet and take any employment I could find, I'd expected to feel like a failure. And I had. I'd been a failure who couldn't crack it in the Navy or keep the menial job I'd found afterward.

What I hadn't expected was the constant stress. The fear that I was one dropped glass or late arrival away from having nothing. I'd even tried using an American accent at work so nobody would realize I was Mexican, but I couldn't keep it going for hours. Or I'd let the accent slip, and then people would really look at me weird. And I'd fucking hated it anyway. I was proud of who I was, damn it.

At least at the High-&-Tight, most people were there to get drunk and/or laid. The bar I'd worked in before had been more of a blue-collar place, and I hadn't gone a week without some drunk redneck going off on me about how I was stealing an American's job and he should report me. There'd been plenty of other racist shit in there, but it was the part about reporting me that had scared me shitless.

It had also ultimately been why that boss had fired me. After helping himself to his usual forty percent of my tips—to make up for what I wasn't giving Uncle Sam, he'd claimed—he'd casually told me not to come back. He'd had a few threats about ICE and couldn't risk getting busted with an undocumented immigrant on the payroll. Thank God one of the bartenders had been leaving to go work at the High-&-Tight, and he'd put in a good word for me with the sympathetic owner. Hank hadn't been keen on hiring someone without a green card, but he'd taken pity on me because I was a veteran.

"Ain't right for a man who's been shot at for his country to be screwed by it," he'd said.

I agreed, even if we seemed to be in the minority.

"I can do this," I murmured to the steering wheel. "This has happened before, and I got through it, and I'll get through it again." It always felt like more than I could handle, but *I got through it*. Every time.

Thank God it was a weekday. Fridays and Saturdays, the club would be packed and the music would be loud and the lights would be flashing so much that just thinking about it made me break out in a cold sweat. On a Wednesday, it would be more like a normal bar—fairly quiet with people just hanging out and drinking, maybe shooting some pool or dancing. I'd gotten used to the crack of pool balls. It was a distinctive sound, and over time, I'd convinced my fucked-up psyche to tune it out. Now if I could just do the same thing with slamming doors or someone dropping a heavy box, maybe I could get through a shift without losing my shit.

I'd go. And I'd be okay. Somehow, I'd fucking be okay.

CHAPTER 13

MARK

The day had dragged as only a day packed with staff meetings could drag. It was finally over, though, and I didn't even bother changing into civvies when I left—uniform and all, I was out of there.

I had just stepped off the quarterdeck when my phone buzzed in my pocket. For a second, I hoped it was Diego calling about seeing each other tonight—we hadn't made plans after he'd canceled last night—but it wasn't him. It was my ex-wife.

"Hang on," I said, and I lowered my phone while I took the ramp the rest of the way down to the pier. Once I was landside and out of the noisy throngs of everyone else trying to leave for the night, I put the phone back to my ear. "Hey, what's up?"

"Hey," Angie said. "I just wanted to let you know we got an offer on the house. It's a few grand under the asking price, but the realtor says it's probably the best we're going to get in this market."

I closed my eyes and exhaled. One step closer to our married life being dissolved. "Okay. Good. Can you email the paperwork to me?"

"Already did. If it looks good as is, I'll sign everything and submit it tomorrow."

"Perfect." Since I was so far away, Angie had a limited power of attorney and could sign on my behalf for anything relating to selling the house. Our lawyers and realtor had raised a few eyebrows over it, but I trusted her, and it would make things a hell of a lot easier this way. "Are we actually going to make money on the place?"

"Oh yeah. Not as much as we'd like, especially once we split it, but enough to pay for the divorce and still have enough left for down payments on new places."

"Good. Just keep me updated, okay?"

"I will," she said. "How are things otherwise? How is . . . what's that town called?"

"Anchor Point. It's nice, actually. Pretty quiet."

"So you're not bored?" There was a note of teasing in her voice. She knew how restless I could get in sleepy little towns.

"Not as bored as I thought I'd be, no."

"Really?" Angie paused. "So what's her name?"

I almost choked. "What?"

"Oh, don't try to bullshit me." She laughed. "Come on. Spill it."

"Um." I cleared my throat. "There's no 'she.'"

"Uh-huh. Sure there's— *Ooh*. So what's *his* name?"

It was my turn to laugh. "You're good at this. And his name's Diego. I met him a couple of weeks after I got here."

"Yeah?" There was a bright smile in her voice. "And it's going good?"

I couldn't help smiling myself. "Yeah, so far." My smile started to fall. "He's got some hang-ups with the military, though. Didn't even want to go out with me at first."

"What kind of hang-ups?"

"I'm still kind of getting that out of him. When he's ready to tell me, he will. For right now, I'm trying to be . . . cautiously optimistic, I guess? Like it's a good sign that he's still seeing me?"

"Or he's really enjoying the sex."

Heat rushed into my face, and I glanced around as if one of the Sailors nearby might've overheard.

Angie giggled. "I can hear you blushing, you know."

"Of course you can," I grumbled.

Another laugh. "Seriously, though—maybe he just wants to get laid and move on."

I tried not to be disappointed at that thought. "I don't know. Maybe. I mean, I'm enjoying it too, so there's that."

"Well, see how it goes," she said. "And maybe, I don't know, *talk* to him if you're not sure?"

"Yeah, after I bench press the ship, right?"

She laughed. "Oh, come on. You're not *that* bad at communicating. Not anymore." A few months ago, there would have been some venom behind the words, but her voice was light and warm. We *had* gotten better at communicating, after all. Both of us. Now I just had to apply that to Diego somehow.

I cleared my throat. "What about you? Met anyone yet?"

"Meh. I've been trolling around on Tinder, but apparently the only thing that's good for is amassing a collection of dick pics."

I snorted. "Is that right?"

"Yeah. And guys really don't appreciate it when you message them back with advice on how to angle the camera or use lighting to at least give the illusion of some size."

I laughed again. "If it were anyone else, I'd ask if you really did that, but knowing you . . ."

She giggled wickedly.

We chatted for a few more minutes before she said, "Okay, I'll let you go."

"All right. Take care. I'll look over that paperwork as soon as I can."

"Perfect. Good night, Mark."

"Good night."

After we hung up, I stared at the darkened screen of my phone. It still blew my mind that we'd managed to end things this peacefully. In fact, from the moment she'd dropped the divorce hammer, all the conflict between us had seemed to evaporate. Sure we were both bitter about things, and we'd both done things we couldn't come back from, but the divorce petition had been like a cease-fire. Now that we weren't fighting to keep our marriage from collapsing, we weren't fighting at all.

On one hand, we should have done this years ago. It would've saved us both a lot of heartache and wasted time. On the other, if we'd gone our separate ways back then, we'd have hated each other. By the time we'd finally separated, we'd matured, and we'd also exhausted ourselves, and neither of us had had any fight left at all. The discussions about dividing things up and selling the house had been civil. Those conversations had been the calmest parts of my life over the last few months, and when all was said and done, we'd buried the hatchet enough to be friends.

It was probably a better outcome than either of us deserved, given how terrible we'd been to each other during certain periods of our marriage, but I was grateful for it.

Phone in my pocket, I continued down the pier toward the parking lot. I hurried home from the base, stripped out of my uniform, and showered. Then I left again, stopping at a burger joint some guys at work had recommended, and picked up a takeout order.

When I walked into the High-&-Tight, it only took a second to find Diego, and the instant I laid eyes on him, all my thoughts about the house and the divorce were gone.

His face lit up when he saw me. When he saw the bag in my hand, I thought I could hear his mouth start watering.

"Hey," I said when I was close enough to be heard. "You have a break coming up?"

He glanced at the bag, then at me. "Yeah. I..." He looked around. "Let me check with my boss. I can probably take off for a few."

Just as I'd hoped, his boss let him slip out. We went into the bar's back room, which was half storage and half break room.

"Oh, man, that smells great." Diego peered into one of the bags. "Is that a bacon cheeseburger?"

"No." I pulled one out and handed it to him. "It's two bacon cheeseburgers."

He laughed softly as he took one of them, and I sat down with the other. We didn't talk much while we ate, which normally didn't bother me. He wasn't just quiet, though. He seemed... distant. And kind of edgy. If he wadded the burger wrapper any tighter in his hand, he was going to turn it into a diamond.

What the hell was going on?

"Maybe," Angie had said, *"I don't know, talk to him if you're not sure?"*

Okay, so she hadn't been talking about this exact scenario, but the advice worked here. I wasn't going to figure Diego out just by watching him.

I washed down a bite with my soda and ignored my sudden nerves. "You okay tonight?"

"Yeah, yeah." Diego waved a hand. "I'm good. Why?"

"I don't know. You just seem kind of... tense?"

He chewed his lip, staring down at the wrapper he was compressing. His hand loosened, tightened, loosened again. Then he shook his head. "I'm good. It's... just been a long day."

Why did that sound like an understatement? And if he was understating it, then maybe that meant he didn't want to talk about it. I was concerned, but I didn't want to be pushy. Finally, I settled on, "How's your knee?"

He cut his eyes toward me, and weirdly, his posture relaxed. Like he was relieved by the change of subject. "It's good. Better." He extended his leg, then bent it again, as if to prove it. When he met my gaze again, a smile—a shyer one than I was used to seeing on him—came to life. "I can move it enough to do everything I need to do tonight." He followed it with a playful wink.

I grinned back, but it felt kind of . . . weird. "Are you sure you're game for tonight?"

"Yeah." He tensed. "Why wouldn't I be? I told you, the knee's fine." He bent and straightened it again.

"I know, but . . ." *But something doesn't feel right.* "You said yourself you've had a long day. We can always take it easy tonight."

His forehead creased. "You don't want to fool around?"

"I didn't say that." I put my hand on his thigh. "I just want to make sure *you* want to."

Diego held my gaze for a moment, and when he smiled this time, it seemed more sincere. He covered my hand with his and leaned in a little closer. "Don't worry about it. If I don't want to, you'll know. Promise." He kissed me lightly, then scowled at the clock on the wall. "Damn. I should get back to work."

Disappointment mingled with uneasiness in my chest. "Already?" I glanced at the clock. We'd been here almost half an hour. "Wow. Time flies."

"Yeah, it does." He lifted his eyebrows. "Did you want to meet up tonight? After my shift?"

"You tell me."

"Of course." He touched my face and moved in for another light kiss. "After the day I've had? You're exactly what I need."

That settled some of my nerves. He'd sounded like he meant it, and even though his eyes were tired, they gleamed with lust.

So I grinned and squeezed his thigh. "You know where to find me."

"I do. And I'll be there as soon as I can."

"Can't wait."

CHAPTER 14

DIEGO

After my shift, I couldn't get out the door fast enough. I needed to grab a shower and get to Mark's. I could've showered at the club, but I needed to go by the apartment anyway to stash two foil-wrapped sandwiches and containers of steak fries in the fridge. God, what a relief to have some food for the next couple of days, even if I did feel a little guilty about it. Since Mark had brought me lunch, I hadn't technically *needed* the free meals my boss allowed every four hours. But given how little there was in my tiny fridge and how little cash I had to put anything in it, I didn't feel *that* guilty.

And thank God the cooks never questioned me; they were in similar boats financially, and one of them even had kids to feed. I didn't know how he did it. I was just grateful he never ratted me out to Hank for abusing the free-meal privilege.

With the food in the fridge and my conscience only kind of nagging at me, I peeled off my clothes and got in the shower.

The water was hot but not quite hot enough. I still felt cold all over. Still shaky. Still not quite together.

Maybe I should cancel tonight. I needed to stay home. I needed to be alone with my thoughts and my nightmares and the aches and pains and panic that were flaring up. Not that they ever went away completely.

Except I didn't want to be alone—I wanted to be with Mark. When he'd come into the club tonight, he'd had no idea how much he'd settled me. Because suddenly there was a meal I didn't have to worry about affording. There was company who didn't judge me and actually went out of his way to be with me. After being on edge all day, I'd been able to breathe for a little while, and I wanted more of that.

And besides, the best thing to pull me back together had always been to focus on living my normal everyday life, and the fact was, my normal everyday life included being with Mark. I wasn't avoiding my problems by going to him—I was living in the now.

So I got out, got dressed, and headed over to his place.

The long kiss hello didn't feel quite right.

The playful glances on the way up the stairs? Those took more work than they should have.

Then we tumbled into his bed, and his arms were around me, and I knew this was a mistake. His kiss was hot and his hands were all over me, but now that I was doing something that should have made me wild, I realized how utterly numb I was. How hollowed out and bled dry I was from being pounded into the ground by my past trauma and present anxiety. Sex? I was better off trying to balance an aircraft carrier on my chin.

But how the hell was I supposed to bow out tactfully?

Fuck it. I could do this. Once I got into it, I'd be fine, and I would get into it. I would. Any second now. Even if my heart wasn't in it, my body could catch up. Right?

"Missed you last night," Mark murmured against my lips.

"Missed you." It wasn't a lie. I had missed him. I'd just spent more time missing being sane and safe and wondering what it felt like to not be on edge. Maybe this was what I needed—to lose myself in someone who'd hold me and make me feel good.

I held him tighter and kissed him deeper, tapping into every reserve I had for energy and enthusiasm. I could do this, damn it. If nothing else, I could get him off and make sure he went to sleep satisfied.

We rolled onto our sides, still kissing and groping. Every time his hand drifted toward my cock, though, I'd casually redirect it. Not slapping it away or grabbing his wrist—just guiding him toward my nipple or my ass or my leg.

Then his hand slid beneath the back of my jeans, and he pressed against me, and there was no way he missed how there was only one boner between us. His.

Cold panic and hot embarrassment shot through me, but then resignation settled in.

I wanted him. I wanted us to be naked and fucking, and I wanted to come in him or all over him or down his throat . . .

But it wasn't going to happen. My body just wasn't into it.

Mark broke the kiss. "What's wrong?"

Damn it. Unlike me, the jig was up.

I pulled back but didn't look at him. "I'm sorry." Squeezing my eyes shut, I legitimately wished the ground would open up and swallow me. Couldn't we have waited a little longer for my mental shit to start interfering with our sex life? Son of a bitch.

"Diego." He touched my shoulder. The unscarred one. I tried not to think about whether that was deliberate, and it made my skin crawl even more to think he was avoiding touching the scars out of disgust, but I was also kind of glad he *wasn't* touching them. I didn't know what I wanted him to do. In a voice so soft it almost made me cry, he asked, "Are you okay?"

"I'm . . ." I raked an unsteady hand through my hair. It was damp, and I hoped it was still from my shower and I hadn't really broken into a sweat. We'd barely even done anything.

"You're shaking." Mark touched my face, and when our eyes met, his were wide. "What's wrong?"

Fuck. There was no point in trying to hide anything from him, and I didn't have the energy to come up with a lie.

"It's, um . . ." I wiped a hand over my face, but it didn't help. Not when I couldn't stop the shaking. "I had a bad night last night. Nightmares and shit. It's from . . ." I shuddered. "From being in combat."

"PTSD?" he whispered.

"Yeah."

"Have you ever seen a psychologist about it?"

I jerked my head up and glared at him. "How the hell would I pay for that?"

Mark's lips parted. He blinked. "You . . . you have VA benefits, don't you?"

I started to shoot back the answer, but then I remembered Mark didn't know my story. Or my predicament. Heat rushed into my cheeks, and I felt like an ass for biting his head off. Lowering my gaze again, I rubbed my neck. "I'm sorry. I didn't . . ." Fuck, I was too exhausted to even put it into words. "I'm sorry." I closed my eyes and pushed out a breath. "I didn't mean to snap at you, and God I *want* to be into this tonight, but I—"

"Hey. Come here." He wrapped his arms around me. My pride wanted me to pull back and insist I was fine, but damn it, I couldn't help sinking into the warm comfort of his embrace. Mark kissed my forehead and murmured, "We don't have to do anything tonight. If you're this rattled, you're not going to enjoy it."

"But I don't want you getting blue balls just because I'm—"

"Diego." He tipped up my chin and looked right in my eyes. "We'll fuck again when we're *both* into it. If it wasn't obvious, I do enjoy being with you even when we have clothes on." He kissed me softly. "You want to just call it a night?"

I felt guilty as hell, but his suggestion made the fatigue soak deeper into my bones. Calling it a night was pretty much my only option. I started to draw back. "Yeah. Let me get dressed and—"

"No." He tugged my arm. "I meant call it a night here." He ran his palm up my back. "With me."

"Really?"

"Yeah." His smile was sweet. "Sex isn't the price of admission for sleeping in my bed."

I swallowed, not quite believing him.

He kissed me gently. "I mean it. Even if you didn't want to fool around tonight, we can just sleep. I . . ." His cheeks colored a bit, and his shy smile pushed *all* my buttons. "I like having you here, you know?"

I moistened my lips. "I like being here."

"Then stay." He squeezed my hand. "I'll have to take off early in the morning, but you know where the coffee is. Just make sure you lock the door on your way out."

"Okay. I will." I chewed the inside of my cheek. "Fair warning—when this happens, I usually get nightmares. Bad ones. Especially when I'm . . . When it's been . . ." Clearing my throat, I tried to roll some tension out of my shoulders. "Just . . . I might, uh, flail. Yell. That kind of thing."

"I know," he said with a shrug. "You've done it a few times."

I blinked. "I have?" *Fuck, I thought you'd slept through those.*

"Yes. And it's okay." It sounded almost patronizing, but then he added, "During deployments, when we were in port, a buddy and I used to get hotel rooms so we didn't have to sleep on the ship. He'd done three tours in Iraq." Mark brushed a strand of hair off my forehead and emphatically repeated, "It's okay."

I studied him, waiting for the other shoe to drop. There had to be *some* way this was a deal breaker for him. Whatever we were doing, it was way too new to weather something like this.

But he just cradled the back of my neck and pressed a tender kiss to my lips. "Should we get ready for bed?"

Speechless, I nodded.

In minutes, we were down to our boxers and curled up under the covers in comfortable silence. Mark had his head on my good shoulder and his arm slung across my stomach, and that bone-deep chill I'd been trying to shake off for days was no match for his body heat. His warmth was soothing. Maybe I didn't have what it took for sex tonight, but I was apparently starving for affection and contact, and Mark was giving it to me in spades just by lying against me.

The more he relaxed and the more his breathing slowed, the more I relaxed too. It was hard to panic and get lost in the past when there was someone right here who was calm and serene. There were no bullets, no mortars, no screams—just the easy, steady breathing of a man falling asleep while he held me protectively.

As he drifted off, I kept stroking his hair.

How can you be everything I've tried to avoid and still be perfect for me?

I closed my eyes as a sick feeling settled in my gut.

When are you going to see what a train wreck I am . . .

. . . and leave?

The room was still dark when Mark got up to go to work. He kissed me on the cheek, and I was just awake enough to catch something about "text you later" and "see you tonight" before he was gone.

I slept for a few more hours. By the time I rolled out of his amazingly comfortable bed, I felt a lot better than I had in the last couple of days. Still kind of shaky, and now with some nerves about how long Mark would keep me around, but I'd rested, and that made all the difference in the world.

While I showered in his bathroom, I tried to recall if I'd had any freak-outs last night. I knew I'd had nightmares—the fear still skittering through my veins was a dead giveaway—but had I woken him up? I couldn't remember. They must not have been that bad, then. At least not for me. Hopefully they hadn't been for him.

I made it through the day on autopilot. I was more rested now, which helped contain the feeling that I was about to start climbing the walls. The anxiety was better as long as I didn't think too much about last night's failure to launch.

It wasn't the first time that had happened—just the first time it had happened with Mark. One guy had ghosted me afterward. Another had accidentally sent me a message on Grindr that was supposed to go to someone else. Something to the effect of *That guy I was fucking last night turned out to be a limp-dicked basket case.* A third hadn't been so great with things like social cues and knowing when to make a joke; the full-page Cialis ad he'd cut out of a magazine and given to me had been the end of our little fling.

If that part of last night didn't bother Mark, then he'd have questions about the other part. The part where I was shaking and distracted and warning him about nightmares. He'd spent enough time with me and we'd talked enough that he had to be putting the pieces together. It was just a question of how long he'd hold out before he finally brought it up.

Turned out the answer to that was—not long.

That evening, after I'd finished an early shift at the High-&-Tight and gone over to Mark's place, we were standing in his kitchen, making uneasy small talk while we sipped coffee, when he went there.

"I'm curious, but you don't have to answer." He watched me, and his voice was soft as he asked, "What happened?"

My skin crawled under my clothes, and I tried not to squirm. As much as I didn't want to talk about it, I suddenly wanted him to know. Like I needed him to know something had actually happened and I had a right to be this traumatized, and I was a fucking idiot for even thinking that because—

"Hey." He touched my wrist and stilled the shaking I hadn't noticed. As he gently took my coffee so it didn't slosh all over us both, he added, "I mean it. You don't have to answer. I'm sorry."

I shook my head. "No, it's okay." Releasing a breath, I turned my hand over under his and laced our fingers together. I wondered if he noticed how damp my palm was getting. "If we're going to be doing . . . whatever it is we're doing, it's only fair you know what you're up against."

His brow furrowed.

"It's, um . . ." I cleared my throat, gently freeing my hand so I could fold my arms across my chest as if that could keep away the inevitable chill. "Okay, so the burns." I tilted my head, letting my chin indicate my scarred shoulder. "I was in a convoy that was ambushed."

Mark shuddered. "Always convoys, wasn't it?"

I nodded. "Convoy detail is scary as fuck. You can sit around the base for days and nothing will happen, but the minute you leave in a vehicle . . ."

"Yeah, that's what I've heard. Iraq or Afghanistan?"

"Afghanistan." I took a deep breath and lowered my arms to my sides. "We hit a small IED. Not enough to kill anybody, but it was enough to destroy one of the wheels on our Humvee." I sighed, absently wiping my hands on my jeans. "So, we had to stop. We knew it was a trap, but I mean, we still had to unfuck the disabled vehicle before we could keep moving."

Mark shifted as if he was getting as twitchy as I was. He probably knew exactly where this was going.

"My buddy and I were posted as guards while they worked on fixing it." I licked my lips, wondering when my mouth had gone dry. My heart was beating faster, an echo of the scared shitless feeling I'd had while I'd stood there next to our crippled vehicle. I could still feel the desert sun biting into my exposed skin and burrowing through my layers of protective gear to heat everything underneath until I was sweating like crazy. I'd had to take my glove off for a minute to fix the strap on my rifle, and I'd burned my finger on the sun-heated barrel of the M5. I'd sworn, stuffed my stinging hand back into the glove, and not had a clue just how minor that pain was about to be.

"Diego?" Mark's hand brushed mine, startling me back into the cool, comfortable room. "You don't have to talk about this if you don't want to."

"I can. It's okay." How long had I been drifting in my own thoughts?

"You sure? You're sweating bullets."

I wiped my hand over my forehead, and I wasn't sure what bothered me more—how wet my fingers were or how badly they were shaking. I thought about cutting off my own story, but I'd started. I was already shaky and queasy. Might as well see it through so I didn't have to work myself up to it again.

I took a deep, unsteady breath. "So, the insurgents . . . they distracted us with another explosion and some gunfire. While we were focused on that, they rammed the Humvee with a car. I was trying to help one of my guys who'd been injured, and the fuckers did it again." I tapped a finger on my knee. "That's how I jacked up my leg. And while someone *else* was trying to get *me* to safety, they threw in a projectile. I'm not even sure if it was a grenade or another IED or what, but we saw it coming and tried to take cover. We didn't have time to get far, so I got hit with a bunch of shrapnel and burned the fuck out of my shoulder." My scarred skin itched under my T-shirt. I sighed and couldn't help running my hand over the spot where the swallow used to look pretty damn awesome. "Pissed me off that my tattoo was wrecked. That fucker *hurt*, you know? And now it's messed up."

He grimaced sympathetically. "I bet. Is there any way it can be redone?"

"Not on this side. I'll have to get what's left removed, and then maybe get a new one on the other side. I mean, they can tattoo over scars, but the skin is so rough right there . . ." I shook my head. "It would look like shit." Scowling, I muttered, "It already does."

Mark ran a hand up my back, and to his credit, he didn't try to insist the tattoo looked fine.

I didn't want to talk about my tattoo, so I went on. "My first tour wasn't even that bad, to be honest. We took fire a few times, but we were mostly hot and bored. The second time, I knew as soon as they put me on convoy duty that it was going to be hell. And it was. Since we came back, four guys from my unit have killed themselves and one has tried. To be honest, I think my head was fucked up before I got hurt."

"Was it?"

I nodded. "It was my second tour, so, you know, I'd already seen a lot. Shit goes down in war zones. That's the way it is. The nightmares sometimes come from the explosion, but also from what happened about three months before that."

His eyebrows rose, a silent bid for me to continue but with unspoken permission to stop if I wanted to.

I continued. "The short version is we were in a village. One where there'd been some heavy fighting. We were trying to flush out a cell of insurgents, but we got ambushed and got pinned down, and one of my buddies took a shot to the leg. High caliber. Lot of damage. We had two of those QuikClot bandages on him—the ones that can stop even really bad bleeding—and it wasn't enough."

"Jesus," Mark breathed. "That must have been a hell of a wound."

"It was. Even after the firefight was over, he needed a medic, but then *they* got pinned down." I pushed out a ragged breath. "One of the other guys, he and I did everything we could with what we had, but my friend bled out while our medics were taking fire two hundred yards away." I shook my head slowly. To this day, I could still hear Samson calling out for his mom, his cries getting weaker by the minute until he fell quiet for good. "I've never felt more helpless in my life."

Mark shuddered hard.

"You ever been to combat?" I asked.

"Not boots on the ground, no. It's always been shipboard ops."

"You're lucky." I wanted to resent him for his cushy-ass career. Usually it made me want to grind my teeth to dust when someone sailed through the Navy, collecting ranks and benefits and never once worrying about being shot or blown up. Officers especially. An officer ordered guys into combat without ever noticing the irony that he was paid three or four times what they were and he wasn't getting shot at.

But I didn't feel that way about Mark. I didn't want him to have been to a war zone. I really didn't *wish* it on anyone, but I also didn't resent him for avoiding it. The thought of him being in the Sandbox and being terrified and hoping nobody heard him crying at night—no. It just made me want to wrap him up in my arms and protect him from everything.

It was my turn to shudder. I cleared my throat and kept talking. "So yeah. That's what happened. The recovery after the explosion was pretty miserable, but fortunately I don't remember the first couple of weeks. Between the burns and the three surgeries on my leg, they kept me sedated pretty hard." I laughed even though my skin was crawling. "Guess if you get messed up enough, they break out something stronger than Motrin."

Mark didn't laugh.

I sobered too. "Anyway, they tell me I was awake off and on that night, and I remember bits and pieces of landing in Kuwait, but the next thing I clearly remember after the explosion was waking up in Germany. I'm, uh, kind of thankful for that."

"I can't imagine," he whispered, "but I believe it." He shrugged away a shiver. "How long did it take to recover?"

"The burns and the skin grafts took a few weeks. There were some . . . setbacks. But they were mostly healed in a couple of months. It was my leg that took for-fucking-ever."

"Yeah?"

I nodded. "Four surgeries in six months, plus rehab." Bitterness crept into my voice. "Which of course meant I couldn't run, so I missed two PRTs."

Mark's eyebrows shot up. "They penalized you for missing PRTs because of injuries?"

"Officially, no. I had waivers and all that shit." I rolled my eyes. "But tell that to the computer running the Perform to Serve numbers. It was the only explanation my chain of command could think of for why my numbers were too low."

His jaw went slack. "You . . . you got kicked out through PTS while you were laid up from *combat* injuries?"

I pressed my lips together and nodded. "Yep. I was all set to reenlist, and suddenly the computer said, 'Fuck you.' Next thing I knew, I was a civilian with nightmares and a gimp leg."

He stared at me, eyes round and lips apart.

I avoided his gaze. "At least the Navy realized PTS was garbage and phased it out."

"But not before they'd let go of too many good Sailors." His voice sounded hollow and full of shock. "Jesus." He paused. "But you have access to the VA, don't you?"

Still not looking at him, I shook my head. "Not unless I want to risk getting deported."

"Deport— What?"

I exhaled, shoulders slumping. "I don't have a green card. I'm . . ." I chewed my lip, then finally looked at him through my lashes. "I'm undocumented."

Mark tensed but said nothing. His wide eyes asked me to elaborate, though.

I looked away again. "I found a job right after I got out, but they laid me off. My green card expired, and I couldn't find another job. Not another legal one, anyway." This whole conversation was exhausting. I slid a hand through my hair as I pushed out another long breath. "I was going to apply for naturalization while I was in, you know? But then I went to combat, and then I was laid up, and . . ." I waved my hand in the air. "I thought I was reenlisting, so I didn't think I needed to hurry."

"Holy shit." He slumped back against the couch.

"Yeah. And I mean, I *am* eligible for VA benefits. I can go to the VA clinic, and I'm probably even eligible for some disability." I made myself meet his eyes, and my voice wavered as I said, "But there's no telling who's willing to help me and who will report me and get me shipped out of the country. It's happened to people like me."

"Fuck. I . . . had no idea that happened to people." He swallowed, returning my gaze. "I definitely understand now why you don't like the military."

I bristled. "Yeah. Kind of hard not to be pissed at the Navy when I'm still trying to pick up the pieces seven years later."

Mark blew out a breath. "Jesus." He was quiet for a moment. We both were. Then, his tone a little cautious, he said, "I can see why you don't even like dating guys on active duty. But . . ." His voice was softer now. "Why are we still doing this? I mean, I want to, but if it bothers you that I'm in the Navy . . ."

It did. I couldn't pretend it didn't. But it didn't bother me enough to send me out the door, so I slipped my hand into his. "I'll deal with it. The Navy is a thing that . . ." I shook my head. "It is what it is. But I do want to be with you."

Mark smiled uncertainly. "Me too."

"So let's just do what we've been doing—play it by ear."

"I can do that." He brushed my hair out of my face. "You want to take it easy again tonight? Because you look exhausted, and I'm pretty beat myself."

I smiled and pressed my cheek against his hand as I nodded. "Yeah. I'm good with that."

Returning the smile without the uncertainty this time, Mark put his arms around me and kissed me. As we stood there in his kitchen, wrapped up in a long kiss, I definitely wasn't far enough out of my funk to suggest anything frisky, but this felt good. Really good.

Slowly, I relaxed into his embrace, just letting myself be relieved by his arms around me and his solid presence keeping me upright.

God, I'd needed this from someone for a long, long time. I knew no one had the power to unfuck what war had done to my mind, but right now Mark held me like he would absolutely keep me standing until this days-long episode was over and I had my equilibrium back.

And right now, I couldn't imagine anything I needed or wanted more.

CHAPTER 15
MARK

After we'd settled into bed, Diego dozed off pretty quickly. That wasn't a surprise; he'd seemed wrung out earlier to the point that I'd wondered how he was still standing.

I was wide-awake. Relaxed and comfortable, but wide-awake. I gazed at Diego's silhouette, my mind going a million miles an hour as I tried to process everything he'd told me.

Knowing the story behind all his scars, his PTSD, his limp . . . Shit. Nothing I could have speculated compared to the truth, and the realization that Diego had been through all of that was hard to swallow. I got the feeling he was as self-conscious of the trauma as he was of his scars. Did he have any idea how strong he was?

Christ. The more I got to know the man behind the dirty talk and insatiable lust, the more I wanted to know. Even the stuff he didn't like.

Which was why the fear in his eyes last night and in the kitchen tonight had damn near broken my heart. He hadn't said it, but I'd heard it: *Do you still want me?*

God, yes, I still wanted him. I wanted more of him than I already had. When I wasn't around him, I counted down the minutes until we were back in the same place. And not only because I was horny. When I thought about him, I thought about *him*, not just having sex with him. I didn't care if we were naked. Hell, we could be fully dressed and watching the Eagles win, and I'd be happy. I just wanted him there. All the time.

I swallowed. Was this what falling for someone felt like? Not that we'd been doing this long enough for anything that strong to be happening, but . . . maybe we had? Because I didn't remember ever feeling like this. Not even for my ex-wife. I loved Angie, and I'd certainly been in love with her when we'd gotten married, but I was pretty sure even time and bitterness couldn't have tempered the memory of feeling something for her that compared to what I'd been feeling for Diego.

I had no idea what to make of these feelings. Maybe I'd been alone too long—my marriage had been nothing if not lonely. That had to be it. I wasn't falling for him; I was in love with not being alone.

Beside me, Diego squirmed a little, muttering in his sleep. I didn't know if he was dreaming or just getting comfortable, but I held him tighter anyway.

He stilled, and his breathing wasn't slow and deep anymore. A hand curved over my shoulder. "You're awake?"

"Sounds like you are too."

He scrubbed his other hand over his face, his skin hissing across his stubbled jaw. "I am now."

"I didn't wake you up, did I?"

"Huh? No." He pressed a kiss to my forehead. "You didn't do anything."

"Okay. Good."

We were quiet for a moment. Then he sighed. "I'm not falling asleep."

"Neither am I."

"Stupid brains."

"No shit."

We both chuckled.

"Might as well not fight it, right?" I asked.

"Might as well."

I pulled away long enough to flick on the light. We both flinched, but as our eyes adjusted, we settled on the pillows, facing each other.

And my heart fluttered.

Oh God. No, this was more than being in love with not being alone. Holy shit.

Diego ran the backs of his fingers down the middle of my chest. "I wasn't keeping *you* awake, was I?"

"Not really."

"That's not a no."

I caressed his cheek. Why lie to him? "I guess I was thinking about everything you told me." *And everything I probably shouldn't be feeling for you. Not yet at least.*

He exhaled. "Sorry."

"Don't be. I'm just sorry the Navy left you out in the cold like that."

He didn't say anything, but I could feel him tensing all over. After a moment, though, he started to relax, and he met my gaze again. "Can I ask you about . . . past things? *Your* past things?"

"Like what?"

He propped himself up on his elbow, his eyes filled with both satisfaction and curiosity in the warm light from the bedside lamp. "You were married before, right?"

I nodded, thumbing the divot on my third finger. "Yeah, I was."

"What happened?"

I *really* didn't want to talk about it, but Diego had poured his heart out earlier. Seemed only fair for me to tell him about my past. Even the parts that might make him look at me differently. If my emotions were getting in this deep this soon, then it was better to tell him about my dark sides now in case he decided to cut and run.

I played with the edge of the sheet while I tried to figure out how to put my turbulent marriage into words. "What happened was we were terrible at being married to each other, and everything that came with the Navy . . ." I thought for a moment. "The weird thing is that the Navy is what almost tore us apart in the beginning, and it's the only thing that kept us together as long as we were."

Diego cocked his head. "How does that work?"

I took a deep breath. "Well, when we first got married, we . . . I guess we were ready to be married, but we weren't ready to be married to the Navy. I was deployed almost immediately, and the separation really got to her. Whenever I could call, we'd fight. When I got home, we kind of got back on the same page, but then I ended up going to school for a few weeks in another state, and by the time I came back, the ship was starting workups. We deployed again a year after the first deployment ended, and I was gone probably half that year."

Diego absently smoothed the sheet. "Separations are rough."

"They are. When I was finally stationed on shore for a while, and we got some counseling, we got back on track, but then . . ." I stared at the ceiling. Even after all these years, it was hard to put my finger on exactly when things had started going downhill. Or if they'd been going downhill since day one and just picked up speed. "At some point, we both gave up. I honestly don't know which is worse—the fact that we cheated on each other, or that we didn't care when the other found out."

Diego blinked, his hand stilling on the sheet. "You cheated on her?"

My face burned. "Yeah. Not my proudest time. I . . . had back-to-back deployments. I'd barely gotten back from one before I was transferred to another ship just in time for it to deploy, and that turned into an extended deployment. So out of eighteen months, we saw each other about eight weeks. Total. We were already on shaky ground, and being apart that much . . ." I sighed, shaking my head. "Like I said, I'm not proud of it. Neither is she. And we came back from it, at least for a while. The last four years we were married were probably the most solid we ever had."

He furrowed his brow. "Then why did you split up?"

I laughed bitterly. "Well, for one thing because being the most solid four years of our marriage doesn't say much. The years *before* it were . . ." I grimaced. "But the ultimate deal breaker was that I was going to retire." The furrow deepened, so I went on. "I was getting close to my twenty-year mark and was still a commander, so I figured, that's it. I'm done. Two weeks after I told her I was planning to retire, she told me she was leaving. I guess the idea of having me home all the time made her realize she didn't want me there at all. And . . . I realized I didn't really want to be with her either." I paused. "It was a lot more amicable than it sounds. I think we just spent so much time either apart or fighting that we didn't even know each other anymore."

Diego's lips quirked like he was mulling it over. "How long were you married?"

"Would've been nineteen years this June. Then ironically, a week after we filed the papers, I found out I'd made captain and they were sending me to the *Fort Stevens*. And . . . here I am."

"You got slam orders?"

I nodded. "Most people don't get them for an XO spot, but the boat had just lost half the upper chain of command to some disciplinary action, and I was a captain who needed orders. I had less than eight weeks to report for duty."

He studied me. "So, three months ago, you were a married commander on the East Coast, and now you're a captain on the West Coast with a guy in your bed?"

Chuckling, I shrugged. "Guess so, yeah."

"Whoa."

"Tell me about it."

He chewed his lip for a moment. "When we first hooked up, you said it had been a while." He narrowed his eyes like he was trying to read me. "Did you . . . have boyfriends while you were married?"

"Well . . ." I focused on his hand, watching his fingers idly playing with a crease in the sheet, and exhaled. "I did cheat on her with men a couple of times, yes. But after we got past all the cheating, she and I . . . Well, she was the last person I had anal with, let's put it that way."

Diego's eyebrows rose. "Your wife topped you?"

I nodded. "When we were coming clean about things after that rough patch, I admitted I'd been with a couple of guys. Thought she'd get pissed off even though we'd both been cheating, but she was more curious than anything. That conversation ended in a trip to the sex shop, and the next thing I knew, she was doing me with a strap-on."

"Did she like it?"

I laughed. "Probably more than she liked me."

He eyed me as if he wasn't sure how to take that.

"Angie was pretty adventurous sexually. She actually wanted to peg some of her boyfriends before me, but none of them would go for it."

Diego grinned. "She sounds like a cool lady."

"She is. And I mean, the shit that I did while I was married to her . . . like I said, I'm not proud of it. We were awful to each other for a long time, and it's a miracle we made it out as friends." I blew out a breath. "If anything, I wish we'd split up years ago. It would've been better for both of us to move on instead of trying to force something that wasn't going to work. I'm just glad we're still friends. She's someone I want in my life even if we're not married."

"That sounds a lot like me and my ex."

"Really?"

Diego nodded. "I mean, he's married now, and we're still really close friends, but we had a thing for a little while. Fuck buddies, basically. But when it seemed like it might get serious, I called it off because he's military."

Something in my gut flipped. He really wasn't kidding about the military being a deal breaker.

"When things started getting serious."

Shit. Maybe I needed to rein in my emotions, if that was possible.

He must've seen something in my eyes—uncertainty, maybe—and he sighed. "I know, it sounds stupid. But I—"

"No, it doesn't. Especially not after everything you told me earlier."

He squirmed like he didn't want me to notice him shuddering. "Can I ask you something a bit *more* personal?"

I studied him, not sure what could be more personal than what I'd done to my marriage. "Go ahead."

He held my gaze. "Has the Navy been worth it?"

Oh. Now that was a question I had to think about. *Really* think about.

It took a while before I could come up with an answer. "I don't know. I really don't. I've had a good career, and I'll be—" I stopped myself from mentioning I'd be set for life after I retired. That was a raw nerve for Diego, and I didn't want to step on it. "It's been good, you know? But it hasn't been . . . free. In some ways, it cost me my marriage. I've missed out on big milestones with my family." I slowly let out a breath. "My sister's first husband passed away about ten years ago. Really aggressive cancer. He lived about two months after he was diagnosed." Even after all this time, mentioning my brother-in-law's death threatened to choke me up. "I was at sea. Called to talk to him and my sister after he was diagnosed, but . . ." Sighing, I shook my head. "I couldn't be there. I couldn't even go home for the funeral."

Diego murmured something in Spanish. Something that sounded deeply sympathetic.

"She got remarried a few years ago," I went on, "and I couldn't be home for that either. It's . . . hard, you know?"

"She understands, though, right?" Diego asked softly. "Why you aren't there?"

I nodded. "She does, but it's still put a strain on things between us. We were close growing up. Then I wasn't there while her husband was dying, and I wasn't there when she got married again. She doesn't resent me as far as I know, but it does make it feel like we're really distant. More like two classmates who were super close in school and say hello at their class reunions but don't really have anything to do with each other anymore." I laughed bitterly. "My sister is pretty much an acquaintance because the Navy kept me away from home so much, and my ex-wife is one of my best friends because the Navy isolated us from everyone else. Fucking ironic."

Diego whistled. "That's the Navy in a nutshell, isn't it?" He sounded even more bitter than I had.

"Yeah. Kind of is." I swallowed, then looked into his eyes. "I get why it's a deal breaker for you. I really do."

"You know, I keep trying to tell myself it's still a deal breaker, but I don't want it to be. And I don't . . ." He held my gaze for a moment before he slid toward me. Cupping my cheek, he whispered, "I don't think it is."

And then he kissed me.

It was a chaste kiss, gentle and light, but it sent warmth through my whole body. I wasn't getting turned on—I doubted either of us had the energy for anything like that tonight. It was just so comforting to be touched this affectionately after I'd laid bare all my sins. I'd had no idea how much I needed that comfort until I had it.

Diego held me closer, the kiss still soft and undemanding, and I draped an arm over his waist, basking in his body heat and his embrace. I hadn't realized until tonight how afraid I'd been of being rejected for everything I'd done during my marriage. Like someone might be interested in me but then take off the minute they realized I'd spent a few years as an unrepentant adulterer. I'd practically convinced myself Diego would be gone. Right when I was finding my emotional footing too.

But here he was. He'd bent—hell, broken—his own rule to be with me, and now he knew I'd cheated on my wife, and he was *still* lying beside me and kissing me. Maybe I had finally done something right.

Eventually, he broke away and met my gaze again. "We should probably try getting some sleep."

"Yeah, we should." I trailed my fingers down his cheek.

"Get the light?"

"Okay." I paused, then slid my hand up into his hair. "In a minute."

Diego didn't object.

CHAPTER 16
DIEGO

The conversation didn't help me sleep. Not that I'd expected to sleep, but now I had a different excuse for lying there staring at his ceiling.

Knowing how much the Navy had affected Mark's life, I felt like a dick for ever making the Navy a deal breaker. Yeah, the Navy had burned me, but it wasn't like anyone made it through a career or even a four-year enlistment without paying some kind of price. Divorces. Injuries. Alcoholism. PTSD. Suicide.

A buddy of mine had been one of those Marines with the Semper Fi tattoo and matching bumper sticker on his pickup. Married, kids, two combat tours under his belt. He'd loved the Marines, but they didn't need him anymore after a sniper in Afghanistan cost him the use of his right arm. Now he was divorced, depressed, and unemployed. Last I'd heard, the only thing keeping him from drinking himself to death was that he couldn't afford to buy food, never mind booze.

Then there was the senior chief at my last command who'd sailed through the ranks and had one of those careers every enlisted guy hoped for—as long as you ignored the two divorces and forgot that he dropped dead of a heart attack a month before the end of our Afghanistan tour.

So it wasn't like I was the only one who'd been damaged by the military. And the damage could have been *a lot* worse. Mark's ex-wife could have been a widow.

I shuddered.

I hated what the military did to people. I'd watched it happen to other people, and it had happened to me. It had happened to Mark. Okay, Mark had lucked into an XO job after getting promoted by surprise, but he'd also lost his marriage and missed his brother-in-law's funeral and his sister's wedding. Nobody came off active duty unscathed.

So how the fuck was I supposed to deal with Mark? He and the Navy were as tied together as I was to my scars. Like it or not, they weren't going anywhere.

But I didn't want to go anywhere either. I'd already decided I liked him—a lot—even before he'd seen this side of me without flinching.

I gazed at his profile in the darkness. Maybe giving military men a second chance hadn't been a bad idea.

So why couldn't I shake the feeling this was eventually going to blow up in my face?

Because everything eventually did.

I sighed. No, I was not going to be a grouchy pessimist about this. Mark was a good guy. I barely even thought about the military when we were together, and I wasn't going to let the military fuck this up. I wasn't going to let *myself* fuck it up.

I want this to work, I decided, and ran my hand up his shoulder. He murmured in his sleep but didn't wake up. *We can do this.*

My heart sank a little, and I couldn't resist giving his shoulder a gentle squeeze.

Yeah. We can do this.

As long as my ghosts don't scare you away.

Fuck.

Fuck, I hated days like this.

My heart wouldn't stop racing. Every sound made me jump out of my skin. My shoulder itched. Everything itched.

It had been a week since that text from my boss had set off a PTSD chain reaction. I'd mostly come back down from it, but it took a while, and after an episode like that, I was usually on a hair trigger for a while. Things that didn't normally set me off could kick me into a panic attack in seconds. Like a few years ago when I'd had a really bad episode a week before the Fourth of July. No amount of noise-canceling headphones or blasting music could keep away the sounds of fireworks and the memories of exploding artillery.

This time, I'd thought I was in the clear. Close to it, anyway.

I'd been wrong.

This morning, on my way home from Mark's, I'd had a near miss at an intersection. Brakes had squealed and gravel had flown, and somehow we hadn't hit each other. In the chaos, I'd caught the briefest glimpse of a cell phone flying through the other car. Texting, probably. That would explain why they'd blown the stop sign.

We hadn't made contact. After a moment, the other driver had waved an apology, I'd waved back something to the effect of *yeah, okay* instead of a well-deserved finger, and we'd gone our separate ways, me muttering every insult I could think of in English and Spanish.

A block later, I'd barely been able to hold on to the wheel because my hands had been sweating so badly. Then they'd started shaking. So had my knees. I'd finally had to pull over and pull myself together, and even now—hours afterward—I was shaky.

It wasn't because I'd almost been in a wreck. That had worn off pretty fast.

It was the glint of a windshield in my peripheral vision.

Something about the angle, the distance, the speed—something had tripped the synapse that had never forgotten the vehicle the insurgents had used to ram my disabled convoy.

Hours later, I was still ready for the explosion to follow. The concussion. The heat. The pain. The dark. Every time there was a sudden noise or jerky movement, or someone dropped something or slammed a door, I jumped out of my skin.

It was a slow night, fortunately. Tuesdays usually were. Not a lot of people or activity or orders—all good.

Mostly good, anyway. At one point, a flashback had almost gotten the best of me, but I'd shoved a hand into the ice bin and concentrated on the cold. The ache tugged my focus back into the present. The past was still holding on, but the deeper the chill set in, the less the desert could keep me.

Breathe. Focus on the cold. Stay here. Just breathe and—

Someone slammed a bottle down on the bar, and if I hadn't already been paralyzed by the flashback trying to close in, I'd have instinctively taken cover.

At least someone had tipped me off about using cold to anchor myself. Had I gotten that from the internet? Or one of my friends who'd actually had therapy? I couldn't remember anymore. Couldn't remember much of anything with any kind of clarity except desert . . . blood . . . gunfire . . . a broken chaplain at the end of his rope . . .

I shook myself. I slipped an ice cube out of the bin and closed my fingers around it before I headed into the back.

My hand was wet, but so was the rest of me. My shirt clung to the sweat on my shoulders and along my spine. A cold drop slid from my hair, down the back of my neck, and under my collar.

I desperately needed to strip off these clammy clothes and take the longest, hottest shower my apartment could offer. Of course, that would have to wait—my shift wasn't over for a while. How long? I was afraid to check the time. I didn't want an actual tangible number. Maybe if I just kept my head down and did my job, I'd be pleasantly surprised when the place was suddenly empty and we were cleaning up. A man could dream.

By closing time, I'd barely been able to stand.

I went home afterward instead of going to Mark's, which sucked. I desperately wanted to spend the night next to him.

Tonight, though, I didn't have it in me to even get to his place. I'd need to shower and change clothes and then drive again, and just thinking about all that made my eyelids heavy. I was wrung out, and my body hurt all over from being on edge. Especially my knee. The knee that had never been the same after that vehicle had rammed the convoy.

No, definitely not going to Mark's tonight. I needed sleep. And there would be nightmares—bad ones—so it was just as well I wasn't going to be next to him. They'd be worse tonight. They fucked with my sleep, but they didn't need to fuck with his.

So I'd texted him, bowed out, and gone home to pass out.

The next day was my day off, so I spent a few hours doing everything I could think of to calm the panic that wouldn't stop jittering under my skin. My landlady had a list of things she needed done around the house, and I did what I could, which pretty much meant fixing the sliding glass door that was sticking in its track and picking up the dead leaves that had finally fallen from the big maple in the backyard. The Christmas lights would have to wait another day or two. Being up on a ladder when my knee gave out or a flashback kicked in would be . . . bad.

Especially since my knee still wasn't doing so hot. Everything still ached, but that old injury was acting up like a motherfucker. Not enough to keep me from working tomorrow night, but it was going to be annoying for a while.

Days like this I wished like hell I could go down to Newport and visit the VA clinic. I had veteran benefits, after all, and those places knew how to help combat vets who were fucked in the head like me.

But I knew of two guys who'd gone to the VA and wound up getting reported and deported, so I was too scared to go.

Sometimes I wondered if that was the worst thing that could happen. Except I didn't have the money to make my own travel arrangements, so I'd be at the mercy of whatever the US government gave me, which meant they could dump me off in Tijuana or something and wish me the best of luck. Wasn't like they'd send me *home*. There wasn't even any guarantee they'd send me to the same border town where they'd dumped my family off when *they'd* been deported. Not that I wanted to go there. Juárez *had* been getting better, enough that I'd been tempted a few times, but now my mother and brother warned me the crime was getting worse again. It was bad there. No matter how much I wanted to be near my family, they urged me to avoid the place they hadn't been able to leave.

At least I knew my way around Anchor Point, and I had a place to live, some kind of income, and a truck that usually ran. In a good month, I could even spare a little money to send to my family. I'd be fucked if the government dumped me off in some border town with whatever I could carry.

So, I stayed away from the VA. In every aspect of my life, from my job to my health care, I flew as far below the government's radar as I possibly could. God knew how long I could keep that up, especially since some days were a lot harder than others. Days like today.

I'd be all right, though. One way or the other, I *would* be all right.

I was still off-kilter when I got off work the following night and headed to Mark's. Better, though. Not great, but better.

All the way to his house, I concentrated on breathing and keeping myself as calm as I could. The less he noticed, the less we'd have to talk about it. Just had to keep it under the surface. Out of his sight. Out of the way. Easy.

Yeah, right.

Keeping everything as hidden as I could, I walked up the concrete path to Mark's porch and climbed the wooden steps as I took a couple of deep breaths. I could do this.

Before I could knock, the door opened, and Mark appeared with a cute, asymmetrical smile on his lips. "Hey." He put a hand on my hip and kissed me hello.

Forcing a smile, I said, "Hey."

We exchanged glances, and though he was still smiling, I didn't like the furrow in his brow. It was like he was reading me. Seeing what I was trying to hide. I fought the urge to swallow nervously.

Then he gestured into the house, and as we stepped inside, he said, "Listen, um . . ."

I braced.

"It's been a really long day," he said quietly, almost sheepishly. "Would you be opposed to a low-key night?"

"Low-key, how?"

"Just pizza and a movie, maybe?" He shook his head. "I think that's about all I've got."

I almost breathed a sigh of relief. "No. Pizza and a movie sounds kind of nice, actually."

Mark smiled. Then he picked the remote up off the coffee table and handed it to me. "Here. See if there's anything on Netflix. I'll go order us a pizza. Any preference for toppings?"

"Not really. Just no fish."

"So, the extra anchovy special is out?"

I wrinkled my nose.

He chuckled, then headed to the kitchen.

I exhaled. Oh thank God. He didn't know I was a mess, but he wanted a chill night? Fuck yes.

While he was out of the room, I did a search for comedies. I was glad he'd let me pick out the movie. I had a mental list of films I could handle even when I was at my most brittle, and a much longer list of films I couldn't. Before the other day's near fender-bender, I would have been okay with some action or sci-fi movies. Now that I was this edgy, I had to keep it to movies without explosions, gunfire, car chases, any kind of crashes, or shit jumping out at me. Which sucked—I fucking *loved* horror movies. The more twisted, the better. When my PTSD wasn't being such an asshole, I could practically binge-watch shit like that. On a night like this? Not so much.

I settled on *Grown Ups*. It wasn't one of my favorite movies, but I'd seen it enough times to know it wouldn't trigger anything.

Once the movie was queued up, I went into the kitchen where Mark was wrapping up his call.

"Forty minutes? Sounds good. Thanks." He hung up and turned to me. "They're a little busy tonight. You okay to wait?"

"What else are we gonna do?" I half shrugged. "Go down there and tell them to hurry up?"

He chuckled, snaking an arm around my waist. "I've yelled at enough people today, so I'll leave that to you."

"Yelled at people?" I raised my eyebrows. "What happened?"

Mark groaned. "The ship has, shall we say, a disciplinary problem." He rubbed his eyes. "I spent almost all day doing XOI." Dropping his hand to his side, he shook his head. And yeah, he looked tired. "It'll be the same shit tomorrow. I'm glad we don't have any aircraft aboard right now, because I promise you I would have a pilot explaining to me why he was drawing dicks in the sky."

I laughed. "Damn. Do they send you guys all the fuckups or something?"

"No, but the upper chain of command was almost entirely fuckups before me and the new CO got there. So now we get to unfuck all of it." He waved a hand. "Anyway. It's work. It can stay at work. I'm just glad to be home with you so we can relax."

Warmth radiated through me. Even after I'd been such a train wreck . . . "Yeah. Me too."

We hung out in the kitchen until the pizza finally arrived. Then we settled in the living room with the box, a couple of beers, and paper plates balanced on our knees.

We ate while the movie played, and when the pizza was gone, we settled back against the couch to finish watching the movie. Mark slung an arm around my shoulders, and I leaned into him.

And damn . . . I felt pretty fucking good.

There was no magically making this feeling go away, and there'd be more nightmares tonight for sure, but spending the evening like this—relaxing without anything that might trigger me—would sure as shit help. Having Mark's warm, solid presence wouldn't hurt either.

By the time the credits rolled, I had relaxed against his side. Hell, I'd pretty much melted into it. Enough that I was getting a crick in my neck. I sat up and stretched.

Mark's hand ran up and down my back. "Feeling better?"

I turned to him. "What?"

"You were having . . ." Mark hesitated. "An off day, I guess?"

I swallowed, staring at him. "How did you know?"

He trailed his palm along my spine. "Gut feeling, I guess?"

"And it didn't bother you?"

"It . . ." He cocked his head. "Of course it bothered me. I don't like seeing you hurting. But it wasn't going to make me chase you out, if that's what you mean." He said it like that was the most absurd thing he'd ever imagined.

"You wouldn't be the first."

Mark scowled. "Yeah, no. Not gonna happen."

"So . . . all this." I gestured at the pizza box and the remote. "That wasn't because you had a long day?"

"Oh, I had a long day." He smiled, looking tired. "But I think you had a longer one."

I wanted to be embarrassed or even annoyed that he'd caught on and that he'd suggested a low-key night for my benefit, but I wasn't. It was actually a relief that he hadn't made a big deal out of it and didn't seem even a little bit bothered by the relaxing, almost boring evening I'd desperately needed.

So, I returned the smile. "Thanks." I slipped my hand into his. "This was definitely what the doctor ordered."

"I figured." He sat up and kissed me softly. Nodding toward the TV, he asked, "Want to watch something else?"

Want to keep things low-key and boring?

God, yes I do.

I shrugged so I didn't seem too eager. "Yeah, sure. Sounds good."

He handed me the remote. I started scrolling through his Netflix queue, then checked out what channels he actually got. When I paused on one, the familiar logo in the corner of the screen made me chuckle. "You actually get AFN at home?"

Mark eyed the screen. "Huh. Guess I do. I didn't even know that was on there."

"You pay close attention to things, don't you?"

He rolled his eyes and elbowed me playfully. "Shut up."

I snickered.

The American Forces Network was military produced, so some of the commercials were a little amateurish, but they had a few good shows and occasionally good movies. Tonight, they were showing a marathon of sitcoms that weren't great, but also weren't full of triggery shit.

"Want to watch this?" I motioned toward the screen with the remote.

"I'm game."

I set the remote on the coffee table, and we cuddled up together to watch the show.

A few times, I almost drifted off next to Mark. I was exhausted from the PTSD flare-up, but I really was a lot more relaxed now. Still tense, but more settled. When I laughed, I didn't have to force it. When I spoke, I didn't have to fight to keep my voice steady.

God, what a relief. After being on the edge of falling apart for days on end, I was finally feeling like myself again.

Right up until the suicide prevention commercial.

The instant I saw the man in camouflage staring at a mirror with a pistol in his hand, I froze. So did Mark.

Then he lunged for the remote, but not before the screen turned to a misty combat scene—a flashback for the guy with the gun—and suddenly there was smoke and flying dirt and people screaming and—

Black.

The screen went dark so fast I jumped.

It was too late, though. Even with the TV off and my eyes squeezed shut, the images were burned into my brain. Just a few seconds of a commercial, and my mind was flooded with memories.

My ears rang.

My throat burned from screaming.

My mouth tasted like a mix of blood and smoke.

Couldn't . . . get enough . . . air.

"Diego?" Mark's voice cut through. "Can you hear me?"

I nodded but didn't speak. I couldn't breathe. My throat was too tight, and my lungs . . . something was wrong with . . . my chest hurt. Was I having a heart attack? Oh fuck, I was. I was fucking dying. Couldn't breathe . . . couldn't—

"Diego." His voice was firmer. "Look at me. Come on."

I lowered my hands—when had I brought them up to my face?—and forced my eyes open. On some level, I knew where I was, but I was still surprised when the desert sun didn't try to blind me and there was nothing around me except Mark's simple, sleek furniture.

And Mark. Eyes intense. Brow furrowed.

"Just breathe. I'm right here. And so are you." His strong arm around my shoulders did more than the soothing tone of his voice. I concentrated on that touch. On the weight of his arm. On finding . . . some fucking . . . *air*.

I rubbed at my chest like that might do something. "Fuck . . ."

"I should take you to the ER."

"*No*." My pulse surged just thinking about it. "There's n-no way I can afford . . . I can't . . ."

Mark blinked. "Diego, if you're—"

"You going to pay for it?" I snapped shakily. My teeth were chattering, and I clenched them as I growled, "And make sure they don't turn my illegal ass in?"

His lips parted, and he stared at me. As much as I hated myself for it, I prayed he actually had a solution. It probably was a good idea to see a doctor right now. *Was* I having a heart attack? Was I about to?

But then he closed his mouth and dropped his gaze.

And the panic cut even deeper. The whole world was closing in around me, my own body was failing me, and the one person who was still calm and collected didn't know what to do either. Shit. Shit, I was going to throw up. And then choke because my throat was too . . . Oh God . . .

My vision started to tunnel and my hands were starting to tingle. Fuck. I leaned forward to put my head between my knees. That didn't help me breathe, but it kept me conscious. I thought. Maybe?

Strong fingers kneaded the back of my neck. "I'll pay for it." His tone was pleading. "I'll give them a fake name for you. Whatever. It's . . . I'd rather see you getting treated and make sure you're not going to drop dead."

I shuddered. It was tempting, but it had only been a couple of months since I'd finally paid off the *last* time one of these freak-outs had landed me in the ER. I knew how much that shit cost, and I wasn't having Mark cough up that kind of money. I didn't want to owe him like that.

"No," I finally said. "I'll . . . I'll be okay. It's . . ." I squeezed my eyes shut as I tried to pull myself together. "No ER."

Mark didn't say another word. Or if he did, I didn't hear it. For what seemed like days, we stayed there on the sofa, my head between my knees and his hand on the back of my neck, and I just tried to breathe and not pass out. My heart was pounding so fast and so hard, I could barely tell one beat from the next. The *thump-thumps* blended together like helicopter blades blurring. Helicopter blades blurring. Helicopter blades. Helicopter.

"Can you hear me, Ramírez?"

". . . need a medevac . . ."

". . . Ramírez? C'mon, man. Stay with— Incoming!"

Sweat rolled down my face.

No, it wasn't sweat.

I swiped at my cheek and sniffed.

An arm around my shoulders kept me steady. Mark didn't speak, but even as my brain darted back and forth between the past and present, he was *there*. Strong, solid, quiet, and warm—he just stayed still and stayed with me, and I anchored myself to him as I tried to ride this out.

Slowly, I steadied myself. My pulse was maybe halfway back to normal. Cold sweat slid down the back of my neck and under my shirt. When I cautiously opened my eyes, the tunnel vision had widened.

I released a long breath and leaned back. Mark went with me, and he held me gently while the panic attack subsided. It would be a while before I felt completely grounded again, but the worst of it was over. The fear that I was having a heart attack was gone, and that usually meant I was on the way to okay.

Still jittery, I looked around to orient myself. The living room was still and quiet, and my trigger-happy psyche wanted to turn it into that room in Kuwait where I'd ridden a morphine high until sliding into that dark tunnel that had ended in Germany. I didn't remember enough of the place in Kuwait to make sense of it, only that I'd been terrified and loopy and . . . there'd been pain, but I couldn't place it. Couldn't say what had hurt or how it had hurt. Only that I'd been in hell. Right now, I remembered the walls being the same powder blue as Mark's living room, but I knew that was just my head filling in the blanks.

I was here. In Mark's living room. In Anchor Point. Kuwait and Afghanistan and Germany were half a dozen years and a million miles away. I was *here*.

Finally, I licked my parched lips and turned to Mark. "I'm . . . I'm okay."

His brow pinched. He put a hand on my leg and squeezed gently. "You sure?"

I nodded. "Yeah. Sorry about that. I . . ." How *did* I get here? My gaze drifted to the TV. Enough of the commercial flickered through my mind to remind me what had set me off, but I tamped it down before it sent me spiraling again. "That commercial. Caught me off guard, I guess."

"I know." He grimaced and shot the TV a glare. "I completely forgot they've got some of those commercials now."

"It's okay." My mouth was so dry it was almost painful. "You'd think they wouldn't show that shit on a channel like that."

Mark scowled, nodding.

I started to speak again, but the dryness made me want to cough instead. I managed to croak, "You mind if I—" I coughed.

"Need something to drink?" He was already on his feet.

"Thanks."

While he was in the kitchen, I took a few more slow breaths to center myself. This feeling was weirdly miserable and amazing. I hated the shakiness and the queasiness, but I fucking *basked* in the feeling that the worst was over. This was the calm after the firefight. When the adrenaline was crashing, the sweat was drying, the blood was pumping, and I was an impossible mix of restless and lethargic. I couldn't move, but I couldn't stop shaking. The fear was gone. The bullets weren't flying anymore. I wasn't okay, but I would be, and just knowing that was enough to make me almost sob with relief.

Mark's soft footsteps pulled me out of the fog, and I looked up as he sat beside me with a glass of water.

"Thanks," I said again and took the glass. After a careful swallow, I added, "I'm sorry you had to see all that."

"Don't be. But are you sure you shouldn't go see someone? Just to make sure you're—"

"I'm fine, Mark." I met his eyes, hating myself for the pitiful sound of my voice. "This happens sometimes. It's pretty terrifying until it's over, but I'll be fine." I swallowed past the tightness in my throat. "And I don't want to owe you that kind of money. Or get . . ." My shoulders sagged just thinking about the hell my life could turn into if someone at the ER gave my paperwork the side-eye.

He sighed, and I thought he might argue. He didn't, though. After a moment, he spoke in barely a whisper: "They'd really deport you? From a hospital?"

"They'd . . ." I sighed. "They'd get the ball rolling, let's put it that way."

Mark studied me. "How does that even work? I mean, does someone just grab you and drop you over the other side of the border?"

"Not quite. There's a process. And it takes some time, but not much." My voice was still shaky, but better. "They say you get thirty days to get your shit together and leave the country. But you have to go on your own dime, and I don't have that kind of money." I raked unsteady fingers through my sweaty hair. "So I'd have to let them send me, and I don't . . . I don't know if they'll get me somewhere close to home, or if they'll just dump me off in Tijuana or Juárez or something.

The really, *really* scary parts of Tijuana or Juárez. That's what happened to my family."

Mark stiffened. "Your family was deported?"

"Yeah. My mom lost her job because she was taking too much time off to take care of my dad while he had cancer. After my dad died, my brother tried to keep them afloat, but then he got laid off, and . . ." I exhaled. Just thinking about it was heartbreaking. Exhausting. Fucking excruciating. "Someone in their apartment complex reported them, and the next thing we knew, my mom, brother, and grandmother were in Juárez." Closing my eyes, I sighed. "And sometimes I think I should just let ICE deport me. I could find some way from wherever they dump me to where my family lives."

"Do you *want* to go there?"

I chewed my lip. "I'd like to be with my family, but they keep telling me to stay away from Juárez. It's getting bad again. The crime, I mean. And they're barely scraping by anyway. I try to send them money when I can, but sometimes I . . ." I exhaled. "Honestly, all I want is some fucking stability, and at this point, I don't give a fuck which side of the border I'm on." My throat tightened, and my voice was thick as I added, "But I don't know how to *get* that stability, you know? I don't know where the fuck I should go right now. Or where I *can* go. This country doesn't want me, and . . ." I sniffed.

Mark gathered me in his arms and stroked my hair. "Hey. Easy. You don't have to make that decision tonight."

All the air rushed out of my lungs. It was such a simple statement, but it shook away some of the panic that had been holding on. Eyes squeezed shut, I slid a hand up his arm and let myself melt against him.

I *didn't* have to make a decision tonight.

Tomorrow was anybody's guess—every damn day was—but no one was knocking down the door tonight and throwing me out of the US, and I grabbed on to that comfort like the rock that it was.

Mark held me close and kissed the top of my head. "Neither of us is going anywhere tonight. I promise."

I just nodded against his chest. Most days, I could cope. It was stressful, and there was never a time when my situation wasn't gnawing at me, but it was kind of like being in combat—you eventually adjusted to the possibility of getting mortared or shot at with no warning, and you ate and slept and shot the shit with your buddies because what the fuck else were you supposed to do?

But some days . . .

I shivered.

"You okay?" he asked.

"I will be." I lifted my head to meet his gaze. "And I'll be better in a few days. I promise."

"I know." Mark kissed me gently. "There's no pressure from my end, okay? I'm not going anywhere, and I'm not over here tapping my foot or anything."

I closed my eyes and released another breath. I felt like kind of an ass for being so relieved that he'd said it. I should've known he wasn't like that, so why the fuck did I need reassurance?

"Diego," he whispered, cradling my face in both hands. "This isn't some flaw or personality quirk, you know? You came back from Hell. I'd be worried if you *didn't* have some PTSD from that."

I opened my eyes and gazed into his.

He smiled. "Just tell me how I can help when it's bad. Or how I can avoid making it bad. Or worse."

"Thank you. I really appreciate it." Sighing, I leaned into him again. I'd only meant to make some contact, but once I'd started, I couldn't stop. I moved all the way in and rested my forehead on his shoulder, and I loved how he felt against me. I loved how *I* felt against *him*.

I let my eyes slide closed. Sleep threatened to take over. That wasn't surprising; now that the panic attack was over, the way-too-familiar exhaustion was tugging me down. "So tired."

"I'll bet you are." His fingers carded through my hair. "You want to go to bed?"

I looked up at him. "You want me to stay here?"

He blinked. "Did you think I was going to kick you out?"

We held each other's gazes for a few seconds.

Then he took my hand and brought it to his lips. "When you came over tonight, I wanted you to stay. That hasn't changed."

Wordlessly, I nodded.

"Are you sure you're all right, though?" he asked softly.

"Yeah. I'll be fine." I wasn't sure if I was telling him or myself.

He ran a hand down my back. "But if you're not, just say so. Okay?"

I nodded again. "Thank you."

CHAPTER 17
MARK

"**I** see you in my office like this again," I growled at the two kids standing at attention in front of my desk, "you're not going to like what happens. Am I clear?"

"Yes, sir," they said in unison.

I shifted my glare to their lead petty officer, who was also standing at attention, but not quite as rigidly. To the two seamen, I said, "Dismissed. AT1, you stay here."

The LPO swallowed hard. His men didn't look at him. He didn't look at them. After they'd left my office, his posture stiffened a bit more.

I folded my hands on the desk and stared at him. "This is the fifth time in ten months that people from your shop have been to XOI. You want to tell me why that is?"

He set his jaw. "I don't have any excuses, sir. The assistant LPO and I will look into it, though."

I regarded him silently for a long moment, deliberately making him uneasy. I waited until he shifted his weight. Some color bloomed in his cheeks too. This wasn't someone accustomed to being put on the spot. He was a young LPO—no way he'd been in more than ten years—and from what I'd gathered when I'd first arrived, the Aviation Electronics Department had had almost as much turnover as the upper chain of command. Odds were he'd inherited the disciplinary mess just like I had. It wasn't his fault, but it was his responsibility to get it squared away, and I needed him to know I wasn't joking.

"I'm going to make you the same promise I made your two junior Sailors," I said flatly. "I see you in my office like this again, it's not going to end well."

The AT1 nodded grimly. "Yes, sir." It came out as little more than a croak.

"Dismissed."

He couldn't get out of my office fast enough. I had a feeling he was going to go catch his breath, then march into his shop and give those two junior Sailors an earful for making *him* get an earful. That was what I would've done.

Alone in the tight confines of my office, I tilted my head to one side, then the other, trying to work out some tension. It wasn't the idiot Sailors and disciplinary bullshit that had me wound up, though. It was the man who'd been sharing my bed.

I couldn't get last night out of my head. Diego's episode had scared the hell out of me, and the things he'd said afterward had burrowed under my skin and wouldn't move. I'd been certain he was either going to pass out from hyperventilating or have a goddamned heart attack. The ER had seemed like the most common sense place to go. I wouldn't have minded if the doctors had rolled their eyes and told us it was just a panic attack. At least I'd know he was okay.

But even in the throes of a panic attack, even while he'd clearly been struggling to catch his breath and rein in the demons from his past, he'd had the presence of mind to reject my suggestion. His inability to get medical treatment when he needed it was so ingrained in him, it had cut through a fucking *panic attack*.

I rubbed my eyes with my thumb and forefinger. A military veteran. With combat-related PTSD. And he couldn't afford to get treatment. Or risk someone noticing he was illegal.

What if he really did have a life-threatening emergency? What if he got hurt at work? Or got into a car accident? I knew ERs were required to stabilize anyone who came through the door, but then what? How long before he'd be booted out of the hospital for his inability to pay? Or escorted out of the *country* because he didn't have a damn green card?

I dropped my hand to my desk and swore into the silence of my office. It wasn't right. It wasn't fair. What the hell could I do about it, though?

Not a damn thing, apparently. I hadn't even been able to take him somewhere to get help last night. His situation? I didn't even know where to start.

Make sure he was okay, maybe. I wanted to text him, but my cell signal wasn't so hot on the ship. They must've been running some of the radar equipment today. Always scrambled the shit out of my reception. And anyway, he might've still been asleep. It was only 1100, after all, and he'd barely slept last night. I'd give him a couple more hours before I went down to the pier to send him a message. I had left a note under his phone telling him to call me on the ship if he needed anything. So far, nothing.

Restlessness was starting to make me itch, so I got up and left, the hatch clanging shut behind me. Not far down the passageway, I knocked on another.

"It's open," Captain Hawthorne said gruffly.

I stepped inside. "Hey. You got a minute?"

"Sure." He put a thick binder down and removed his glasses while I took a seat in front of his desk. "How'd XOI go?"

I grunted. "They'll be coming to see you if they set foot in my office again."

"Repeat offenders?"

"One of them. And they're both from a shop that's about to install a revolving door in my office."

Hawthorne scowled. "What the fuck is going on down there?"

"Don't know." I shook my head. "I put the fear of God into the LPO, though. He doesn't straighten shit out in a hurry, they'll all be hearing from me."

"Good, good."

We both fell quiet for a minute. The disciplinary mess wasn't really a shock. The *Fort Stevens* had had a rough couple of years. Morale was in the toilet. Couldn't really blame the crew, though. It was hard to keep people in line when they knew damn well their last CO had gone down for bribing people in security to hide the results of his drug tests. The CO before him—along with the XO I'd replaced and several other members of the brass—had been busted taking part in the prostitution ring a lieutenant had been running. From what I'd heard from people who'd been here for the worst of it, discipline had pretty much crumbled in the enlisted ranks before any of that had even started. A chief had gone to jail in some port or another for beating up a local national. Federal agents had apparently escorted a master chief off the ship in handcuffs after *"something you honestly don't want to know about, Captain."*

Yeah. This place was a mess. Which meant Hawthorne and I had to pull it all together, especially with a deployment coming up in the spring. We weren't going to be popular anytime soon, but we *would* get this crew back in line.

Assuming I kept my head in the game, anyway, and that had been a struggle lately.

"You all right?" Hawthorne asked.

"Yeah. I . . ." I scrubbed a hand over my face. "I'm curious about something."

He made a *go ahead* gesture. "Sure. What's on your mind?"

"You heard about immigrant vets getting deported after their time is up?"

Hawthorne shrugged. "If their green cards expire, sure."

"And there's nothing we can do about it?"

He studied me. "You got someone under you who wants to get citizenship?"

"I'm, uh . . . Not someone in particular. And it's someone who's not in anymore."

Immediately, Hawthorne shook his head. "Nothing we can do if he's been discharged."

I blinked.

He shrugged again. "Look, Sailors and officers have plenty of opportunity to apply for naturalization while they're in." He sat back, shaking his head. "If they don't go through the available channels while they're on active duty, ain't much we can do once they're discharged."

I pursed my lips. "So it doesn't bother you? Someone getting out after serving and then getting booted out of the country?"

"I'm not thrilled with it, but as long as there are options available while they're active, I don't have a lot of sympathy for people who don't take advantage."

Gritting my teeth, I asked, "And what if they're discharged before they have that opportunity?"

"Then either they fucked up and got kicked out early, or they're full of shit." The harsh tone offered no sympathy or flexibility. "There's no way someone can't find time to fill out some paperwork in four years."

Okay, a few weeks ago I'd have agreed he had a point, but now it didn't sit right with me. Diego had been to combat. He'd been wounded. He had PTSD bad enough to be triggered into a panic attack by a TV commercial. And he'd had every intention of getting naturalized, but by the time he'd recovered enough to be functional, the Navy was showing him to the door thanks to a computer algorithm.

Before I could say something, Hawthorne gave a disgusted sneer. "What's really fucked up is these illegals who still want VA benefits."

"You don't think they should have them?"

"Fuck no, I don't."

I blinked. "Why not? They earned them."

"And they also earned a shot at becoming citizens. If they don't use that, and they're not going to pay taxes and work legally like everybody else . . ." He shook his head. "Then no, I don't think they should be getting benefits other vets have to jump through hoops to get."

I shifted uncomfortably. "So, what if—hypothetically—a wounded vet was kicked out under Perform to Serve? Before he'd had a chance to get his citizenship squared away?"

Hawthorne scowled. "PTS was a flawed program. It's a damn good thing they scrapped it. The Sailors who were discharged under it? It's a shame, but . . ." He waved a hand and sighed. "Look, it isn't like they would've been kicked out overnight. The first PTS score wasn't final. But if the second one said they were out, then . . ." Another shrug.

I swallowed.

"And it wasn't like people didn't know about PTS." Hawthorne rapped a knuckle on his broad steel desk. "If I were an immigrant and knew that shit was hanging over my head, I'd be filling out my immigration forms right away. What excuse does someone have to wait until the last second?"

"Besides combat-related convalescence?"

Hawthorne cocked his head, and his eyes narrowed a little. "This isn't a hypothetical, is it?"

I tried not to shift noticeably, but I probably failed.

"This can't be one of your Sailors." He studied me intently. "What's going on?"

"Just a . . ." I thought fast. "Friend of a friend. Got kicked out under PTS while he was recuperating from combat injuries."

"And he was an illegal?"

"He wasn't at the time, but his visa expired after—"

"How long was he in?"

"Eight years."

Hawthorne shook his head, a faint sneer on his lips. "Then he's got no one to blame but himself. In eight years, he could have done that paperwork. If he isn't motivated enough to fill out some forms, the Navy doesn't need him and neither does this country."

"And there's nothing we can do." I sounded even more resigned than I felt.

"Once they've been discharged, they're not our problem anymore. Not our jurisdiction and not our responsibility." *Case closed*, I could almost hear him adding.

So I just nodded. "All right. I was just curious."

We talked for a few more minutes, but then he needed to get to a meeting. I had one in an hour, which meant I had some time to slip off the boat and see if Diego had messaged me.

On the way to the quarterdeck and the ramp that would take me pier-side, I fought to quell a sick feeling that had started during my conversation with the CO. Convincing him he was wrong was probably a lost cause, but I didn't like the idea that the Navy could and would do nothing for Diego. Except . . . what could they do? If he'd been discharged recently, maybe, but it had been several years.

Hawthorne's comments about illegals grated on me more than anything. Someone who'd served shouldn't have *been* illegal. Period. Why veterans weren't automatically granted citizenship, I would never understand. A non-US citizen veteran being denied health care for his war-related injuries? That was some bullshit.

I made a mental note to see if any of the personnel on my ship were in danger of falling into Diego's circumstances. Even if Perform to Serve had rightfully gone the way of the dinosaur, it didn't hurt to make sure people were prepared in case they decided not to reenlist. At the very least, I could put out a memo urging any immigrants under my command to come talk to me about making sure the proper paperwork was filed if citizenship was something they wanted.

I'd do that after my meeting. First things first, though, I needed to check on the man who'd spent the whole night tossing and turning next to me.

Down on the pier, where my signal was stronger, I took out my phone. I was more than a little relieved to see a text from Diego.

Hey. :) Feeling better today. Thx for last night.

I smiled as I read and reread his words. Then I wrote back, *You're welcome. Glad to hear it.* After I'd sent that message, I added, *See you tonight?*

As soon as Diego started typing, my heart flipped. I silently begged him not to say no. Even if he was still off-kilter tonight, I wanted to be with him. At least then I could see for myself that he was all right. Close to it, anyway.

Then he stopped typing. Shit. What did *that* mean? Was he trying to let me down easy somehow? Had I done something wrong? Fuck, maybe I'd been too pushy about the ER thing. He'd been busy falling apart and I hadn't been willing to let it go, so he'd had to argue with me while trying to get his head together.

I winced at the memory. Oh crap. I'd handled that all wrong, hadn't I? Now how the hell did I—

He was typing again. A few seconds later, a message came through: *Sorry. Boss called. Tonight sounds good. After closing ok?*

I smiled like an idiot and wrote back, *Can't wait.*

CHAPTER 18
DIEGO

Today was better. Much, *much* better. The ghosts had scattered. They'd be back eventually—they always came back—but for now, they were gone, and I was grounded in the present where I belonged. I made it through my shift without falling apart. By the time I was on my way to Mark's, I was damn near twitching, but it was a new kind of restlessness. Or at least one I hadn't felt recently.

I was horny.

Not just horny. I wanted Mark. We hadn't had sex in days because I'd been too much of a wreck. After last night, I should've *still* been a wreck, but I wanted him. Especially after he'd swung by the club earlier to bring me dinner and check on me. He'd only been there a couple of minutes, but something about seeing him tonight, about the look in his eyes that said he was concerned and he cared and *maybe even still wanted me*, was driving me insane.

You're going to know—tonight—*how much I want you.*

So as soon as he let me into the house, I grabbed him and kissed him hard. He hesitated at first, stiffening in my arms, but then he must've decided to follow my lead. Wrapping his arms around me, he gave as good as he got. His fingers raked through my hair, and we held each other so tight and so close I could feel his erection growing under his jeans.

"You're—" He licked his lips. "I didn't think you'd be in the mood tonight."

"Neither did I." Christ, I was out of breath. "But I have been ever since you showed up at the bar."

He stared at me, and I thought for a second we were going to stop and pick apart exactly why that moment had made me so hungry for him. Instead, he cradled the back of my head, drew me in, and kissed me even harder than before. No more talking. No more questioning. I tugged him toward the stairs, and he groaned against my lips as he followed me.

We stumbled a few more steps until we hit the bannister. Then I broke the kiss, and we hurried up and into the bedroom.

"I want you naked," he growled. The commanding tone made my spine prickle.

I grinned against his neck. "Do you?"

"Uh-huh."

"Maybe you should do something about it."

He exhaled sharply, then shoved my shirt up and off. His nails raked down my bare skin, making my breath hitch. Clothes came off, even if they were a bit stubborn about it. I swore if I could tear denim with my bare hands, there'd be nothing left of those jeans. I couldn't, though, and after some swearing, they were on the floor along with his boxers.

We finally sank onto the bed, completely naked and holding each other close. It had only been a week or so since we'd done this, but the heat of his skin against mine was as intoxicating as it had been the first time.

I moved to straddle him but flinched as a bolt of pain shot through my leg. Fuck. Just what I needed—my stupid leg to act up now that my brain had finally calmed down. Okay, plan B.

"I've got a better idea." I moved onto my back and started stroking myself. "Get me a condom and get on."

Mark's eyes widened, but he quite clearly had no objection to the idea. He handed me a condom, and as I put it on, he poured some lube in his hand. When he started stroking it on me, I damn near lost it.

"Fuck, Mark . . ." I bit my lip, arching my back as he pumped my dick. "Get . . . get on, damn it."

He didn't even bother teasing me. He straddled me, and then he was easing himself down onto my cock, taking me in one long, slow stroke until I was all the way in.

"Oh God," I breathed. "That's . . . *Oh God.*"

"Mmm, yeah." He planted his hands on the mattress on either side of my head, and I ran my palms up his arms as he found a steady rhythm with his hips. A low moan escaped his lips, and then "Fuck, you feel good."

"You too. And you look . . ." I slid my hands down to his thighs. "Ungh. Christ."

I was fucking *drunk* on him. Completely overwhelmed by all these sensations—being inside him, being under him, his hot skin and his hard, perfect thrusts—and ready to break down and cry from the sheer joy of not being scared. Because for the last several days, I'd been scared. Constantly. Of my own mind. Of my past. Of losing Mark. Of never feeling normal again. Of losing what little stability I had.

And right now—even if it was just until we were done fucking—I wasn't scared of anything. That void where all the fear had been was full of warmth and lust. It was just him and me, bodies and sweat and whispered curses, and I was flying as he took my cock again and again.

"Oh God," I moaned. "God, Mark, I'm . . . Yeah, that's . . ." I slid my hands up his chest, palms gliding across the slick sweat and fingers parting the thin dark hair. "I'm gonna come."

"Yeah?" he panted. "You close?"

I nodded because I'd forgotten how to talk. Fuck it. Didn't need to talk. He knew. I dug my teeth into my lip and my heels into the mattress and lifted my hips, meeting him every time he came down.

"Oh yeah," he growled. "You are so hot. Love . . . love watching you come apart. *Jesus*, Diego."

I tried to speak, but he added some twist or roll or whatever to his hips, and that was all I could take. I yelled something that might or might not have been in Spanish, and as I came, Mark kept right on going, clenching hard around my dick and riding me fast until I couldn't take any more.

He lifted himself off my cock but stayed on top of me.

"C'mere," I ordered, and as he came down to kiss me, I closed my hand around his dick. He met my lips with a low groan. I slid my other hand behind his neck and kept a tight grip as I kissed him deeply and stroked him. His hips rocked like he was still riding me, and hot huffs of breath rushed past my cheek as he seemed to get even thicker and harder in my hand.

He broke the kiss, and his head fell beside mine. He fucked into my fist and groaned into my ear. "Fuck yeah, baby . . . God . . ." Then he shuddered hard, and my strokes were suddenly slick with cum, and he thrust a few more times before he collapsed over me. "*Fuck*."

"We should . . ." I murmured. "We should definitely do it like this again."

"Uh-huh." He brushed a breathless kiss across my lips. "Shower?"

"Sure. Soon as I can stand."

It was a good five minutes before either of us was steady on our feet. We finally made it into the shower, though, and the hot water felt good. Good, but not nearly as good as Mark's body. Both at the same time? Fuck yes.

We didn't paw at each other or try to get things started again. We just stood there under the running water, my cheek resting on his shoulder while he nuzzled my hair. And it was amazing. It was perfect. My skin had finally stopped crawling, and I loved the way it felt to be pressed against him. The PTSD episode had been long and horrible, but standing here in the shower with Mark, body satisfied and tingling after my orgasm, I felt like the episode was really *over*.

"Doing all right?" he asked after a while.

"Yeah." I pulled back and met his eyes. It was weird how things between us *weren't* weird. There was no pity in his expression. Concern, yes, but also other things. Warmth. Need. Lust. Christ, it was like he hadn't had a front row seat to my breakdown. It was like . . . he still saw *me*. And he still wanted me.

Mark cocked his head, a few drops of water sliding down the side of his face. "What?"

Oh shit. I'd been staring. And spacing out. I cleared my throat. "I, um, I wasn't expecting any of this tonight."

He touched my face. "Why not?"

"I don't know. I . . ." Avoiding his gaze, I brushed some wet hair out of my face. "After the last couple of days, I didn't think you'd . . . I mean, it's not really a turn-on, you know?"

"*You're* a turn-on." He said it simply and matter-of-factly. "You turn me on. You always do."

I looked at him. "Even after . . ."

"Of course. I . . ." He blinked a few times, then slid his wet hands over my hips. "What kind of question is that?"

A valid one after you saw me melting down yesterday.

He must have seen the worry in my eyes, because he leaned in and kissed me. "Yes, you still turn me on. And yes, I still want you just like I did a week ago." His forehead creased. "Why are you so surprised that I'm still into you? What kind of men have you been dating?"

"The kind that don't get it, I guess." I half shrugged as I brushed my dripping hair off my forehead. "Can't really blame them, you know? They don't understand. It's got to be scary the first time you watch someone have a panic attack, right?"

Mark averted his eyes, but he nodded. "Yeah. It is."

"Between that, the nightmares, the way I can be edgy for days at a time, and all the things that can trigger me?" I grimaced. "I get it, you know? When someone can't handle it? Because *I* can barely handle it. I just don't have a choice."

"I can handle it." He pulled me in closer. "And no, it's not easy to watch," he said so quietly it barely carried over the shower, "but it's not going to send me running."

I still watched him, trying to convince myself he was just blowing smoke, but his eyes and his voice were so fucking sincere. I smiled. "I thought you said something about being bad at relationships."

He laughed before claiming a gentle kiss. "Well, my track record isn't so good."

I shrugged, wrapping my arms around his waist. "I'm not complaining."

"Good. Because I'm not either." Then he kissed me again.

It would have been easier if he had been shitty at relationships. Hell, that was probably part of the reason I'd let myself get this involved with him in the first place. Because in the back of my mind, I'd expected him to fuck it up.

But he wasn't fucking it up.

In fact, he was making it really, *really* hard to not fall in love with him.

The bedroom was quiet. In the distance, the ocean crashed against the coast, and I could feel the thump and the roar more than I could hear them.

Here, the heater hummed in the background, and Mark snored softly beside me. Not loud enough to keep me awake—I couldn't sleep anyway—and not annoying. I kind of liked it, actually. I liked listening to him sleeping peacefully next to me.

Nightmares weren't a problem tonight. Those would require me to actually sleep.

I glanced at the clock. It was almost five on a Saturday morning, so he wouldn't be jumping out of bed in the next few minutes. At least that meant one of us could sleep.

I pulled my attention from the clock and looked at him. I'd been watching him a lot tonight, and my mind kept going back to the night we'd told each other about our shaky pasts. That night, I'd started making peace with the idea of having a boyfriend who was military. Of really doing this. I'd been scared as hell he wouldn't stick around once he saw just how bad my time in combat had screwed me up.

But he had.

When we'd started out, I hadn't liked the idea of getting too close to someone who was military. Now that I *was* close to him, I was even more sure the other shoe was going to drop. I'd gone down the road my instincts had warned me about, and it was going to catch up with me sooner or later.

Before Mark and Dalton, I'd resisted service members because I was too bitter to go anywhere near the military. Their uniforms, their jobs, the familiar white ID cards that showed whenever they took out their wallets—it was all too poisonous, and I hadn't wanted anything to do with it.

I hadn't been *scared*, though.

Now I was. Even that night when I'd worried about him seeing my demons, I hadn't been scared like this. What if what finally pulled us apart wasn't him or me at all? What if neither of us screwed up, and shit still fell apart?

Eyes closed, I pushed out a breath. I couldn't shake the feeling that sooner or later, the Navy was going to happen to us. I didn't know when. I didn't know how. It wasn't like anyone could order him not to date me. Somehow, though, the fact that Mark had uniforms hanging in his closet was going to fuck this whole thing up. Right?

So why didn't I worry about it when we were actually doing something together? When I was lying awake at night and working myself into a panic, I worried about it. When Mark and I were fooling around or watching a movie or eating . . . it didn't cross my mind. Huh.

Maybe that meant I really was getting over some of my issues with the military. It would be a cold day in hell before I could drive past NAS Adams without muttering things I would never say around my mother, but maybe I could handle Mark in his uniform without being overcome with bitterness. That was a start, wasn't it?

And was it enough?

My heart beat faster. I couldn't resist sliding closer to him and draping my arm over his waist as I buried my face in his neck. He mumbled something and wriggled back against me. After feeling around blindly for a second, he found my hand and laced our fingers together. In no time, he was asleep again. I wasn't sure if he'd ever been awake, or if he'd been on autopilot.

I smiled and pressed a kiss to the back of his shoulder. Second-guessing my rejection the night we'd met had been one of the smartest things I'd ever done. Now I just had to get past all the reasons I'd rejected him in the first place. He was Navy. That was the way it was. The only thing standing between us was my hang-ups.

If we had any hope of making this thing work, I had to let that shit go. Yeah, the Navy had fucked me. I had scars on my body and in my mind that would never be gone, and I'd lost my career and my stability, but that wasn't Mark's fault. None of it was. The only thing I could blame him for was how I'd been feeling these days, and that was mostly good.

I *was* scared, though. Not of facing the Navy—of losing Mark. To my own hang-ups or to him getting tired of the landmines in my head or . . . anything.

I closed my eyes and sighed. Mark shivered, probably from my breath across his neck. In his sleep, he murmured again, then brought our joined hands up to his chest and held them there.

I'd already let my past keep me from someone I absolutely could have loved. Losing Dalton had made me rethink my hang-ups about the military, but it was Mark who had me wanting to actually make peace with my past. Not because the Navy collectively deserved any kind of forgiveness, but because it was the only way I could give myself completely to Mark.

And . . . I wanted to. My throat tightened as that realization sank in. It was true, wasn't it? I had no idea where this thing between us could go, only that my past wouldn't—*couldn't*—be the reason it crashed and burned. Even before the military had screwed me over, I'd never wanted someone to have as much of me as I wanted to lay at Mark's feet.

That terrified me. And thrilled me. And worried me. And excited me.

You're something else, Mark.
How do I keep you?

It was weird being the one off work and waiting for Mark. He'd gone to the ship's Christmas party the other night, but I'd been at the club, so I hadn't really been waiting around for him.

Tonight, the bar was closed. Hank might have worked us all into the ground, but his club was always closed on Christmas Eve and Christmas Day.

I'd been seriously surprised when Mark had told me he wanted to go to the Christmas Eve service at the base chapel. And *he'd* been surprised when *I'd* told *him* there was no way in hell I was going to that, and not because it was on-base. He'd sort of sheepishly admitted he'd assumed I was Catholic, and I'd admitted I hadn't expected him to be religious at all. The things you learn about the men you date.

He'd left for church an hour or so ago, and now I was kicked back on his plush sofa, scrolling through his Netflix queue while dinner cooked in the other room. It felt kind of domestic—like we were living together and I was cooking while I waited for him to get home from work. I kind of liked it too.

After he'd left, I'd called my family like I always did on Christmas. My mother was the only one home, so I'd call again tomorrow when everyone was there. I needed to call more often anyway; though now I remembered why I didn't call as often as I should—because I was always homesick when I got off the phone.

Not for Juárez. I'd never been there and, from what my family had told me, had no desire to go. But I missed my family.

I'd lived north of the border since I was fourteen, and I hadn't been back to my hometown of Rioverde in almost fifteen years. Even that had only been for a couple of weeks after my grandfather had died. If I went there now, I probably wouldn't recognize it, and anyway, I had no one there now. Everyone I knew and loved in Mexico was in Juárez, begging me to stay away.

So like I always did, I got off the phone feeling homesick and depressed. And on top of that, guilty. I'd promised my mother I'd go to Mass because it was Christmas, but that lie was better than hurting her with the truth. I couldn't tell her that my boyfriend was at church right now and I wasn't because I didn't believe anymore.

My parents had raised me Catholic, and I'd taken my faith for granted for almost thirty years. It would break my mother's heart to know I'd lost my faith entirely in a single day, and it would hurt her even more to know why. How did a son explain what it was like to walk in on the chaplain and find him drinking and crying in blood-smeared camouflage? Or how quickly faith could crumble to ashes while a sobbing, bloody chaplain admitted he couldn't reconcile the God he loved with the horrors he'd seen?

"I've always known the world was corrupted by sin," I could still hear Father Perez saying between gulps of whatever'd been in that bottle, *"but where is God when boys who aren't even old enough to drink have to die in pain in a desert for a lost cause?"*

Two weeks later, someone had found his body at the edge of our camp. No one had ever told me exactly how he'd killed himself, but what he'd said in his suicide note got around pretty fast.

Whatever hell God sends me to for ending my own life can't be any worse than where I've already been.

That line alone had almost brought several of us with him.

I shuddered at the tangled mess of memories and took a few slow, deep breaths to keep the panic from surging up again. I was doing good. I needed to keep myself like this—calm and present.

But I couldn't keep my mind out of the desert. Out of the things I'd seen, done, and felt. Sometimes I thought that last conversation with Father Perez had been more traumatic than the explosion that had nearly killed me or the day I'd tried like hell to hold a friend's wounds together while we'd waited for medics who never came.

My peripheral vision darkened. I gripped the remote tighter, willing myself to stay here. This wasn't the time for a flashback. Not on Christmas, for fuck's sake.

I shook myself and got up to go check the pot on the stove. Or at least move around and shake off some of this nervous energy. Damn it, this was what happened when I had time alone to think—I *thought*. I didn't need to do any more of that today.

I kept myself busy, and I was just taking the noodles off the heat when the front door opened. A second later, Mark appeared in the kitchen doorway. He was wearing a suit, not his uniform, and damn he looked good in it.

"Hey." He inhaled deeply through his nose. "Oh my God, something smells amazing."

"Don't get too excited—pasta with store-bought sauce."

"Mmm, carbs," he said in a Homer Simpson voice. Then he put a hand on the small of my back and kissed my cheek. "You weren't too bored here by yourself, were you?"

Not when I've got my demons to keep me company.

"Not at all." I started pouring the noodles into the colander to drain them. "How was the service?"

"Meh." He shrugged. "The chaplain's got a monotone, so half the congregation was dozing off."

"Oh, that must've been the Protestant guy. Haines, right?"

"Yeah. You've met him?"

"He did my ex's wedding right before I met you."

"And you went?"

"Of course I went."

Mark's eyebrows rose. "You went *on-base*?"

"For my friend's wedding? Hell yeah." I chuckled. "I'm not a monster."

"Fair enough." He shrugged out of his suit jacket. "It's a shame the boat's chaplain didn't do the service tonight. I like him, and he probably wouldn't put me to sleep."

"Yeah?" I poured the noodles back in and splashed some olive oil on them. While I mixed in the oil, I said, "I'm . . . kind of surprised you *go* to church."

Mark loosened his tie. "Why's that?"

"Don't know. Just didn't expect it, I guess?"

"Eh." He pulled off the tie and draped it over his jacket, which he'd hung over the back of a chair. "To be honest, I'm one of those half-assed Christians who only goes to church on Christmas and Easter." He paused. "I mean, I'm a believer, don't get me wrong. I'm just a slacker when it comes to going to church." In a stage whisper, he added, "Don't tell my mom."

I laughed halfheartedly. I kind of expected myself to resent Mark for still having some faith, but more than anything, it surprised me. I remembered how much comfort I'd found in my religion back when I'd still had it. In fact, I missed that comfort. Why the hell would I hold it against him if he could still find it?

He appeared beside me and rested his hand on my back. "By the way, sorry I, uh, assumed you were Catholic. I—"

"Mark." I shook my head. "It's not like you assumed I eat babies or something. I get it—I'm Mexican, so people think I'm Catholic. And up until a few years ago, I was."

"Oh. But you're not anymore?"

"No. It's . . ." The prickly feeling that had come with thinking about Father Perez started crawling up my neck again. I rolled my shoulders and shook my head. "It's a long story. But no, I'm not Catholic anymore. I guess I'm an agnostic or something. Not really an atheist, but not a believer either."

"Oh," he said again, eyebrows up. I could tell he was curious, but he didn't push it. Maybe someday I'd tell him the story. Not tonight, though. I'd need a few drinks to go there out loud.

I cleared my throat. "Ready to eat?"

"Yeah. Definitely. Just, um . . ." He gestured at his white dress shirt. "Let me change out of this before I get sauce on it."

While I dished out the food, he jogged upstairs to change clothes, leaving me alone with my thoughts again.

Mark had it all. He still had his faith. He still had his career. He still had a closet full of uniforms because he was still military.

And it . . . didn't bother me? It should have. Up until recently, it had, but now it didn't. Suddenly, it was like poking at an old, fading bruise, expecting it to hurt, and being pleasantly surprised when it didn't. In fact, now that I thought about it, it was getting harder and harder to hold anything against the military when it was the reason Mark was in Anchor Point. If not for the Navy, we'd never have met.

That thought sent a prickle down my spine.

I never would have met him.

Well, fuck that. If the Navy had brought me Mark, then maybe I could be a bit less hostile toward it. There was still shit in my past that happened because of the military. I didn't see myself putting military bumper stickers on my truck or using my old uniforms for anything except rags to detail my truck, but the hostility wasn't burning quite so hot anymore.

Footsteps shook me out of my thoughts, and Mark came back into the kitchen in a pair of jeans and a black sweatshirt.

I raked my eyes over him, and we both grinned. Yeah, he looked good. He always looked good.

"Thanks for making dinner." He kissed me softly. "Merry Christmas."

I smiled. "Merry Christmas."

As we sat down to eat, I glanced at one of the many Navy-themed plaques he had hanging on the wall. For once, the sight of an anchor didn't make my teeth grind.

Call it a Christmas miracle—maybe I could live with the Navy after all.

CHAPTER 19

MARK

After dinner, we were both full enough that we'd fall asleep if we sat on the couch to watch TV, so Diego suggested we go down to the pier.

"Not the one on-base," he said, apparently seeing the bewilderment on my face. "The one downtown."

I blinked.

Diego smiled. "Grab your jacket. I'll drive."

Minutes later, we were in his truck, headed down to Anchor Point's waterfront. I hadn't expected anything to be open, but to my surprise, there was hardly any place to park. The pier Diego had mentioned—a long wooden one that had what looked like a permanent carnival—was bright with Christmas lights and crawling with people.

Craning my neck, I stared out the windshield. "I didn't even know this place was here."

Diego laughed and gave my thigh a gentle squeeze. "You really haven't spent much time out in town yet, have you?"

"No, because I've either been on base or in bed with you."

"Fair enough."

He lucked out and found someone pulling out of a parking space about two blocks away. When the other car had gone, Diego snagged the spot, and we got out.

The night was brisk, especially with the wind coming in off the Pacific, but we just tucked our hands in our pockets and nestled our faces into our coat collars.

Christmas and carnival music mingled in the air. The closer we walked to the pier, the more I could smell everything from gingerbread to hot apple cider to something with pumpkin spice. Tiny colorful lights were hung from every surface and strung along the entire length of the pier, glittering against the black void of the ocean and sparkling on the gently rolling waves.

"They didn't used to open it up on Christmas," Diego said as we strolled into the fragrant, noisy, brightly lit chaos. "I heard someone talking about it the other day, though. So . . . seemed like something worth checking out."

"Yeah, I'd say it is. Kind of reminds me of the Christmas markets they do in Europe."

"You been to one?"

I nodded. "Angie and I went to Austria for Christmas one year. We must've spent two entire days at the market in Vienna."

What was happening on the pier had definitely been modeled after one of those markets. In between the games and carnival rides, rows of booths had been erected, and people sold craft items like wreaths and ornaments. At least half a dozen were hawking candles, and there was definitely no shortage of mistletoe. A couple of twentysomethings had an edge on the mistletoe market thanks to their signs: *Humanely trapped wild mistletoe. Corn-fed organic mistletoe. Gluten-free mistletoe.*

I damn near bought some.

One lady had framed needlework, which I usually wouldn't have noticed, but Diego glanced at one and laughed. "I think you need that one for your office."

I read the delicate, flowery lettering out loud: "'Take Your Bullshit Someplace Else.'"

We both snorted, and the lady smiled sweetly at us as we continued reading the similarly snarky work. I was tempted, but I didn't want to carry anything right now, so we told her we'd be back and kept walking.

As we did, Diego's elbow brushed mine. We exchanged glances, both smiling. A few steps later, another brush. The pier was way too crowded to walk any farther apart, and . . . who was I kidding? There was nothing appealing about putting more space between me and Diego.

But what about shrinking the space a little more?

I cleared my throat, creating a tiny cloud in the air. "Question."

"Hmm?" He turned to me, eyebrows up as we kept moving with the crowd.

"Do you have any objection to . . . um . . ." I glanced down at our arms, which were dangerously close to touching again.

He was quiet for a second, but then a sly smile appeared on his lips. "Any objection to someone looking at us and guessing we're a couple?"

My heart thudded at the last word. We were, weren't we? Mute, I nodded.

Diego's smile turned to something warmer, and he shook his head. "No. I don't. What about you?"

My tongue was suddenly sticking to the roof of my mouth, so instead of speaking—and potentially saying something stupid—I freed my hand from my coat pocket and wrapped my arm around his waist.

Somehow, I was still surprised when he didn't shy away.

And I was even more surprised when he wrapped his arm around me in return. We exchanged glances again, both smiled, and kept walking.

I didn't notice much of the crafts for sale after that. I was too caught up in being this close to Diego, openly telling the world I was his and he was mine. The thrill made my head spin. I was distantly aware of a few dirty looks from other people, but I just didn't care. After too many years of being starved for affection in a doomed marriage, the weight of his arm across my lower back warmed me more than a gallon of that hot apple cider could have. If someone from the ship saw us and realized I was with a man, fine, because that meant they'd know I was with *him*. With Diego.

Yep, I'm queer, and yep, he's with me. Isn't it awesome?

We stopped in front of a booth selling small wooden ornaments with designs burned into them. Behind the counter, the seller was carefully burning a detailed reindeer into a small round disc of pale wood. We silently watched him work, and it was impressive how quickly and precisely he made those dark lines.

Diego picked up one of the ornaments. Then he let go of me so he could turn it with his other hand. The cool spot where his arm had been was jarring. Like it had been hours, not just a few minutes, since he'd put it around me.

Kind of like how I swear you've been in my life longer than a few weeks.

My own thought jarred me, and my heart sped up as I watched Diego inspecting the tiny ornament. It was this weird feeling of *where have you been all my life?* and *you've been here right from the start.* My divorce, the loneliness, the long years of doing stupid shit like cheating—it was all a distant memory now because Diego was here. Because of course he was.

I stared at him. The twinkling lights above the booth picked out some of his gray hairs and the edges of those scars beside his eye. I remembered being intrigued by those and wanting to know the story behind them, because that would be a step closer to knowing the *man* behind them.

And now I did. I knew the story. I knew the man. I knew his scars and lines and the way he smiled, and how dizzy I could get from his playful laugh or wicked grin. It was hard to imagine him ever being a stranger.

Oblivious to me, Diego put the ornament back on the rack. Then he turned to me. "Ready?"

"When you are."

He smiled, and we started walking again.

He didn't put his arm around my waist this time, though. Instead, he laced our fingers together. As we strolled through the thick crowd, his thumb ran back and forth across mine, and I wondered if he knew what that was doing to my pulse. Or what he was doing to me just by being here.

I stole another look at him, and my heart gave a little somersault as Christmas lights danced across his features and that serene smile. He really was stunning, and not just in the way that had stopped me in my tracks the night I'd first laid eyes on him.

Early on, I'd wondered if I was discovering what falling for someone felt like.

Tonight, I knew how it felt to realize I'd already fallen.

"If anyone peeks in your windows," Diego said the next afternoon, "they're going to think we're the most pathetic couple of bachelors they've ever seen."

I laughed, but I couldn't argue with him. If not for the pitiful tree glittering in the corner of the living room, no one would have guessed it was Christmas Day. The coffee table was covered in munchies and beer bottles, and we had a Star Wars marathon playing. Not the prequels, of course, since Diego refused to acknowledge they even existed. Just the three originals and the two newest ones.

We were both dressed down in sweats and T-shirts with the logos of our respective football teams. Neither of us had bothered to shave. We didn't look like slobs, but we sure as hell weren't fit for a church service. Not that either of us was planning to go to one today.

We'd both called our families earlier to wish them a merry Christmas. My parents had filled me in on the latest drama in their retirement community, where my dad was constantly battling with his neighbor over some issue involving a tree and my mom's bridge club had developed a rivalry with the people who played dominoes down at the clubhouse. My dad had asked about the ship, and my mom had fretted about how I was doing since the divorce, and I'd just smiled as I'd run my fingers through Diego's hair and insisted I was doing fine.

I couldn't have repeated a single thing Diego had said while he was on the phone with his family, but admittedly, I'd listened just because I loved hearing him speak in his native language. That, and someone on the other end could make him laugh in a way that made my heart melt. Completely relaxed, not in the least bit self-conscious—God, he was beautiful.

After we'd made our respective calls, we'd settled in for the laziest Christmas imaginable.

With the credits rolling on *Return of the Jedi*, I got up and collected the empty bottles. "You want another one?"

He looked into the one in his hand. "Might as well top off before the next movie starts." He got up and followed me, bringing the empty Doritos bag too.

"Let me know when you want actual food," I said as I put the bottles in the recycling bin. "I've got some frozen pizzas."

Diego chuckled. "That is one festive Christmas dinner."

"I know, right?" I pulled a couple of beers from the fridge. "Hell, I'm just happy I'm not stuck on board tonight."

"You usually have to work on Christmas?"

"Used to. Doesn't really happen anymore, but when I was a junior officer it did." I popped the lid off one bottle and handed it to him. As I opened the other, I added, "You know how it is."

"Oh yeah. I was on duty three Christmases in a row."

"Jesus, really?"

Diego took a swig of beer as he half shrugged. "Luck of the draw."

"I hear that." I sipped my own. "Anyway, if it's a choice between eating on the ship and having some sad frozen pizza at home? Easy."

"Especially if you can have a beer with it."

"Precisely." I motioned toward the freezer. "So anyway. Holler if you want me to start preheating the oven."

"Will do. I think I'm good for a while, though. I don't know if Doritos count as lunch, but . . ." He waved a hand.

"Hmm, yeah. Point taken." I wasn't miserably full or anything. I just didn't need to eat anytime soon. We started to head back to the living room, but I paused and put my free hand on his hip. "By the way, in all seriousness, I was expecting to spend Christmas alone this year. It, um, turned out a lot better than I expected."

Diego smiled. "Yeah. Same here." He lifted his chin and kissed me softly. "Just don't tell my mom I did a Star Wars movie marathon with my boyfriend instead of going to Mass on Christmas."

"Long as you don't tell mine."

"Deal."

We clinked our beer bottles together, then shared another quick kiss before we continued into the living room.

"So." I dropped onto the couch. "*Rogue One*?"

He sat beside me. "Definitely."

I held up the remote, but hesitated. "You're, uh, okay with this one? It's got a lot more combat scenes and—"

Diego smiled, patting my leg. "It's fine. I've seen it before. Thanks, though."

"No problem."

"But wait, weren't we supposed to watch that one before Episode IV?"

I paused. "Shit. I think you're right." Then I reached for the remote. "Meh. Whatever."

Diego laughed into his beer bottle. "You rebel, you."

"To be fair, it is called '*Rogue* One.'"

"And I can't imagine anything more rogue than watching the movies out of order."

I shot him a glare. "I will put on the prequels."

He stiffened. "You wouldn't."

"Try me."

We locked eyes.

After a few seconds, he exhaled dramatically. "Fine. You're a rebel and a rogue."

"That's what I thought." I clicked on the movie and sat back beside him. He'd spent the last three movies curled against me, and he did the same thing now. I loved how we fit together, especially once I let out the recliner. Sitting like this, he could keep his leg fairly straight or propped on a pillow and didn't seem to get too sore.

Even with our combined body heat, the room was cool, so I dragged the blanket off the back of the couch and draped it over our legs. Somehow, that made it feel like we were cuddled even closer than before. I didn't question it. I just sat here and enjoyed his warmth while we watched the movie.

When the credits rolled, Diego shifted a little but didn't get up.

I ran my hand up and down his arm. "Comfortable?"

"Mm-hmm." He stretched, then draped his arm across my stomach. "*Force Awakens*?"

I glanced around for the remote. It was just out of my reach. The only way I was getting it was if Diego moved and let me sit up.

I rested my hand on his shoulder. "It can wait a few minutes."

"Fine by me." He sighed happily.

We stayed like that for a little while, but eventually, he sat up to twist a crick out of his back.

"You okay?" I asked.

"Yep." He turned to me and smiled. "Too long without moving."

"I know the feeling." I tucked the recliner in and sat up myself. Yeah, I was getting a bit stiff too. When I stretched, my back cracked loudly.

Diego laughed. "Getting old?"

"Shut up."

He chuckled and wrapped an arm around my waist. "I told you, I'm going to milk the age jokes until I turn forty."

"And when you do?" I pulled him closer. "You are *never* going to hear the end of it."

He snickered softly but let me draw him in for a kiss. A kiss that kept right on going, until we weren't fighting off laughter anymore but were completely engrossed in what we were doing. Diego's fingers slid up into my hair, and the tip of his tongue teased my lips apart. I ran a hand up the inside of his thigh. He gasped, fingers tightening in my hair.

"If anyone peeks in my windows now," I said between kisses, "I doubt they'll think we're a couple of bachelors."

Laughing, Diego slid his hands down my back. "Hmm, no. Probably not. Think we should give them a show?"

I didn't answer.

But if anyone did peek in my windows, they *definitely* got a show.

CHAPTER 20
DIEGO

The annual New Year's Eve party at the High-&-Tight was legendary. Even some of the people who stuck to the clubs in Flatstick came up to Anchor Point for this, so we had a packed house. It was a great night to be a bartender too—I'd be flush with cash for days even after I sent a nice chunk to my family.

A couple of my coworkers were handing out glittery hats and masks, but they didn't bother offering one to me. They all knew I hated stuff like that. I was the Ebenezer Scrooge of party favors, according to them. I let them think that. It was easier than explaining that I didn't like things on my face or my head because even lightweight paper brushed the same nerve endings where my protective headgear and NVGs had sat.

It was weird, the shit that could send me into a tailspin. One of my friends from the military couldn't handle flashing lights, especially strobes. They didn't bother me at all. Hell, one of my buddies from the war zone had freaked out after someone in a crowd bumped hard into her shoulder. The crowd had already been making her nervous, and something about the impact of his shoulder slamming into hers reminded her of a weapon's recoil, and it had taken three people to get her outside and bring her down from the flashback.

Me? I didn't like anything on my face. Not even sunglasses. If I ever had to start wearing glasses, I was going straight to contact lenses.

Movement caught my eye, and when I looked up from filling a pint glass, my heart went wild. It wasn't a panicked reaction, though. Quite the opposite.

"Hey you." Mark leaned on the bar.

"Hey." I grinned and gave him a *just a sec* gesture. I finished with the customer's beer and settled up. Then I wiped my hands on a towel and turned back to Mark. "Sorry about that." I leaned partway over the bar for a kiss. "Glad you came."

"Me too." His gaze flicked to my lips, then met mine, doing crazy shit to my pulse as the disco lights played in his eyes. "Didn't want you to spend New Year's alone."

"Alone?" I gestured at the thick crowd. "You call this alone?"

Mark slid a hand up my arm and winked. "I have a different kind of not-alone in mind. For later."

I gulped. "Oh yeah?"

"Mm-hmm." He leaned closer, gesturing for me to do the same, and his low growl barely carried over the music: "I want to start the new year barely being able to walk."

The noise swallowed up my whimper, and the room was suddenly ten degrees hotter. In his ear, I said, "I think we can arrange that."

"Good." He kissed my cheek, then my lips, staying there a second longer. When he drew back, he gave me a wink that almost dropped my knees out from under me.

I cleared my throat. "You don't want me to be able to concentrate tonight, do you?"

He just laughed.

Rolling my eyes, I smirked at him. "All right, smart-ass. You want a drink or something?"

"I wouldn't mind a Corona." He took out his wallet, but I waved him off.

"You know I'm not going to charge you for it." I took out the bottle, popped the top, and put in the lime wedge. "Now go dance so I have something to keep me entertained."

Mark chuckled as he pocketed his wallet again. "Am I that bad of a dancer?"

"You know you're not."

Another wink. Then he took the bottle, toasted me with it, and slipped into the crowd.

"That your boyfriend?" Chase, another bartender, asked.

I couldn't help grinning as I nodded. "Yeah."

Chase whistled. "Damn. He's *hot*."

Beaming, I nodded. "Yeah, he is."

Chase eyed me. "Since when do you date guys in the service?"

"Since him, apparently."

He laughed. "Can't blame you. He's a little old for me, but damn, I'd bend all kinds of rules to get with that."

"You have no idea." I'd meant to sound smug, but it came out . . . reverent? As I watched Mark out on the dance floor, I just . . . couldn't . . .

He was mine. Somehow, that man wanted me, and I wanted him, and when the party was over, we'd be going home together. He . . . was *mine*.

"Can I get a vodka martini?" The voice snapped me out of my daze, and I turned to see three guys in sparkly New Year's hats watching me expectantly.

I shook myself, nodded, and started pouring the drink. I could ogle Mark later. Right now, I had tips to earn.

At a little before midnight, Hank cut half the bartenders loose. Those of us who'd worked all night last year got the rest of the night off this year. With a fat wad of tips in my wallet already, not to mention the credit card tips I'd collect from my boss later, I was happy to take an early night for once.

"The countdown's starting!" someone shouted, and everyone crowded around the flat-screen TVs. I didn't usually like being in crowds, but I didn't object as the mass of people pushed me and Mark closer together. We exchanged smiles before looking up at the screen. As we watched the ball starting to drop over Times Square, Mark slipped his hand into mine. I turned, just meaning to glance at him, but once our eyes met, I couldn't look away.

We were surrounded by people, but it felt like we were completely alone. Like we had the entire High-&-Tight all to ourselves, and even with all the noise and activity, the whole world seemed to stand still.

He was military. So recently divorced the ink was still wet.

And I . . .

Was falling for him.

Hard.

Right then, he flashed a smile, and my stomach flipped.

No, I wasn't falling for him—I already had.

He was military, but he was also *Mark*, and that was the only thing that mattered. He was Mark, and I loved him.

Everything I'd spent the other night thinking about came crashing back, and . . . yeah. It *was* time to make peace with the idea of a boyfriend who was military, because Mark wasn't getting out anytime soon and I didn't want to let him go. If I stayed with him, that meant staying with the Navy.

And as I looked up at him, watching the disco lights playing in his eyes and across the flecks of silver in his hair, it was a no-brainer. There was no "if" when it came to staying with Mark. It didn't even matter that we'd only been seeing each other for a little under two months. Every time I met his eyes, I just knew.

We were standing less than ten feet from the spot where we'd met, but it felt like I'd never been here before. We'd met right there less than two months ago, but it felt like I'd known him all my life.

Of course we're here. Of course we're together.

And of course I love you.

"Seven!"

Midnight seemed way too far away. Way too long to wait.

"Six!"

I cradled the back of his neck, lifted myself up, and kissed him. As everyone around us continued counting down, he wrapped his arms around me and parted his lips so I could slide my tongue into his mouth. I held him close, kissed him deep, and midnight came and went without mattering.

Mark ended the kiss as softly as I'd started it, and our eyes met again. Disco lights glittered in his eyes. Music and cheers vibrated the floor beneath my feet.

And my heart was going crazy. While we gazed at each other with that kiss still tingling on my lips, the feeling of being alone in a packed room came over me again.

He brushed my hair back off my forehead. "Happy New Year."

"Feliz año nuevo," I murmured as I went in for a longer kiss. Mark's arms tightened around me, and the kiss deepened just like it had while we'd ignored the countdown.

"Maybe we should get out of here," he whispered.

I didn't say a word. I just took his hand and headed for the door.

I slammed Mark down on his bed and kissed him before he had a chance to recover. He moaned, throwing his arms around me, and rubbed his clothed dick against mine so hard I was surprised neither of us came.

We were sweaty from the club, and probably needed a shower before we did anything else, but I wanted him too much. We'd both be drenched in sweat by the time I was done with him anyway, so it didn't matter.

"Did you see how many people were staring at you tonight?" he asked out of the blue.

"Huh?"

Mark's lips curved against mine. Then he started on my neck. "So many guys there were checking you out."

"R-really?" I could barely remember other men even being there, never mind what they were looking at.

"Uh-huh. Was fucking hot." He nibbled under my jaw. "I wanted to blow you right then and there so they all knew you were coming home with me."

A shudder surged through me, and we both gasped as the motion pressed our cocks together. "That's . . . Oh my God . . ."

"I had the hottest man in the room tonight." His voice was a low, throaty growl now. "And everyone there knew it. And it made me want you so fucking bad."

I whimpered, grinding my hips against his. "Yeah? So what're you gonna do with me?"

He gave a rumbly groan, then flipped me onto my back, pinning my arms to the mattress, and sank his teeth into my shoulder. My hips bucked involuntarily. Fuck, now I *wanted* to come, and I was still dressed.

"Want it rough," he growled in my ear.

A pitiful, needy sound escaped my throat.

He laughed and nibbled my earlobe before he whispered, "Quiero que me des duro hoy."

And I burst out laughing, then clapped a hand over my mouth.

"What?" He lifted himself up, smirking and blushing at the same time. "Did I say it wrong?"

"No." I tried to pull myself back together, but I wasn't doing a very good job of it. "I just . . . wasn't expecting . . ."

As he came down to kiss me, he laughed too, and his breath rushed past my skin, which made me shiver and sober right up.

"Oh God," I groaned. "For the record, if you want me to fuck you like that, all you have to do is say so."

"I did. Just . . . badly. In what was apparently horrible Spanish."

"No, it was all right." I chuckled. "Just caught me by surprise is all. Who taught you to talk that way?"

He blushed again. "The internet."

"Of course." I snorted, trying not to laugh again. "You *googled* how to say 'I want you to fuck me hard today'?"

Mark grinned, not looking quite so embarrassed now. "Apparently I did get it right."

I rolled my eyes. "Yeah, you did. Now get over here so I can fuck you."

He wrapped his arm around my waist and kissed me. We were laughing almost as much as we were kissing, though, which . . . was kind of hot, actually. Maybe I was just dizzy from lack of oxygen, but the longer we kissed and laughed without actually getting anywhere with the condom and lube, the more turned on I was.

Finally, I couldn't wait any longer, and breathed, "Condom."

"Should . . . should probably get undressed first."

I glanced down. Well, shit. He had a point.

"Clothes off, condom on?" he asked.

"Yes."

Once we'd stripped out of our clothes—fucking *finally*—Mark handed me a condom and grabbed the bottle of lube. While I opened the wrapper, he uncapped the bottle and poured some in his hand. After I put on the condom, he started stroking on the lube, and as he did, he looked me up and down. "I don't know if I've told you this enough." He sounded like he was out of breath. "But you are fucking *hot.*"

I grinned, rocking my hips to fuck into his tight fist. "So are you. Especially when my dick's in your ass."

A strangled sound escaped his lips as he shivered, and he tightened his grip around me.

"Fuck," I ground out. Then I batted his hand away. "On your back. *Now.*"

Mark obeyed immediately, lying back on the pillows and spreading his legs wide for me. I fingered him a little, just to make sure he was relaxed and slick, then guided myself to his hole. He bit his lip as I pushed into him. "God, yeah . . ."

I wanted to make a joke about how I'd barely given him an inch, but . . . *God, yeah* was right. The deeper he took me, the more I wondered how I was going to keep from going off too soon.

Mark closed his eyes and exhaled. His fingers dug into my upper arms as he rolled his hips like he wanted to coax me even deeper.

I'm getting there, baby. Don't worry.

I got there. In no time, I was thrusting hard, making the bed creak so loud it almost covered up our voices.

"Oh yeah," he was slurring. "Oh yeah. God, yeah. That's *so* good. So good."

It was, and it wasn't just my body he was overwhelming. The way I'd stared at him from across the room. The way I'd felt while I'd looked in his eyes just before midnight. The way being with him drowned out everything except how good I felt.

"Te—" I cut myself off before *te amo* slipped off my lips. It didn't matter if it wasn't in English; I couldn't say *I love you* now. Not like this. "Te *quiero.*"

Mark whimpered, arching under me. "Fuck, it's hot when you . . . oh God . . ."

"Hmm? When I talk that way?" I slammed into him. "Or fuck you this way?"

"Both." His nails bit into my back, and his whole body tensed as he breathed, "Jesus, both. Don't stop . . . keep doing *both.*"

I moaned against his neck and squeezed my eyes shut as I fucked him harder, and I kept murmuring in Spanish. I didn't even know what I was saying anymore, only that I couldn't stay quiet while I was riding him like this, and he was getting more turned on with every syllable I slurred in his ear.

Then his body jerked, and a hot huff of breath rushed past my shoulder as Mark clenched around me, and we both cried out. He kept pleading—almost sobbing—for me to keep going, and I did because he felt so, so good, and because I loved the way he sounded and felt when he came, and suddenly I was coming right along with him, shooting so hard I almost blacked out.

When the smoke cleared, I had collapsed on top of him. I didn't remember doing it, and I didn't care that I now had cum all over my stomach. I was against him and spent and satisfied, and it was perfect.

I pulled out but lay there for a moment longer just to catch my breath. Once we both had our bearings, we got up and went into the bathroom to clean ourselves off before flopping back onto the bed.

Mark stroked my hair. "Holy shit, that was good."

"Uh-huh." I turned onto my side so I was facing him. "Always is with you."

He grinned, then kissed me softly. He trailed his fingers down the side of my neck. "And that party was pretty— Ow!" He jerked his hand back and shook it. "What the hell?"

"What's wrong?" I pushed myself up on my elbow, heart thumping suddenly.

Mark stared at his hand, then turned it, and I saw the tiny drop of blood beading on his thumb.

I carefully brushed a finger over the place he'd been touching and found the sharp edge. "Oh. Piece of shrapnel. It, uh, happens sometimes."

Mark's eyes widened. "Come again?"

"There's . . ." I gestured at my face and neck. "They didn't get all the shrapnel out. Sometimes pieces come out on their own."

His lips parted. "You're serious."

"Yeah. I've got some tweezers at home. It's fine right now."

"You're just going to leave a little piece of metal in your skin?"

"It's been there for seven years." I shrugged. "Hasn't hurt me yet."

"It doesn't hurt like that?" He gestured at it.

I shook my head. "Not really. Just stings a little."

"I've got tweezers here too." He nodded toward the bathroom. "You're welcome to them."

As much as I didn't want to leave the warmth of his bed, I didn't need him cutting his lip on it or something. Or worse—not wanting to kiss my neck at all.

So, we got up. Mark pulled a pair of tweezers from the drawer and watched silently as I leaned in close to the mirror and tilted my head. I had to run my finger over the fragment until I found it, and it was so tiny, it took three tries to get the tweezers to grab on to it. Then I gave it a careful tug, and the sliver of metal slid free. I dropped it in the trash, then cleaned off the tweezers. As I set them on the counter, I said, "You'll probably want to put these in alcohol or something."

"I can deal with that later. What about you? Are you sure you're—"

"I'm fine." I dabbed at the thin cut with a wadded square of toilet paper. There wasn't a whole lot of blood; I'd done worse shaving. "Okay. Looks like that's it."

He frowned. "You sure? That's it?"

Chuckling, I faced him and snaked my arms around his waist. "It's really not a big deal. It's no worse than a splinter." I kissed him softly. "Sorry for the little, uh, interruption."

"Don't worry about it." He ran his fingers through my hair. "As long as you're good."

"I am."

A little grin played at his lips. "Do I get to brag about that? Rocking your world so hard it knocked shrapnel out of your skin?"

I snorted. "Yeah. We fucked so hard, I fell apart."

"Came so hard you came apart at the seams." We both laughed, and he gathered me up in his arms. We held each other like that for a while, still kind of laughing, but more and more, kissing. When he spoke again, his tone was light, but serious: "Tonight was amazing, by the way."

I couldn't even make a joke about how it was amazing aside from me losing pieces of metal. Not when he sounded so sweet and sincere. "Yeah," I said. "It really was."

Our eyes met again, and we both smiled.

Do you have any idea how much I love you?
"Happy New Year," he said.
I lifted my chin and kissed him. "Happy New Year."

CHAPTER 21

MARK

Sex with Diego was always amazing, but this was by far my favorite part—when the smoke had cleared and we were lying half under the sheets. My marriage had been dead for so long, I'd almost forgotten how much I loved—and needed—this quiet, gentle cuddling in the afterglow. There was a lot to be said for the warm, solid presence of someone who still wanted to touch me once the orgasms were over.

Tonight, we'd landed with Diego on his back and my head on his shoulder. His fingers absently stroked my hair, and I had my arm draped over his stomach. For the longest time, we were quiet and still, and I savored every minute of it.

After a while, he reached up and dabbed at the side of his neck. When he inspected his fingertip, I realized he'd been checking it for blood.

"Still bleeding?"

He shook his head. "No. Sometimes they bleed for a while, but this one stopped."

"Good. And it really doesn't hurt?"

He shrugged. "It stings a bit, but it hurts a lot less coming out than it did going in."

I shuddered. "Jesus. You seem like you're used to that happening."

"I am. It creeped me out the first few times, but eventually, it stops being such a big deal. Especially now that it doesn't happen so often anymore. Since, you know, most of the pieces are gone."

"And no one's worried they'll get into your bloodstream or something?"

"And pierce my heart?" He laughed, shaking his head. "Nah. I mean, I asked if that was a risk, and the doctors didn't think it was anything to worry about." A smirk played at his lips. "I tried to talk the docs into giving me an arc reactor like Tony Stark. You know, just to be safe."

I smirked. "What did they say?"

"They gave me some Motrin."

I barked a laugh. "Ah, good ol' vitamin M."

"The arc reactor would have been so much cooler."

"Damn budget cuts."

"Right?" Diego chuckled. "Seriously, though, it's no big deal."

I frowned. "And it doesn't bother you? With your, uh . . . with your past?"

"Not anymore, no." He touched the spot on his neck again as if it might've sprung a leak in the last minute or so. Then he shifted onto his side and, when I faced him, laid his arm over my waist as he gazed at me. "It used to be bad, but it's gotten better. So I guess . . ." He chewed his lip. "Maybe that means there's hope of me getting over *all* my shit with the military."

"Maybe. Has that gotten better? The whole picture?"

Diego nodded slowly. "It's still hard. The military is still, you know, a sore spot. But I want to be with you, and being with you means being with the military."

I clasped his hand in mine and brought it up to kiss his palm. "I want to be with you too, as long as it's not stressing you out."

"It's not." Diego smiled. "I thought it would, but . . . it's really not."

"Good." I pressed a soft kiss to his lips. "If, um, you *are* feeling better about all of it . . ." I hesitated. "You can say no if you want to, but there's a party coming up. The Hail and Farewell for the outgoing CO from our supply ship." I raised my eyebrows. "If you want to, I'd love to have you as my date."

To my surprise, Diego smiled. "Do I get to damage your uniform afterward?"

I laughed. "Baby, you can rip it to shreds if you promise to fuck me like you did tonight."

"I'll do that anyway."

"Then you can do whatever you want to my uniform."

His smile turned to a devilish grin. "I like the sound of that."

I chuckled, but my humor faded quickly. "All joking aside, are you sure about this?" I stroked his hair. "Going to the party?"

Diego swept his tongue across his lips as he nodded. "Yeah. I want to be with you. I need to make peace with you being in the Navy."

I held his gaze for a moment, not sure what to say. As much as I loved the idea of showing him off to the people I worked with, I didn't want to push him. "You don't need to make peace with it overnight. If you're not ready—"

"Mark." He took my hand and kissed my palm, raising goose bumps all the way up my arm. "If I'm not ready for a dinner party, then I don't have much hope of being ready for anything. I'll be fine."

I hesitated, but finally nodded. "All right. Just . . . say so if you're not fine, okay?" I brushed his hair off his forehead. "We don't have to stick around if it's too much."

"I'll be *fine*," he insisted, and kissed me.

When we broke that kiss, I whispered, "How did you say it in Spanish? Feliz . . . something?"

Diego smiled. "Feliz año nuevo."

"Feliz año nuevo." Then I frowned. "Doesn't sound nearly as good when I say it."

He laughed, curving his hand around the back of my neck. "No worse than my English sounded when I was first learning. You'll get it."

"Yeah? Are you going to teach me to curse too?"

"What?" He snorted. "Why do you want to learn to curse?"

"Mostly so I know what you're saying when we're in bed."

Diego burst out laughing. "How do you know I'm cursing when we're fucking?"

"I can't imagine you're reciting a chocolate chip cookie recipe."

Another laugh. "I might have to try that."

"Oh God." I rolled my eyes. "Just what I need."

Still grinning, he said, "Maybe I'll translate for you one of these days." He ran a finger up my arm. "I kind of like letting you fantasize about what I'm really saying."

I laughed. "That sounds like a cop-out."

He flashed a toothy grin. "Uh-huh. Call it what you want—you know it's hot."

"Yeah, you're right. It is." I brushed my lips across his. "*Everything* you do is hot."

"Oh yeah?" He slid a hand down my side. "Everything?"

"Uh-huh," I murmured as he nudged me onto my back. "Everything."

He made a quiet sound that seemed to be both a huff of laughter and a breathy moan, and then he kissed me. As we tangled up again, my mind kept wandering through our conversation and him accepting my invite. I still wasn't completely sure if that had been a good idea. Maybe it had been too soon to throw that out there? I couldn't wait to walk into that party with him, but only if he really was okay with it. So far, he was. If he changed his mind, then I was perfectly happy staying home. I was perfectly happy doing anything as long as I was with him. Whether we were making out and turning each other on like we were doing now or trash-talking over a couple of beers and a football game. I just liked being with him. Full stop.

I understood why my active duty status had been a deal breaker at first. Hell, the more he told me, the harder it was to believe he'd thought twice and decided it *wasn't* a deal breaker. That he'd stuck with me this long when the Navy had worked him over so hard, and that now he was willing to go with me to a Navy function.

Was I pushing too hard? Was this going to blow up in my face somehow?

Diego moaned as he stroked my hair, and we rolled again so I was on top of him. The warmth of his arms around me and his leg hooked over my hip made me dizzy, but not enough to completely drown out my thoughts.

I didn't have a great track record with relationships. Truth was, I had no idea what I was doing.

I don't know how to make this work.

I pressed a kiss behind his ear.

All I know is that I want it to.

And that I love you.

CHAPTER 22

DIEGO

I tugged at my tie on the way up Mark's front steps. I didn't wear this suit often, and it was weird to be wearing it now. It fit right, and the material was soft and comfortable—more than I could say about the shoes—but I was used to jeans and T-shirts.

Oh well. It was just one evening.

I rang the doorbell and continued fussing with the tie and cuffs until footsteps came jogging down the stairs inside. When Mark opened the door, he had a towel around his waist and droplets of water on his chest and shoulders. "Hey. Sorry." He kissed me quickly as I stepped inside. "Got home late."

"It's all right. You want me to wait down here while you get dressed?" I winked. "So we don't end up being even later to the party?"

He bit his lip, but nodded. "Probably a good idea." He looked me up and down and grinned. "*Especially* when you're dressed like that."

"Mmm, and when *you're* dressed like *that* . . ." I playfully tugged at his towel.

Mark laughed, swatting my hand away. "Behave."

"Why?"

He quirked his lips. "Good question."

I chuckled, and I knew if we kept this up, we really would wind up with that towel on the floor. So I let go and nudged him toward the stairs. "Go. We gotta get out of here."

He pouted briefly, then leaned in to kiss my cheek. "Help yourself to anything in the fridge. I'll be down in ten."

"Take your time."

We exchanged smiles. Then he headed up the stairs and I went into the living room.

Mark's cover was sitting on the coffee table beside his wallet and keys. The sight of it made my hackles go up, but I silently talked them down. It wasn't a big deal. My bullshit with the Navy was far enough behind me that it was time to get over it. That started tonight.

Well, it had started a while ago, back when I'd decided to see Mark even though he was Navy. Tonight, I'd be in the same room with all the shit I'd left behind when I'd been discharged, and I would handle it. I'd be fucking fine because it had been long enough, and Mark was worth it.

I pulled my gaze from his cover and wandered to the wall where he'd recently hung up some framed photos. Family, by the looks of it.

On a bookshelf, there was a small photo I hadn't noticed before. It was him with his arm tightly around a petite redhead. He was in his dress whites, and still a lieutenant commander, so it must have been several years ago now. Possibly around the time I was discharged, but I tried not to linger on that thought.

They were embracing in front of an aircraft carrier. It looked like a homecoming—lots of people hugging in the background, with flowers and balloons and service members in their dress uniforms. His arm was around her shoulders, wedding band gleaming in the sunlight, and they both smiled for the camera.

This must have been his ex-wife during one of those rare happy times in their marriage. I stared at the picture, waiting for the surge of jealousy, but it didn't come. In fact, I felt the opposite of jealousy, if there was such a thing. My boyfriend had a photo of himself and his ex-wife on display, and I . . . I *liked* that. Whatever shit they'd been through, they'd come out on the other side as friends, and he'd made peace with it enough to have a picture of the two of them in his house.

In fact, I kind of wanted to meet her. Maybe not now, but someday. I was curious about this woman who'd been through hell and back with Mark.

Heavy footsteps came down the carpeted stairs. Then dress shoes clicked on the hardwood floor, and I turned around just as Mark appeared in the living room doorway.

Oh.

Wow.

Okay, yeah. This was a good start if I wanted to get over my issues with the Navy.

He'd be even hotter if I put him on his knees and—

I cleared my throat as I looked him up and down. "You know I'm going to be tearing that off you later, right?"

"I'm counting on it, sweetheart." He hooked a finger in my waistband and pulled me closer. "When you're ready to leave, you just let me know."

"Mmm, I will." I slid my hands up the almost-black suit jacket, letting my fingers catch on the gold buttons. "Can't promise we'll make it to dinner."

Mark groaned, squeezing my ass through my slacks. "Maybe we *should* just stay home."

Oh, that was tempting, but I'd said I would go, and it wouldn't look good for an XO to not show up.

"No." I shook my head and straightened his tie. "We'll have plenty of time when we get home. Let's go."

"We will. But first . . ." He took his hands off my ass, wrapped an arm around my waist, and kissed me. I wondered if he'd meant for just a short kiss. More than a peck, but maybe not *this*. Whatever. I wasn't going to argue if he wanted to tease my lips apart and slide his tongue past mine.

He drew back and our eyes locked. Oh fuck. He was too sexy for words. That uniform needed to be on his bedroom floor right now, and he needed to be . . . hell, I didn't care. Under me, on me, in me, over me—just get me naked and do stuff to me. Now.

He muffled a cough and broke eye contact. "We should go."

"Right." I cleared my throat too. We both fussed with our jackets, and I wondered if he was also trying to accommodate a hard-on. Good thing we still had to drive over to the party. Neither of us was in any condition to be walking into mixed company.

As I got in the passenger seat of his car, I unbuttoned my jacket. "You know I'm fucking you senseless when we get home, right?"

"I sure hope so." He sounded sultry and a little breathless. "Think we'll make it past dinner?"

I raked my eyes over him. "If we do, we'll probably wind up screwing in the restroom."

Mark just shivered and put the car into reverse.

Mark drove us down to the Holiday Inn. It seemed like kind of an anticlimactic place to have a big military function, but I supposed there weren't a lot of options in town. Not without going on base, anyway. Yeah, the Holiday Inn was fine with me.

We got out of the car, and I buttoned my jacket. I hadn't worn this suit in ages, but it still fit nicely. Guess poverty was good for something; though if my mother saw me now, she'd lose it.

On the way inside, Mark put on his cover, adjusted it, and then offered me his elbow.

I regarded it uncertainly. "You sure? You're in uniform."

"It's okay." He smiled. "Long as we're not making out or anything."

"Damn it." I took his elbow and smirked. "So much for the dance floor, right?"

"Are you kidding? We just have to wait until everyone else is drunk."

"I love the way you think."

We exchanged glances and continued inside.

As soon as we stepped through the banquet hall's double doors, it was déjà vu. Military functions had a certain look about them. A certain vibe. Navy décor didn't change much—a lot of blue, gold, and gray, with anchors and chains and pictures of ships. This event was on the formal end of the spectrum, with service members in dress uniforms and civilians in evening wear. Kind of reminded me of the Navy Ball, actually, aside from the *Hail & Farewell* banner on the wall.

The cocktail hour was still going, so most people were milling around with drinks in hand, waiting in line at one of half a dozen bars, or crowding around small tables. A few were already wobbling and getting loud. Yep—Navy function.

As we made our way through the crowd, it was kind of surreal to be wandering in a sea of uniforms.

Just like Navy décor, the uniforms hadn't changed much. Not the dress uniforms, anyway. Enlisted still wore the classic Sailor suit. Officers still wore suits like Mark's. The insignia was all the same too. I could still tell ranks apart at a glance, and I could even remember some of the rate insignia on the enlisted uniforms—master-at-arms, corpsmen, aviation techs, nukes, boatswain's mate.

I didn't see anyone with my old rate—aviation ordnanceman—and didn't look too hard to find one. I still missed my old job—the one I'd done before volunteering for boots-on-the-ground combat—and that was a wound that didn't need salting.

Mark and I found an empty chest-high table, and he turned like he was going to say something, but paused. He cocked his head. "You all right?"

"Yeah." I cleared my throat. "Just a little déjà vu, I guess."

Frowning, he slipped an arm around my waist. "Anything I should be concerned about?"

"No. No, I'm good. It's just been a while since I've been around this kind of crowd." I touched his arm. "I'll be fine. Promise."

He seemed uncertain for a second, but then he smiled and kissed my cheek. "You want me to go grab a couple of beers?"

"Sure." I reached for my wallet, but he stopped me. I was about to get annoyed, but he shook his head.

"Open bar."

"Oh." I relaxed. "Okay, then. Um, I'll have whatever you're drinking." I smirked. "So, Corona, right?"

"Am I that predictable?"

"Hey, you like what you like." I shrugged. "Who am I to judge?"

"The bartender who probably silently judges everyone based on their drink order?"

I laughed. "Am *I* that predictable?"

Mark chuckled. He gave me a quick kiss, then headed for the growing bar line.

I stayed at the table and just kept taking in my surroundings. This *was* really weird, but I was determined to be okay with it.

Before I could get too lost in my own thoughts, someone tugged at my elbow. "Excuse me, could we get another round over here? Bud Light?"

I blinked "What?"

The man—a very large commander—held up an empty bottle. "Bud Light? Another round?" He gestured at five other people, all of whom watched me expectantly from their table.

"I, um . . ." I cleared my throat and nodded in the direction Mark had gone. "The line is over there, I think."

"But aren't—" The man straightened. "Oh! God. I'm sorry. I thought you were one of the waiters."

I gritted my teeth. *Of course you did.* "It's all right," I said with a forced smile.

I hoped he'd go away, but instead, he extended his hand. "So since you're a civilian, are you a contractor or are you here with someone?"

I grudgingly shook his hand, but I wasn't quite sure what to say. Mark had been openly affectionate, and he was here with a male date, so I assumed he was out. I figured he hadn't brought me as his date to pretend we were roommates or something. Still, I—

Mark picked that moment to materialize beside me anyway, his hand coming to rest on my back. "Hey, Harrison. I see you met my boyfriend." The pride in his voice made my heart flutter, and I was probably blushing.

"Your— Oh. He's here with you?" The commander smiled, gave my hand one more pump, and then let go. "John Harrison. This is my wife, Erika." He introduced us to the others at the table before turning to me again. "So where are you from?"

Oh yay. This conversation.

"Mexico." I took a deep swallow from the Corona Mark had brought me.

"Oh yeah?" John grinned and nudged me. "Better stick with us. You don't want to get tangled up if ICE goes after the staff."

"*Commander.*" The growl in Mark's tone made my hair stand up.

The man blinked innocently. "Hey, I'm just saying." He gave Mark a very unprofessional clap on the shoulder. "If *I* thought he was a waiter, then . . ." He trailed off into a shrug.

Mark's glare finally cut through John's boozy haze. The commander mumbled some kind of goodbye and herded his wife toward the bar.

Once they were out of earshot, I muttered, "Somebody must've been pregaming."

"Uh-huh." Mark rolled his eyes. "I think he and I will have a little *chat* on Monday." He said it in what must've been his XO voice—harsh, low, and full of *do not fuck with me*. It gave me a goose bumps.

What would it take to get you to use that voice in bed?

I shook myself before I wound up with an embarrassing hard-on. That probably wasn't the impression Mark needed either of us to make tonight.

With our drinks in hand, we wandered around the room, and he introduced me to so many people I would never remember any of their names. At one point, we stopped beside a couple who looked like they were in their late forties or early fifties.

He and Mark exchanged greetings, and then Mark gestured at him as he said to me, "This is Captain Hawthorne. My CO. And this"—he turned to his CO as he put an arm around my shoulders—"is Diego. My boyfriend."

I smiled as I shook the CO's hand. It was seriously never going to get old hearing Mark call me his boyfriend.

"Nice to meet you, Diego." Hawthorne introduced me to his wife, Dana.

He and Mark made a little small talk while Dana and I sipped our drinks. As I watched them banter, it was kind of weird to realize Mark was so laid-back with his commanding officer. When I'd been in, the rank of captain had been so far above me I'd get a nosebleed just thinking about it. But they chatted like peers.

Because they *were* peers.

Because even though Hawthorne was the CO, Mark was the XO. He was *also* a captain.

Whoa. I was dating a man who was the same rank as his CO.

That was . . . kind of hot, actually.

I tried not to leer at Mark's uniform. There'd be time for that later.

Right then, the CO turned to me. "So where are you from, Diego?"

My good spirits sank.

This again. Hooray.

"Mexico." My cheeks burned, and I wasn't sure why. How many times was I going to have to answer this question tonight?

His eyes narrowed a little, and he slid his gaze toward Mark. Something passed between them, something unspoken but vaguely hostile. Then Hawthorne faced me again. "Oh yeah? What part of Mexico?"

I tried not to squirm under the couple's scrutiny. "Rioverde. In San Luis Potosí." That was met with blank looks, so I added, "It's about a hundred and fifty miles inland from the Gulf."

The CO cocked his head. "That near Mexico City?"

"Not really. It's . . ." Explaining Mexico's geography didn't really work. Most Americans knew Tijuana, Mexico City, Cabo, Cozumel, and Mazatlán, and even then, there was no guarantee they'd find them on a map. It was like using streets and landmarks to tell someone how to find something in New York City when they'd never been there. "It might be easier to show you." I took out my phone and pulled up the map. After I'd put in the city and state, the little pin dropped on Rioverde, and I showed him the screen.

He leaned closer, tilting his head back so he could look through the lower part of his bifocals. "Huh. Never heard of that place."

His wife smiled. "We went to Mazatlán a few years back. We thought Mexico was quite lovely."

I smiled back. "It's nice." Or so I'd heard. Then again, I'd also heard that Mazatlán had deteriorated quite a bit. Not that I'd ever been there.

"So do you miss it?" Dana asked.

"Sometimes." *I miss not being an outsider. I miss not being scared of getting thrown out.* "I left when I was fourteen, so it's been almost twenty-five years. It's changed a lot since then." *So has this country.*

"Do you like it here?" Hawthorne asked.

I nodded even as I fought the urge to squirm uncomfortably. They were curious and making conversation, and they couldn't have any idea how hard it was to talk about being homesick for a place I'd barely known. It was also impossible to predict how people would take it if I mentioned how fucking miserable I'd been for the last few years. A conversation could quickly turn into me getting lectured for being ungrateful, told how I should just go back if I hated it this much, and usually catching hell about stealing an American's job. It just wasn't that simple, but it was impossible to convince people of that. And considering it hadn't been that long since someone else had mistaken me for a waiter and made a joke about ICE, I was on edge.

After some more small talk and handshakes, though, Hawthorne and his wife continued mingling, and we returned to our table. I tried to relax, but I couldn't shake off the weirdness of the conversation.

I glanced at the CO's back as I said to Mark, "I have a question."

"Hmm?"

I turned to him. "Why did he act so weird when I said was from Mexico?"

Mark's lips thinned, and he put his arm around my waist, a gesture that felt oddly protective. "I was asking him a while ago about, um, Sailors in your situation. Getting discharged without citizenship. I think he just figured out why I was asking."

My blood turned cold, and I straightened. "Is he going to report me? Mark, he's—"

"Relax." Mark slid his hand up my back and squeezed my shoulder. "He's way too political for that, and he knows it wouldn't look good if he was responsible for a vet getting deported."

"Not even someone like me?"

"No." He held me closer to him. "It'll be fine. I promise."

I chewed the inside of my cheek. I couldn't relax, knowing someone in this room knew my status, and the more I thought about it, the more anger boiled inside me. It didn't even help to tell myself that Mark might very well have been right about Hawthorne. I'd spent enough time around motivated brass to know what he meant when he said the guy was political. At this stage in his career, Hawthorne's image was crucial. He'd get all kinds of accolades for getting a hundred people like me deported, but deliberately getting a combat veteran kicked out of the country would be political suicide. That kind of shit outraged people. Not enough to actually do anything about it besides a few Facebook memes and strongly worded tweets, but they definitely didn't like it.

Something sharp and painful dug in behind my ribs. I'd served my country—it *was* my country—and the only thing keeping a decorated officer from reporting my ass to the authorities was the damage it could do to his image. If he could get away with it, he'd probably be on the phone right now, having me and half the waitstaff unceremoniously escorted off the premises and out of the country.

And he knew about me because Mark had told him.

I glanced sideways at Mark.

You told him about me. How could you?

I tried to tell myself Mark couldn't possibly understand what a betrayal that was, how vulnerable it made me, but it didn't do a thing to cool the hurt and anger rising in my chest. I thought he'd understood how terrifying it was to live like this. I thought he got it. But now this. Fuck.

Someone made an announcement that dinner was about to be served, which jarred me out of my train of thought.

"Ready to eat?" Mark asked.

Not particularly, no.

But . . . fine. We'd have dinner. We'd get through the evening. And afterward, when there was no one around to overhear, we'd talk about this.

"Sure." I forced a smile. Mark and I joined the CO, his wife, and a few other high-ranking officers and their wives at a table. I regarded Hawthorne warily, but didn't say anything. Mark trusted the guy— or at least his political ambitions—so I told myself over and over the captain wouldn't actually do or say anything. Still, I was a lot less comfortable than I'd been when we'd gotten here.

It only got worse as dinner started. While everyone at the table chatted, I looked around the room, and that painful thing dug even harder into my chest.

And I realized what it was—*this* was what I'd wanted. What I'd worked for. A uniform full of ribbons. Sleeves with stripes to commemorate years of service and chevrons showing I'd moved up the ranks. All the pomp and circumstance and ceremony.

I scanned the room, my heart dropping deeper into the pit of my stomach. Aside from what I assumed were some civilian contractors, everyone here was either military or married to it. The whole spectrum of a Navy career was on display. There were E-3s and E-4s who still looked optimistic and unscathed. The kids with their entire careers laid out in front of them. There were commanders and captains like Mark. People early in their careers, people on the verge of retirement—everyone.

Some had spouses or partners on their elbows, so it wasn't like everyone in the room was in uniform, but I felt conspicuous in my suit. Without the stiff material or a row of medals to fuss with. The only evidence left of my career was the pair of shiny black shoes I wore—the one piece of my dress uniform I could still wear. The rest was gone.

I swallowed past a lump in my throat. I was at a Navy function, and someone had mistaken me for a *waiter*. Worse, while everyone else only had to worry about keeping food off their uniforms and not drunkenly saying something stupid in front of a superior, I had to worry about someone tipping off ICE. Either because they thought I worked here or because they'd figured out—thanks to my fucking boyfriend—that in the eyes of the law, I wasn't supposed to be here.

I clenched my jaw so hard my teeth ached. Suddenly, I wasn't so sure I *wanted* to be here. My knee throbbed. So did my head. It was like being in a room with someone I didn't want to even lay eyes on, except every single person was that someone. A lot of people didn't get it when I said the Navy was like an ex-spouse I couldn't escape, but it was true. I'd given it eight years, and when it decided I wasn't good enough and kicked me out, it had taken everything. Left me with nothing.

Coming to this party had been like running into an ex with his new lover. Not someone like Dalton who I loved and adored and wanted to be happy. Seeing him with Chris was sweet, and I was glad they had each other.

The Navy, though. Fuck. All those people wearing ribbons and insignia I should have had.

I didn't want to think about it, but I couldn't stop myself. Fact was, if things had been different, I'd have been an officer by now. Commander at least. Maybe captain, but it was hard to say.

It didn't matter, though. I hadn't stayed in long enough to go to Officer Candidate School. Or hell, even finish my degree. I'd had to put that on hold so I could go to combat. Then on hold *again* while I'd been on my second tour. I hadn't been able to pick it up while I'd been recovering, and I'd been too busy healing to even think about my naturalization paperwork, especially since I'd taken for granted that I'd be reenlisting. I'd had no reason to believe that reenlistment was off the table until it was too late. Until all of it was gone.

Until I had . . . nothing.

These people had—and undoubtedly took for granted—the career and the education I'd been working my ass off to have. Some of these people probably hadn't even been seaman recruits or ensigns back when the Navy had washed its hands of me.

There was a senior chief at another table with red stripes and chevrons instead of gold. From the stripes on his sleeves, he'd been in at least twenty years, but he still had red stripes.

So this was someone who had fucked up. Probably gone to Captain's Mast at some point. Maybe even lost rank along the way. He'd done something, somewhere, and it was enough to keep his stripes red instead of turning gold after twelve consecutive years of good conduct.

He'd fucked up, and he'd still made senior chief, and he'd be able to retire with full benefits whenever the fuck he felt like it because he was already past twenty. He might even make it to thirty. He might even make *master* chief.

The really shitty part? If he'd been in that long, he'd been in when PTS was in effect. Which meant his career had survived the program that had caused the Navy to show me the door.

What did the computers see in you, and why didn't they see it in me?

A lump rose in my throat, and I had to take a deep swallow of my drink just to tamp it down. That senior chief had done something to warrant red stripes, but he still had stripes to wear. I'd busted my ass, done everything I was supposed to do, and even volunteered for two fucking combat tours because everyone told me it would be good for my career. Now Senior Chief Red Stripes was sipping a high-ball in dress blues while I had a fucked-up brain, a fucked-up knee, and a fucking good shot at being deported if the wrong person noticed me.

Or if someone at my own damn table noticed me. Because someone here *knew*. Because Mark had *told him*.

I let my gaze slide toward Mark, and for the first time, the sight of him hurt. It wasn't just an ache in my chest either. Every scar itched, and my knee throbbed, and my head thumped from too many thoughts trying to crowd their way in. Mark was sexy as fuck in that uniform, but that wasn't why I wanted to tear it off him right then. I wanted it gone so he wasn't Navy anymore. So I could look at him and see the man I was in love with, not all the reasons why my life had gone to shit.

But taking his dress blues off wouldn't matter. Yeah, I could have him naked or in civvies for a while, but come Monday, he'd be in uniform again.

And even if he wasn't in uniform, could I trust him now? Could I even fucking look at him?

Maybe.

But not tonight.

I pushed back from the table. "I need to go."

"What?" Mark straightened. "Why?"

I didn't answer.

I just got up, walked out of the ballroom, and kept right on walking.

CHAPTER 23
MARK

"**D**iego, wait!" I called after him.

He spun around, and the tears in his eyes stunned me.

"What's wrong?" I asked as I caught up. "What's—"

"I can't do this, okay?"

"Do what?"

He clenched his jaw and swiped at his eyes. "Look, I tried, all right? I really thought I could handle this. But everything in there?" He pointed sharply at the room. "All of this?" He made a sweeping gesture at my uniform, his lip curling with disgust like he couldn't remember telling me two hours ago how badly he wanted to fuck me in this. "This is what I wanted, Mark. It's *all* I wanted. Everyone in that room has it, and what do I have? Not a goddamned thing."

I stared at him, too stunned to speak for a few seconds before I managed, "Then we can go. Let me get my jacket, and we'll—"

"No," he whispered, shaking his head. "*I'll* go."

"But we—"

"Mark." He pressed his lips together and pushed his shoulders back, but he avoided my eyes. "And it's not just the fucking Navy, okay? It's *you*."

My knees almost wobbled out from under me. "What?"

He looked at—no, *glared* at me, and his voice was even shakier as he said, "How could you tell your CO about me?"

"I didn't tell him it was you! I—"

"Oh, yeah. That makes a huge difference." He rolled his eyes and clenched his jaw. "Don't you get it? He can put two and two together, and if he does, I'm fucked. I trusted you, Mark. I didn't think I had to spell out that you can't fucking broadcast my—" He glanced around, then lowered his voice. "It's not something you can just throw out in a conversation. Not with people getting deported left and right."

"I'm . . ." I exhaled. "Jesus, Diego. I'm sorry." Showing my palms, I added, "You're right. At the time, I didn't think you'd ever meet him, because you didn't want to come to military functions, so it didn't seem—"

"And look at us now," he growled. "But it doesn't fucking matter. There's someone in there"—he gestured sharply at the ballroom we'd abandoned—"who knows what I am, and even if he didn't, I can't stay here. I can't . . . I can't fucking do this, Mark. Whether either of us like it or not, being with you means being with all this shit." He cleared his throat. "Being with you means constantly being around reminders of what I had taken away from me, all because I had the audacity to get hurt doing my job in a fucking war zone. Now I can't even live here legally." He paused, pulling in a deep breath through his nose. "I did everything and gave everything so I could have the career that you and everyone else in there have. Now I'm somebody who gets mistaken for a waiter and probably *would* get picked up if ICE did a raid. And since someone in there knows what I am . . ."

I had no idea how to respond. Nothing he'd said was wrong. Well, it was *wrong*, but factually incorrect? No. And there wasn't a damn thing I could do to change it. He was scared. He was hurt. He was angry.

And there was *nothing* I could do.

Before I could come up with a response, he stepped back. "I can't do this. It's just too much."

My heart fell into my feet. "What . . . what can I do? There's—"

"There's nothing you can do." He sounded exhausted. Like a man who'd been treading water in rough seas for so long, he had no fight left in him. Tone wavering and heavy, he said, "You're Navy. I knew that from the beginning, and I thought I could handle it. I thought—" His voice nearly broke, and he cleared his throat. "Give me one good reason why I should spend another fucking minute around all of *that*." He stabbed a finger in the direction of the party. "Especially when your fucking CO *knows* about me."

"I told you—we can go." I put up my hands. "We don't have to stay here. Just . . . I don't want to lose you."

He sighed, shaking his head again. "I'm sorry. I need—"

"I love you, Diego."

He flinched and looked away.

"I mean it," I said. "I've been trying to figure out how to say it, or when, and I—"

"Don't." He faced me again, and the shine of tears in his eyes hit me hard. "What do you want me to do? Even if I could ignore the fact that you *told* someone about me, the military is . . . it's too . . . Look, I almost got fucking killed for a country that will kick me out the second they realize I'm here illegally. Why would I want to be surrounded by people wearing the same uniform I wish I was still wearing? And the same uniform as the people who said I wasn't good enough while I was still recovering from a fucking *explosion*?" A tear slid free, and as he sharply wiped it away, he muttered something in Spanish.

I cleared my throat. "I don't even know what to say. I'm . . . God, I'm so sorry, Diego."

"I know," he said quietly. "That part isn't your fault. But I just . . . I can't." He swallowed, and after a moment, he whispered again, "I'm sorry."

And then he turned to go.

He didn't stop this time.

Jaw hanging open, stomach churning, I stared at his back as he strode down the hall. Jittery panic shot through me as he neared the door, but what could I say? I wasn't going to physically block him from leaving, especially if it hurt him this much to be here. To be with me after I'd inadvertently—but unmistakably—betrayed his trust.

The door shut behind him. I couldn't hear his footsteps, and suddenly it was like he'd never been here at all. Like I'd been standing out in this hallway alone, and the last few weeks of falling in love with him had all been in my head.

Except he had been here, and those weeks had happened, and . . . Fuck.

What do I do? What can I do?

Nothing. I couldn't go after him. I couldn't go back to the party that had salted his wounds. I couldn't fucking move.

Because Diego was gone.

I didn't sleep that night. I didn't do much of anything the next day. Had I been this shell-shocked and lost after Angie had dropped our divorce papers? Christ, no. I vaguely remembered getting choked up when I'd realized what they were, but it had been more relief than sadness. It had been like being handed a cease-fire after fighting for too damn long.

Last night had come out of nowhere.

Except . . . it hadn't.

Sitting back in my La-Z-Boy, feeling anything but relaxed in the comfortable chair, I swore into the silence of my empty living room. I was too restless, and I desperately needed some air, so I went outside. I leaned on the deck and stared out at the ocean. The Pacific was rough today, with whitecaps dotting the gray water from the shallows all the way to the horizon. A thick blanket of clouds halfheartedly dropped some misty rain. This was what everyone had told me to expect when I came to this part of the country, especially this time of year, and yeah, it was depressing as hell. Kind of fitting for my mood. A bright, sunny afternoon would almost be insulting at this point.

The cold, salty air was pleasant, but it didn't make me feel any better. As I stood there and let the mist settle on the back of my neck while the wind played in my hair, my mind kept going back to last night.

I should've let him tear off my uniform and take me to bed. Yeah, it would've been bad form to miss the party, and Monday might've been a little awkward at work, but I'd still have Diego.

But . . . for how long?

My heart fell. It had only been a matter of time. Sooner or later, he'd have realized Hawthorne knew about him. Even if that hadn't been an issue, there was still the Navy. If the Navy was that big of a sticking point for him, we could only avoid it for so long. If it hadn't been last night, it would've been . . . well, sometime in the future when I was even more attached to him. When watching him leave would have hurt that much more.

This couldn't be how it ended, though. Maybe he'd slept on it, and now I could properly apologize and we could adjust some boundaries a little, and—

That would explain why he hadn't called.

My heart sank even deeper into the pit of my stomach. If things were okay, or at least not as bad as they'd seemed last night, he'd have called. Right? Unless he really was that angry. Which . . . fuck. Could I *blame* him?

Fuck. I needed to talk to him. Now that we'd both had a chance to clear our heads and get some distance between us and last night, we needed to talk. If he was still firm and this was still over, then . . . then I'd figure out how to deal with it. But first I needed to know.

Blood pounded in my ears as I took out my phone and called him. It rang twice on the other end. Then, "Hey."

The sound of his voice—his soft, tired voice—almost bowled me over. "Hey. Um." I gulped. "Can we talk?"

His end was silent for a while. Long enough I thought he might've hung up. Then he exhaled. "Okay. We can talk."

I moistened my lips. "Look, first things first—I'm sorry about Captain Hawthorne. I talked to him because I was trying to understand what happened, and if there was anything that could be done."

"What do you mean?"

"Like, was there anything he or I could do for someone who'd been fucked over by PTS and wound up in your situation."

He was quiet for a moment. "Is there?"

I sighed. "If there was, I'd have done it. Honestly, though, that's the only reason I mentioned it to him at all. I'm sorry. I really am. I was trying to help, and I . . . I'm sorry."

More silence. Then a heavy, resigned sigh. "I guess I can understand that. Just don't do it again, okay? Please?"

"Of course. I promise." And yet again, silence, this time because I didn't know what to say. He'd asked me not to fuck up again, but did that mean there was a *chance* for me to fuck up again? Finally, I managed, "What about us? Are we really done?"

Diego didn't answer for a few painfully long seconds. "I don't know how we *can't* be. I thought I could live with you being in the Navy, and I've been trying really hard to not care about it, but last night . . ." He paused, then cleared his throat. "I just can't do it."

A lump rose in my throat. "We don't have to go anywhere near the base. Or any functions. It's—"

"It's still too much." His tone sounded like he was pleading with me to understand. "I thought I could do this. I was wrong. I tried to tell myself I could tough it out until you retired, but last night . . . everything there was my entire *life*, Mark. And everyone there has all the things I wanted. They still have careers. They're not going to get thrown out of the goddamned country if someone asks to see proof they're allowed to be here."

"I get that. I really do." I squeezed my eyes shut. "There's always retirement if—"

"*No*," Diego said sharply. "Mark, you *just* made rank. You retire now, you get commander's pay. I'd stay in if I were you, and I don't want you giving up your career for me."

"But that means we can't make things work between us. Right?"

Diego sighed. "I didn't want it to mean that. I promise I didn't. But we both know being with you means being with the Navy. Especially as high up the chain as you are, and with a deployment coming up?" Another heavy breath, and his voice didn't sound quite steady when he continued. "It's just part of your career. I said for a long time I wouldn't date military men. And I made an exception for you because that's how bad I wanted to be with you. But I didn't realize how much it still hurts—" He cleared his throat again. "I can't deal with it, you know? Seeing everything that was taken away from me because I got hurt doing my job." He paused. "You understand, don't you?"

I closed my eyes. "Yeah, I do." My heart sank as I said the words. I did understand. I wanted to find some magic way around it, but there wasn't one.

"I forgive you for the thing with your CO," he said sadly. "But the rest . . . I can't. I'm sorry."

I exhaled. "So am I."

Silence again hung on the line. I didn't know what to say—I didn't dare rub salt in either of our wounds by telling him I loved him again—and I couldn't read his mind through our cell phones. I probably wouldn't have been able to read him if he were standing right there in front of me. Or maybe, I realized with a sinking feeling, I'd be able to read him, but I wouldn't like what I saw.

"I need to go," Diego said. "I have to get ready for work."

I wiped a hand over my face. "Okay." There was another long, uncomfortable pause before we murmured a couple of uneasy goodbyes.

And then he was gone. Again. Still.

The wind continued to blow. The rain was starting to fall faster.

Then the ships in the distance started to blur, but it had nothing to do with the wind or the rain.

After work on Monday, I found myself out on the deck again. I didn't remember the steps I'd taken to get here, only that I'd come home, changed out of my uniform, and wound up here. Somehow, I had a Corona in my hand, but one sip of that had soured my stomach. It tasted too much like the night I'd met Diego.

I could go to the liquor store, but I wasn't even sure I had the energy to go back to the fridge, never mind drive into town. Was I even safe to drive? I'd made it to and from work without killing anyone, so maybe. Probably best not to chance it, though. As it was, I'd been a million miles away all day. I was pretty sure I'd spent most of the day wandering aimlessly around the ship. Nobody had questioned me. If the XO wanted to go belowdecks or follow the passageways as far aft as they would go, he probably had a reason for it, and nobody besides the CO would say a word.

Now I was home. Alone. Outside. With a drink I couldn't stomach and a head full of thoughts I couldn't sort out.

Thumbing the label on the Corona, I turned and gazed at the base. It was another dreary day, and the misty rain made the ships harder to see than usual, but if I squinted, I could see the glowing white *9* amidst all that gunmetal gray.

I was starting to understand, on a much more personal level than before, Diego's hatred of the Navy. If it hurt me this much to look at the base and ships that represented the barricade between me and him, then yeah, I could absolutely understand why it was so hard for him to be around anything that reminded him of what he'd been through. My career had been a good one, and most of my years in the Navy had been smooth sailing, but just driving onto the base this morning had made me sick with anger and sadness. Yeah, he had every right to need some distance from me if I came with a whole fleet of reminders of his past. And his present.

It made it easier to understand why he'd left, but it sure didn't make our split easier to swallow. Breakups were so much easier when I could either blame the other person or blame myself. When someone had fucked up. My ex-wife and I had both run up long lists of sins, and we'd done more wrong than right. The endings of the few short relationships I'd had before her had been easy to define too. Too much fighting. She cheated. He refused to be with someone who was closeted, and I couldn't be out because—

Because of the Navy.

I closed my eyes and pushed a breath out my nose. This wasn't the first time, was it? That had been a short relationship back in my late teens. A guy whose name I couldn't quite remember. Charlie? Chad? Even his face seemed blurry. All I really remembered was some hot, secretive sex, and then a huge fight before I headed off to an ROTC drill. We'd dated two, maybe three weeks. Barely a blip on my timeline. I probably hadn't thought of him in a decade, but I was sure thinking of him now.

There was no telling what would have happened with that guy back in my ROTC days if DADT hadn't been in effect. If I could have been out, would we have lasted? It was impossible to say. And our relationship—if you could call it that—had been so short, the breakup had been more disappointing than painful. I didn't remember ever feeling any ill will toward him. We'd broken up, I'd gone to my ROTC drill, and I was pretty sure I saw him with another guy a week or so later.

Had I even had the awareness to be pissed off at the Navy at the time? I was pretty sure that back then, things like DADT were just par for the course. Being out of the closet and in the Navy weren't compatible, and that was the way it was. If anything, after that I'd just tried to set my sights on women so I didn't have to hide a man.

Twenty-some-odd years later, after a too-long marriage had finally gone the way of DADT, I'd found a man, and I'd fallen for him, and I didn't have to hide him, and . . .

And the Navy had hurt him.

I swallowed, staring hard at the ships and the glow of the base. I'd fallen for Diego like I'd never fallen for anybody, and he was gone because the Navy had hurt him badly enough he couldn't even cope with wearing civvies in a room full of uniforms. It wasn't his fault, and it wasn't my fault, but at the end of the day, it didn't matter whose fault it was because I didn't have Diego anymore.

I tore my gaze away from NAS Adams and glared out at the choppy seas. It wasn't right. This could *not* be the end. If one of us fucked up and the other left, or if we realized after a few weeks or months or years that we didn't like each other after all—fine. But not like this. There *had* to be some way to fix this, but hell if I knew what it was.

So, I took out my cell phone and called the one person who might be able to talk me through this.

"Hey," Angie said. "What's up?"

I closed my eyes. "Do you have a few minutes?"

"I'm just waiting for my dinner to finish cooking, so yeah, I've got some time. What's going on?"

"I need some advice. About Diego."

"Okay? What happened?" It was kind of odd that there was no accusatory undercurrent to the question. No *What did you do?* lacing her words. Shit, maybe we really *had* unfucked our relationship.

She was waiting for an answer, though, so I pushed those thoughts away and told her the entire story. From Diego hesitating to even hook up with me because I was military to the scars he thought made him unattractive to the way the Navy had tossed him out on his ass and left him with nothing.

"Wow," she said when I was done. "So he has all the VA benefits but can't use them?"

"Technically he can, but if someone realizes he's here illegally, he could be deported. I mean, the guy's halfway to a bachelor's degree. Even though he has the GI bill, he can't finish it because he's afraid to even apply for a student visa. And I'm not sure his job would cover his textbooks or anything anyway." Fuck, I was exhausted just explaining it—I could only imagine how much *living* it had taken out of Diego. "He earned all this shit, and just being able to use it would probably make a huge difference in his quality of life right now. But . . . he can't."

"Christ. No wonder he's bitter." She clicked her tongue. "The Navy takes a lot from all of us. For him, it not only took his job, it took away any real shot he has at *any* solid job in this country. And that's *after* he got hurt and traumatized in combat. Would you want to have anything to do with the Navy if it messed up your mind and your body, *and* cost you a chance at citizenship?"

"No, of course not. It . . ." I chewed my lip. "It already cost me enough. I can't imagine how it's been for him." I sank onto one of the deck chairs, ignoring the cold dampness now soaking into my jeans. "I don't blame him, you know? If the Navy had worked me over like it did him, I wouldn't want anything to do with it either."

She was quiet for a moment. "So what are you doing to do?"

"I have no idea." I pressed an elbow into my knee and bowed my head so I could run my hand through my hair. "I don't want to give up and admit he's gone, but . . . what can I do?"

Angie released a long, heavy breath. "I wish I knew."

Neither of us spoke for a long time. Gears ground in my head as I searched for some kind of solution. Something—anything—that might assuage the pain I'd seen in Diego's eyes last night.

And that was the crux of it, wasn't it? Yes, I absolutely wanted Diego back, but the most heartbreaking thing about last night hadn't been watching him leave. It had been watching him fight back tears while I'd pleaded with him to stay. It had been watching him *hurt*.

I looked out at the whitecaps. "Maybe there's a way I can help him."

"Such as?"

"I'm . . . I'm not sure yet. My CO told me there's nothing we can do, but that can't be right. I know the Navy has channels for getting Sailors naturalized. Maybe if I could find a way to push things through for him, that would make up for . . . I mean, it can't fix the last several years, but maybe it could make things easier for him going forward."

"I'd definitely look into it," she said. "You don't sound sure, though. What's stopping you?"

I let my head fall forward. "I don't know."

She was quiet for a moment. "Are you afraid he'll be upset?"

I had to think about that for a minute. "Maybe? Or maybe upset that I didn't do something sooner? Especially since he knows I at least looked into it?" I winced. "Fuck, I *should* have done something sooner.

I should've dug deeper when Hawthorne said there was nothing we could do."

"You can't change it now." The sharpness in her voice wasn't angry. More like she was trying to get my attention and keep me on the rails. "All you can do is move forward. And with his situation, if there's something you can do to help him, I say do it. Or at least find out what you can do, and ask him if he *wants* your help." She paused, and her voice softened a bit. "Do you think that if you do something to help him, he still won't take you back?"

"No, that isn't it. It's . . ." I stared up at the thick gray clouds. "Kind of the opposite, I think."

"What do you mean?"

I took a deep breath. "I'm afraid he'll feel *obligated* to take me back. And I don't want him to. I don't want strings attached, you know?" My throat tightened, and I had to clear my throat to keep speaking. Even then, my voice was thick. "I want him back. God, Angie. I love him. I really, really do. And not having him anymore hurts like hell. But I'd rather not have him at all than have him because he thinks he's obligated to be with me." I closed my eyes and pushed out a breath. "Does it sound as crazy to you as it does to me?"

"No, not at all. You want to help him, but you don't want him to think it's for selfish reasons."

"Yes. Exactly. Because it's not for selfish reasons. I really want—"

"I know you do." There was a soft smile in her voice, one I hadn't heard—or seen—in a long time. As she went on, though, it faded. "I know you're not like that, Mark, but I've also known you for twenty years. He hasn't. And I think he probably knows as well as I do that you don't want to lose him. So, yes, there's a possibility he's going to think you've got an ulterior motive. There might not be any way around that."

Eyes squeezed shut, I swallowed hard. "So what should I do?"

"Help him out anyway. If that makes him pull even farther away from you, then . . . I mean, it sucks, and it'll hurt, but it won't change that you did the right thing."

The lump in my throat was getting more stubborn by the second. I would move heaven and earth to fix what the Navy had done to

Diego, but I wasn't going to pretend I didn't wish there was a way I could still have him.

My ex-wife went on, "If he had anyone else in his life who was willing or able—especially able—to do this, they would have by now. If he could have done it himself, he would have by now. You're in a unique position because of your rank, and you can fix how the Navy screwed him."

"I know." The words came out as barely a croak.

"I'm not really telling you anything you didn't already know, am I?"

"No, but that's fine. I think I just needed someone to tell me I wasn't being an idiot."

She laughed softly. "So you call your estranged ex-wife?"

"Come on." I chuckled. "You were my estranged *wife*. You're not so bad as an ex-wife."

"Gee, I'm touched." But her tone was light, and we both laughed again.

We talked for a few more minutes before we hung up. Then I stared out at the ocean again. It was still gray and choppy, the ships still partially obscured by misty rain, but it didn't look so bleak now. Or maybe I just didn't feel so bleak. So powerless.

I took a deep breath and let it out slowly. Tomorrow morning, I'd get to the boat early, and I'd start making some phone calls.

And hopefully I could do something about Diego's situation.

CHAPTER 24

DIEGO

Three days after I'd walked away from Mark, I was getting stir-crazy in my apartment. I had to work tonight, but not for a few hours, and I needed a distraction until then.

I sent Dalton a text: *Hang out?*

He replied almost immediately, *Gotta work at 7, but free till then. Come over?*

I was out the door before I'd even responded that I was on my way. When I got to his apartment, I parked in the usual guest spot and headed up to their front door. I loved that Dalton lived off-base now. We could hang out at his place instead of making do with mine.

In the kitchen, either Dalton or Chris had left a camouflage blouse draped over the back of a chair, and I tried not to look at it. On a good day, the sight of a uniform made me flinch. Today, it was enough to make me sick.

Dalton pulled a couple of sodas from the fridge, and we sat on his couch.

"Chris at work?" I asked.

He nodded. "At least I'll see him during shift change."

"Better than nothing?"

"Yep."

"Think you guys will be on the same shift at your next command?"

Dalton rolled his eyes. "*God*, I hope so. Working opposite shifts gets old fast."

"I believe it." I didn't know how they did it. Dalton was on nights, Chris was on days, and even though they had the same days off, their sleep schedules were staggered.

That was just part of their jobs, though. Initially, working separate shifts had meant they could stay together even after Chris was promoted to Dalton's supervisor. Now that they were both E-6s, they were peers, which meant they couldn't be busted for fraternization. Plus they were married. But of course, their department only had so many E-6 jobs available in each shift, so they were *still* on separate shifts.

Such was life in the Navy.

My heart sank. Mark was probably at work right now. He'd be off a little after I went to work. Similar schedules to Chris's and Dalton's, except I couldn't blame the Navy for the time we were spending apart.

Just me. Just my own damn head, and my own fucking issues, and . . . *Fuck*. How did Chris and Dalton do it? They knew it was worth it, that was how. They'd had their relationship tested by the Navy. They'd had to choose between love and careers, and they'd fought until they'd had both, because they'd known damn well *it was fucking worth it*.

And me? I couldn't make it through a stupid party.

Walking out the other night had been a mistake because it meant walking away from Mark. Seeing all those Navy people and all that Navy shit? That had hurt. Every second since I'd walked away from Mark? Fuck. *That* had hurt like hell.

Except I hadn't had any other choice. Sitting there in that Holiday Inn ballroom, surrounded by reminders of the life I couldn't have because I'd had the audacity to get too close to an IED and not be fully recovered by the time I was up for reenlistment? Fuck that.

There was no avoiding any of that if I was with Mark. Even if I never had to attend another military function, dating Mark meant dating the Navy. That was how things were.

Which meant there wasn't any point in trying to make it work. No matter how much it hurt to let him go, it still hurt way too much to be anywhere near the Navy. Subjecting myself to that shit had cut deep, and even now I started getting choked up just thinking about it.

Not that I could stop thinking about it. Any of it. I couldn't get that senior chief or his red fuck-up stripes out of my head. I couldn't stop thinking about the younger guys who were already a rank or two ahead of where I'd been when I'd been kicked out.

And I couldn't unsee Mark standing there in that fucking uniform and telling me he loved me. I also couldn't pretend that even while I'd been hurt and furious, part of me had wanted to stay there and tell him I loved him too.

I'd *had* to walk away, though. I had to stay away too, regardless of the fact that I'd forgiven him for the shit with his CO. I couldn't stick around no matter how much I wanted to.

Because . . . the Navy.

The fucking Navy.

All the blue and gold and gray. The uniforms. The reminders of everything I'd lost. No, everything the Navy had *taken* from me. Just thinking about it made my teeth grind. A few times, I'd thought I was overreacting. After seven years, I needed to move on and stop being so damn bitter about the Navy.

Except I *couldn't* move on. Not when everything in my life was constantly hanging by a thread. Not when my chain of command hadn't lifted a finger—and probably couldn't have done much anyway—to argue with that computer algorithm that had decided I wasn't good enough to stay in the Navy, leaving me without a visa and without access to treatment for two combat tours' worth of damage.

Move on? My ass. The Navy had done way too much damage to me and to my life, and I wasn't apologizing for refusing to let that go.

But how the hell was I supposed to let Mark go?

"Hey." Dalton nudged my knee. "What's going on?"

I didn't bother trying to play stupid. He knew me too well. Picking at the seam on my jeans, I said, "I, uh, fucked things up with Mark."

"How?"

I took a deep breath and told him everything. By the time I was done, my throat was aching and my eyes were stinging. "I don't know if I fucked up by getting involved with him at all," I said, voice shaky, "or by letting him go."

"Letting him go. Obviously." Dalton put a hand on my leg. "You know, I seem to recall some wise old asshole telling me not to let the Navy take away the man I loved."

I glared at him. "Are you calling me old?"

"Don't change the subject." He inclined his head. "We had this exact same conversation a few months ago, except I was the idiot who wasn't—"

"Except you could *do* something," I threw back. "And you did. You reported your chief, and he got what was coming to him. What am I supposed to do?"

Dalton chewed his lip. "Honestly?"

"Yeah."

"You need to decide what's more important to you—Mark? Or how pissed you are at the Navy?"

The ache in my throat got even worse. "When you put it like that, it's a no-brainer."

"I figured." Dalton touched my arm. "And I'm not saying all the shit you've gone through will go away overnight. I just think you'll be miserable if *he* goes away."

I chewed my lip, trying to force back the lump in my throat.

"He's not going to be in the Navy forever," Dalton said softly. "If you feel this strongly about him, though, and you let him get away? You're probably going to regret that forever."

I avoided his eyes, but it didn't help because my gaze went straight to the hand on my arm. The wedding band on Dalton's third finger stung. What could we have been if I could've let go of my hang-ups about the military?

And what would I lose if I couldn't let them go now?

But they were real, and they hurt like hell.

So did being without Mark.

Fuck.

I ran a hand through my hair. "The thing is, even if he takes me back, it doesn't change anything. I'm still fucked up in my head and . . ." I gestured at my knee. "How long do you think an XO is going to hold on to a fucked-up undocumented immigrant who pours drinks in a gay bar?"

Dalton rolled his eyes. "Please. That's bullshit and we both know it." He must've seen the *WTF?* in my eyes, because he added, "How long would you have dated him if you'd thought for two seconds he would *ever* kick you to the curb for that?"

Damn. He knew me too well.

"Don't make excuses," he said. "Go talk to him." When I didn't respond, he added, "Diego. Look at me."

I met his gaze, and I didn't think I'd ever seen Dalton's eyes so full of intense determination.

Still firmly holding eye contact, he took my hand. "You're being an idiot. Mark isn't the Navy. He didn't do any of that shit to you. And if you let him go, you're just letting one more piece of you be a victim to everything that happened before." He squeezed my hand so tight it was almost painful. "How much more of your life are you going to lose to that?"

Breaking eye contact, I tightened my jaw and tried to force back the ache in my throat. He had a damn good point, and I couldn't argue with it. The Navy had taken my health, my job, my stability—even my fucking tattoo. And the Navy had Mark, but it wasn't taking him from me. That was me. *My* issues. *My* hang-ups. *My* bitterness. Our relationship didn't have to be over, and I didn't have to hurt like this. All I had to do was get my head out of my ass, learn to live with the Navy, and talk to him.

I lifted my gaze and met Dalton's eyes again.

Or else I can lose him like I lost you.

"I'm sorry, by the way," I whispered. "For letting my shit kill what we had going."

"It's okay." He wrapped an arm around my shoulders and kissed my temple. "I still have you as a friend."

"Thank God for that. But still . . . we could've had something."

"I know. But we both got second chances. I married mine." He gave me a gentle squeeze. "Don't let yours get away."

Closing my eyes, I sighed and leaned against him. I'd been damn lucky with him. I didn't care how far away he and Chris moved—we were staying in touch forever.

In the meantime . . . Mark. This wasn't how it ended. It couldn't be.

I'd talk to him. I didn't know when, and I didn't know what the hell I'd say.

But I'd talk to him.

I was on autopilot at the bar. It showed in my tips, too, so I was trying like hell to get myself together. I couldn't afford to lose tips. A bartender who wasn't friendly and charismatic didn't make money.

But I felt like shit and it was hard not to let it show.

As I wiped down the bar for the hundredth time this hour, I fought away thoughts of Mark, but it wasn't working. Talking to Dalton this afternoon had only made it worse. Now I wasn't just hurting over Mark—I felt like an asshole and an idiot for leaving. Well, not for leaving—I'd been too pissed to stay. Not going back, though? Or giving him a chance when he'd called? Fuck. What was I thinking?

On top of that, I was still terrified that even if and when I figured out how to apologize and get us back together, we wouldn't be able to make it work. Three times since I'd left Dalton's place, I'd tried to work up the courage to call Mark. Each time I looked at his name in my contacts, though, I'd put the phone back in my pocket without dialing. Each time, it felt less and less like there was any chance of having him back.

I quickly wiped my stinging eyes and hoped none of my coworkers or customers noticed. I needed to get my shit together. Part of me didn't see that happening until I smoothed things over with Mark. Part of me suspected it needed to happen before I even thought about talking to Mark. Another part didn't think it would happen at all.

God. I was a mess.

I finished mopping up phantom drips from the bar and tossed the rag underneath where it would be in easy reach. I was about to check my garnish tray when some movement caught my eye. I looked up, and a face materialized in the sparse crowd.

The glass in my hand almost fell.

Mark.

And he was coming right toward me, and he'd already seen me so it wasn't like I could duck out and pretend I wasn't here. I had no idea if that was what I wanted to do, but it didn't matter.

He stopped, the freshly polished bar standing between us like a defensive wall. He'd never struggled to hold eye contact, but he did this time, and his voice barely made it to me as he said, "Hey. Can we talk?"

I pressed my lips together. Fuck, I was not ready for this. I knew what I needed to say, but I was terrified to say it. I had no idea how to explain any of it.

We need to talk, but not now. I'm not ready for this. Damn it, Mark, not now.

Before I could say any of that, though, he cleared his throat. "I just need a couple of minutes. I, um . . . I have something for you." He glanced down, and I realized he had a thick manila envelope in his hand.

I eyed the thing. What was it? A wild card of some sort, and now I was both insanely curious about the contents and seriously dreading finding out what they were.

"Okay," I said finally. Might as well just do this and get it over with. "Hang on."

My boss wasn't on tonight, and the bar wasn't all that busy, so I flagged down Kim, the shift manager.

"I'm going to step out for a minute," I told him. "If you need me, I'll be right outside."

Kim nodded and went back to filling the glass in his hand.

I motioned for Mark to follow me. We went out the front door and around to the side of the building. There were a few people shivering in the parking lot while they smoked, so it was quieter over here.

My heart was in my throat as I turned around to face him. I hugged myself against the cold night. "So, what did you want to talk about?"

Mark took a deep breath and held out the envelope. "This is for you."

I eyed it but didn't take it. "What is it?"

"Just . . ." He nodded toward it. "Please."

After hesitating for a few more seconds, I took it. We stared at each other, not speaking. His eyes flicked toward the envelope. Then mine did. I wondered if he was waiting for me to open it. I was waiting for him to explain what the hell was going on. Maybe that made me a coward, but I wasn't sure I wanted to know what this was.

Finally, Mark swallowed. "The Navy did you wrong, Diego. I can't undo that. There's nothing I can do to get you reinstated. And believe me, I checked. That"—he gestured at the envelope—"was the best I could do."

Now I was curious, so I thumbed open the flap and slid the contents out. There was a stack of what looked like paperwork, a booklet, and—

Application for Naturalization.

My heart stopped. I looked at Mark, unable to speak.

He chewed his lip. "You know where Pass & ID is, right? The building outside Gate Three?"

I nodded, still mute.

"Fill all of that in, and take it to Pass & ID along with the letter on top. They'll get you a pass to go to admin."

My mouth had gone dry, but I managed to croak, "I don't have a military ID anymore. They won't let me on base."

"They will. They already know you're coming."

My hackles went up. "Did you fucking out me to—"

"Don't worry about that." He patted the air between us. "All Pass & ID knows is that you need a temporary base pass, and that it's been authorized by me. Any hiccups, and they're to call me directly. Or, if you're more comfortable, I can meet you there and escort you to admin."

I stared at him.

He pulled in a deep breath. "Every detail is on a need-to-know basis, and once everything is turned in, I'm going to personally make sure it's processed and expedited. Anyone who will have their fingers anywhere near that paperwork knows that if anything is delayed or kicked back for some bullshit reason, they'll be answering to me."

Jaw slack, I glanced back and forth from him to the papers.

"It's still going to take some time," he went on. "There's only so much any of us can do, but we're going to do what we can. In the meantime, I've also checked around for civilian contractor jobs. There are some listings and applications in there." He pointed at the envelope. "If you want to apply for one, we'll help you get your green card."

I swallowed. "Are you serious?"

Mark nodded. "Technically, it might qualify as an abuse of power, but if ever there was a time to pull rank, this seems like it."

My head was spinning. I had to lean against the wall, and I could barely hold on to the papers. "I thought you said there was nothing you could do."

"I dug deeper and called in some favors."

I stared down at the forms in my hand, then met his gaze. "Why are you doing this?"

"Because you served your country," he said. "And the Navy screwed you. Like I said, I can't undo all of that, and God knows I should have looked harder for a solution sooner, but I can at least help you get what you should've had the day you enlisted." He smiled, looking kind of nervous. "Like I said, if I'm going to throw my rank around . . ."

I stared down at the papers. With shaky hands, I looked through them. Application for Naturalization. A letter from Mark on US Navy letterhead stating that this was an important and personal matter, requesting it be expedited, and explaining that no one who'd served his country—least of all someone who'd been wounded in action—should be denied citizenship. Behind that were several applications for on-base civilian contractor jobs, a booklet on obtaining citizenship, and some paperwork for a green card.

My eyes were starting to sting, and the text was getting blurry. "Mark . . . this is . . ."

"It's yours if you want it." His voice was softer than I'd ever heard it. "Even if it's just so you can go to the VA without worrying about getting deported. Or so you can get a solid enough job to save up some cash and go home."

My throat tightened. Home. Enough money to see my family. Maybe help them get back to Rioverde. *Stability.* There was no guarantee I'd even find a job, but there'd be more options now. More options that didn't mean working under the table and praying every day I wouldn't get caught. And I could *finally* go to the fucking VA and see if someone could do something about my knee and these nightmares. After the last few years of trying to pray my PTSD under control and looking over my shoulder and . . .

Just like that, there was a light at the end of the tunnel.

I could barely get enough air moving, but as I held the papers to my chest, I managed to whisper, "Thank you."

"You're welcome. It . . . shouldn't have taken this. The Navy, your chain of command, they . . ." Mark shook his head. "I'm sorry they let you down. I just hope this will undo some of that damage."

Mute, I nodded. I hadn't even known something like this was possible. That someone could use his rank and connections to push things through. That anyone would be *willing* to.

"I'm sorry again. For what I said to my CO, and also for how the Navy screwed you over." He gestured at the papers. "Hopefully that isn't too little too late."

I shook my head. "No, it isn't. I . . . Thank you. I don't even know what else to say."

He smiled, then cleared his throat. "I should, um, let you get back to work. I just wanted to make sure you had all that. If you run into any snags, you've got my number. So just, you know, text me if there's any issues."

"Oh. Uh." I was too shocked and confused to know what to say. "Okay. Thanks."

He smiled quickly, then took a step back and started to go.

Panic broke through the confusion. "Wait."

He turned, eyebrows up.

"You're not . . ." I struggled to form words. "You don't want to get back together?"

Mark sighed. He lowered his gaze for a second before he looked at me through his lashes. "I do. And I came here thinking that was exactly what I was going to try to do. But I can't."

I blinked. "You can't? Why not?"

He stared at the ground for a moment, then exhaled hard. "Because there is no way I can give you that"— he nodded toward the papers—"and ask you to take me back. I don't want strings attached to any of this."

It took a minute for the words to make sense. "So you were just . . . You'll let me go, but you'll still do all of this?" I held up the envelope. "Even without . . . Even if I don't . . ."

"Absolutely. There's . . ." He swallowed, and he didn't meet my gaze as he said, "There was no way I could bring those papers *and* ask you to take me back without making it sound like all of that was contingent on you staying with me."

"It isn't, right?"

"No," he said without hesitation. "I'm going to see all that through no matter what, even if I have to hand walk every piece of paper to where it needs to go."

"What if I said I wanted you back?" I stepped closer, wondering when my knees had started shaking. "And that I wanted you back even before you showed up?"

Mark searched my eyes. "Do you?"

My throat was getting tight and achy, so I just nodded.

He swallowed. "I just . . . I don't want this—us—to have anything to do with . . ." He motioned toward the papers. "I mean it when I say there are no strings attached. I'd . . ." He avoided my eyes, and his voice was soft when he spoke again. "I want you, Diego. And I love you. But undoing what the Navy did to you is more important than me having you, so—"

"Who says we can't have both?"

He chewed his lip. "It's your call."

Our eyes locked. My heart went crazy. This was the part where I had to say everything I hadn't figured out how to say. Shit . . .

So, I took a deep breath and hoped I didn't make things worse. "I've, um . . . actually been wanting to talk to you. And trying to figure out what to say." I couldn't handle the intensity of his gaze, so I watched my thumb play with the sweat-dampened corners of the papers in my hand. "Ever since we met, I've been going back and forth in my head about being with you and being around the military. I knew I wanted you. That's never been a question. But I . . ."

"But it hurts to be around the Navy. I get it."

"No. You don't." I shook my head. "You don't get how much I've been trying like hell to get over my shit with the Navy because I wanted to be with you. The Navy's already cost me so much, and I even told one of my friends not to let the Navy be the reason he lost the guy he loves, and I . . ." I sighed. "That's exactly what I was doing. Because I was too hurt and fucked up to see that being with you is *worth* being close to the Navy. And I mean, what happened will never change. Even with this"—I gestured with the papers—"my situation still happened and I'll still have to live with it. None of that will magically change just because I'm not with you anymore. And not being with you . . ." I swallowed. "That hurts too much."

Mark's lips parted.

"This?" I held up the papers again. "Just sealed what I'd already figured out—that walking away from you was the stupidest thing I've ever done."

"It wasn't stupid," he said softly.

"Yeah, it was." I chewed the inside of my cheek. "Question is, do you still *want* me back? After I left the other night?"

For the first time tonight, Mark smiled, but he still looked sad. "You really think I'd hold that against you? In your shoes, I probably would've done the same thing. I'm honestly not sure I'd have stuck around long enough to even go to that thing."

I blinked. "What does that mean?"

He dropped his gaze. "It means I've been counting myself lucky as hell that you wanted me in the first place. And feeling *guilty* as hell that I put you in that position the other night." He scratched the back of his neck. "I told you I'm not good at relationships, okay? I want to be. And God, I want to be good at this one, because I don't want to lose you. So yeah, I'm kind of amazed you hung on that long."

I couldn't help laughing, and I stepped a little closer. "You really think being with you was 'hanging on'?"

He met my eyes, silently challenging me to suggest otherwise.

"You're an idiot." I reached out, hugged him tight, and tried like hell not to cry as I said, "And I'm an idiot too. I'm sorry I left."

Sighing, Mark wrapped his arms around me. "No. You had every right to leave." He held me closer and kissed my temple. "I should have known it would be pouring salt in the wound if I took you to a function like that. I didn't mean to—"

"I know. But I thought I could handle it." I pulled back enough to look into his eyes. "So it was my fault for agreeing to go."

He brought a hand up and ran his fingers through my hair. "Still. And I should've gotten this paperwork rolling the first time you told me what the Navy did to you. You deserved so much better."

I smiled. "I think I found it." I cradled the back of his head, pushed myself up, and kissed him. I was surprised the papers didn't slide out of my hand, but I was holding on to them almost as tight as I was holding on to him.

When he finally broke the kiss, we were both out of breath.

Panting and shaky, I whispered, "I thought you said you were terrible at relationships."

Mark laughed and pressed a soft kiss to my forehead. "I am. I was. I . . ." He sighed. "The thing is, I've never been good at them. But you make me want to be better at it. You make me want to get it right."

I managed a laugh even as a hot tear slipped down my cheek. "You're off to a damn good start."

He held me tighter. "You deserve it. And the paperwork . . ." He touched his forehead to mine. "I mean it. It wasn't mine to give you. It should've been yours from—"

"Don't." I kissed him hard. "I get it. I really do. And . . . thank you."

"You're welcome. I'd do anything for you, Diego."

The words *I know* lodged somewhere around the lump in my throat.

"And you don't have to go to any military functions. *I* have to go to them, but if you don't want to . . ." He shook his head.

I thought about it, then shrugged. "I don't know. Let's see how I feel when we get there."

"Okay. It's totally up to you, though," Mark said softly. "I really do want to get this right."

I smiled past the emotions trying to bubble up. "Like I said, you're off to a damn good start." I cradled his face and kissed him. " I love you."

And Dios mío, no words had ever been truer than those three. I'd been fighting them so hard for reasons that were justified and stupid at the same time, and now that I'd said them, I felt like I was going to crack from the intensity of pure, sweet relief.

Mark's hand slid up into my hair. "I love you too."

Then he kissed me again, but I only let it linger for a second before I buried my face in his neck and just held him. It was all I could do not to break down. Or collapse. Like the stress had been keeping me so rigid for the last few years that I literally didn't know how to stand on my own now that even some of it was gone. Between the papers in my hand and the man in my arms, I was so overwhelmed I couldn't think straight.

Mark pressed his lips to the side of my neck as he stroked my hair. Neither of us said anything for a long time.

After a while, though, I became aware of the club's bass vibrating the ground under my shoes and remembered where I was. Where I was supposed to be.

Sighing, I pulled back a little and looked up at him. "I have to get back to work."

Mark nodded. "Yeah. Sorry I crashed your shift. I couldn't wait, and I wasn't sure where else I could talk to you and—"

"I'm glad you did." I swallowed. "I'm, um, off at two thirty. Is that too late to come by?"

"Not at all." Mark's smile turned my insides to liquid. "I'll wait as long as I have to."

It was seriously tempting to blow off work and go now, but I knew better. The doors he'd opened for me wouldn't solve everything overnight, and I needed to hold on to this job until I was sure things were coming together. And what was a few hours if this man—this gorgeous, loving, amazing man—was waiting at the end?

He cupped my jaw and gave me one last long kiss. "I'll see you soon."

"As soon as possible."

Then we exchanged grins, and he headed for the parking lot.

After he'd gone, I paused before going inside. I needed a moment to collect myself, so I closed my eyes and released a long breath.

What had just happened? Twenty minutes ago, I'd . . . There hadn't been Mark. There hadn't been any way out of my visa problems or my health issues or . . . anything. And now there was. I had Mark back. I had an envelope full of tickets to unfucking a lot of the things that had gone wrong in my world. None of this would magically solve every problem in my life, but it was a breakthrough that would make some of the uphill fights feel less steep. Like I actually had a shot at getting on my feet in this country and the means to maybe go back to my family. There were *options* now. I could . . . fuck, I could talk to someone about the PTSD and do something about my knee besides store-brand ibuprofen.

All because Mark had pulled some strings I didn't even know existed and made things happen that had seemed impossible.

With any other guy, I might've thought he'd been doing it to get back into my good graces.

I smiled to myself, gazing down at the papers he'd left with me. I had no idea what it had taken for him to get all of this together, or how many cages he'd have to rattle to get it all the way through, but he had. There was no way I could ever show Mark just how much I'd forgiven him and how grateful I was for everything he was doing.

But I could damn sure show him how glad I was to have him back in my life and how hard I'd fallen for him.

I checked my phone. Three hours, and I could go to Mark.

Three hours, and I could go *home*.

CHAPTER 25

MARK

On the way into the High-&-Tight, I'd been a mess. Anxious. Scared out of my mind I was going to say the wrong thing or that I'd already done the wrong thing.

Now, waiting at home for Diego, I was still a mess. What if he changed his mind? What if he didn't show up? What if he gave it some thought and realized he wasn't interested in—

A car engine outside raised the hairs on my neck. He came?

I looked out the front window as the headlights dimmed, and when my eyes adjusted, the familiar shape of his black pickup truck materialized.

He came.

I was at the door before he'd even made it up the front walk, and when he met my eyes in the glow of the porch lights, he smiled brighter than I'd ever seen him smile.

He came up the steps, and as soon as he was at the top, he wrapped his arms around my neck. "Sorry I took so long."

"I could say the same thing," I whispered. "Should've come through for you before—"

Diego kissed me hard. "Shut up. Just shut up." He held me tighter and kissed me again, and I shut up.

And just like that, we were back where I'd needed us to be. Hopefully where he wanted us to be too, and from the way he was holding me—so, so tight—I had a feeling he needed this as much as I did.

Holy shit. He was in my arms. He was kissing me. He *wanted* me again. *He was here.* It didn't matter that he'd said he was coming or that he'd told me he loved me. The proof was in this tight embrace and long, sweet kiss.

Diego gently broke away and touched our foreheads together. "Your neighbors are getting a show."

I have neighbors? "They don't have to watch."

"No, but we might be more comfortable in your bed." He squeezed my ass through my jeans. "No indecent exposure when I take your pants off."

And with that, I was persuaded. I herded him inside, stopped long enough to dead bolt the door, and jogged up the stairs on his heels.

We dropped our clothes and shoes unceremoniously all over the bedroom floor. I hadn't even settled on the bed before Diego was on top of me, straddling me, and he leaned down for a long, deep kiss. Oh fuck. We were here. Naked and kissing, my hips between his thighs and his erection thickening beside mine.

I broke the kiss and stared at him. "You're really here, right?" I ran shaky fingers through his hair. "I'm not hallucinating?"

He laughed, warm breath rushing across my lips. "No. You're not hallucinating. I'm here." He kissed me softly and added in a hoarse, unsteady whisper, "I'm not going anywhere."

"Good." I kissed him, and as I did, I curved a hand around the back of his neck and slid the other between us. Diego moaned into my kiss and fucked into my hand.

"I missed you so much," he breathed, lips barely leaving mine.

"Me too." I gave his cock a gentle squeeze. "Will you do something for me tonight?"

He lifted his head. "Yeah?"

I grinned, trying hard not to smirk. "Quiero que me des duro hoy."

Diego snorted. Then I did. Laughing harder, he let his head fall beside mine. "You are such a dork."

"Would you expect any less?"

"No." He lifted his head and, still grinning, kissed me again. The longer the kiss went on, though, the more our lips relaxed, and the joking faded away as we lost ourselves in one of those intoxicating kisses I'd been addicted to since day one. Our hands slid all over each other's bodies, kneading and tracing and groping and caressing, almost like we needed to touch every inch of each other again to make damn sure this was happening.

"Fuck me," I pleaded. "I want . . . Fuck me, Diego."

He groaned against my lips and kissed me even more frantically. He still wasn't fucking me, even though our bodies were starting to rock like he was already deep inside me, and I was on fire with frustration, but he was kissing me, so to hell with it. I held him tight and breathed him in, and we moved, and . . . Jesus, I loved the things this man did to me.

With a string of breathless Spanish swearing, Diego broke the kiss and lunged for the drawer where I kept the condoms and lube. Oh yes. Oh, fuck yes. My toes curled with anticipation as he fumbled with the wrapper.

Yes, yes, yes. Please. Now.

He was quick as always about putting them on and putting a little lube on me, and when he pushed my thighs apart, I almost came right then and there. The anticipation was driving me insane, and the view? Oh God. Diego. Flushed. Aroused. Hungry for sex. For *me*.

He started guiding himself in but paused, meeting my gaze with a raised eyebrow as if to ask if I was ready for him.

"C'mon," I growled.

The eyebrow came back down, and Diego grinned. With a hand on my hip, he pressed against my hole. He met resistance, of course, but not much—after a moment, the head slipped past the tight ring, and we both grunted.

"*Fuck.*" He closed his eyes and moaned.

The burn and the stretch took my breath away. With no prep besides a few strokes with his lubed fingers, he could have easily made this painful. He was patient, though, easing himself deeper. He paused for some more lube, and as he pushed back in, my back arched off the bed.

"Ungh, Diego . . ." I tried to spread my legs even wider for him so he could get as deep as possible. "Oh yeah . . ."

He murmured something under his breath as he took long, fluid strokes.

My eyes watered. I couldn't tell if it was from the burn or the relief, the invasiveness or the fact that Diego was *here*. All of it, maybe. Probably. Whatever—he took his time, letting me yield to his thick cock, and now the anticipation was driving me even wilder than it had before he'd put on the condom. He was in, but he was still going slow, and I was too far gone to care that it was either that or hurt me.

Diego moaned. Something Spanish, and no doubt dirty, tumbled off his lips as he withdrew. He pushed back in, and I took more of him this time. Then more. I was taking him easily now, and he was moving faster, and before long, skin slapped skin and we both grunted and cursed as he bottomed out with every deep, hard thrust. Yes. Fuck *yes*.

Abruptly, he stopped.

What? No! Keep—

Before I could protest, he panted, "I want . . ." He shivered, then pulled out and sat back on his heels as he made a *turn over* gesture. "On your stomach."

I didn't argue. As soon as I'd turned over, Diego mounted me from behind, and when he pushed back in, the whole world blurred. I'd jokingly asked him to fuck me hard, and I'd meant it, but this? Christ, he felt good. Even better when he sank down on top of me, molding his body to mine. That was almost as amazing as his cock moving inside me. We were touching in as many places as two men could possibly touch, and it was mind-blowing. So intense and hot and sexy it was almost painful, and it was perfect. Everything was. The stretch, the friction, the weight of his body, the breathless Spanish curses—it was all Diego, and it was all perfect, and if it got any hotter, we'd both go up in flames.

It seemed crazy to fall back into sync like this when everything had been in pieces earlier, but it made sense too. Of course we'd made it back to this. Why wouldn't we?

Because makeup sex has never felt like this before.

The last thing I wanted to think about now was my marriage, but I couldn't help comparing this moment to all the times Angie and I had pulled ourselves back together and wound up in bed. Makeup sex had always been hot and a relief, but . . . never like this. Maybe that should have been a sign that my marriage was doomed from the start. Or maybe it was proof this wasn't makeup sex. It wasn't fucking away the remaining tension after a fight. It was like all the walls had come down, and there was no reason to be apart anymore, and now we wanted to be as close as possible.

This, what I had now in this moment with Diego, was nothing if not a sign that we had something worth holding on to. Not because the sex was spectacular—it was—but of this almost painful need to be against him. Feeling his heartbeat, his hot breath on my skin, the friction and slide of our bodies moving together—meant things I couldn't even get my head around. That we'd really found our way back to each other. That he wanted me as badly as I needed him. That if I screwed this up, it was a regret I would take to the grave.

I love you. The words kept echoing inside my head. *Diego, I love you. I love you so, so much.*

All that came out, though, was a whispered, "You feel so good."

Diego moaned. He pressed his lips behind my ear and murmured something I didn't understand. I couldn't even say for sure if it was English or Spanish—I was just too far gone to make sense of anything except his body and his cock and his presence and how close I was to coming. Oh God, I really was close. Right on the edge. Right there. Almost. Just about.

"Harder," I ground out, and Diego rode me harder, and my whole body seized under his as he forced a powerful orgasm right out of me.

More Spanish profanity rushed past my ear. His scruff burned my skin as he buried his face in my neck, and then he shuddered hard, thrusting deep, and he let go of a muffled whimper as he came too.

We slowed to a shuddering halt. He pulled out, gasping softly as he did, but stayed over me, his skin damp and hot against my back.

"In case I haven't mentioned it," he slurred, his accent more pronounced than usual, "I *love* fucking you."

I just groaned.

After a moment, we separated long enough to clean ourselves up, then climbed under the covers together. I held him close and savored his lazy, languid kisses. Now that the more primal needs were out of our system—for the moment, anyway—I could relax into having him here beside me. I hadn't thought there was a way around the things that had pushed us apart. But here we were.

Diego drew back and looked into my eyes. Touching my face, he whispered, "Thank you again. For what you did."

"You're welcome." I brushed a few strands of hair off his forehead. "And you're sure it won't make things weird between us? You're not obligated to be with me because of—"

"Mark." He smiled, running a hand up the middle of my chest. "Did anything about what we just did feel like obligation?"

"Well, no. But I—"

He kissed me again. "Relax. I'm so grateful for what you did, but this"—he gestured at the two of us—"isn't something I'm doing out of obligation. I've spent the last few days trying to figure out how to get back to this." A smile grew on his lips, and it was sweet and sincere, especially as he added, "You just beat me to it."

"Really?"

Diego nodded. "I knew I'd fucked up. And I knew I wanted you back. I just didn't know how to say it." He reached up to smooth my hair. "Then you showed up with all of that, and . . ." His breath rushed out of him and his shoulders slumped. "You blew my mind."

"I was afraid you'd resent me for it, to be honest."

"You were?"

"Yeah. Like it was a way to manipulate you into taking me back, or like I was telling you you couldn't solve your own problems."

He laughed bitterly. "To be fair, if I could have solved them, I would have." His humor—such as it was—faded, and he swallowed. "You have resources I don't. I'm grateful you were willing to use them."

I wasn't sure what to say, and the silence set in uncomfortably.

Then he lowered his gaze and took a breath. "I dated someone a couple of years ago who offered to get married so I could get a green card. I'm not going to do that, though. If I ever get married, it won't be out of pity or because I need some fucking paperwork. *Then* I'd just constantly feel like I owed him something, you know? That would make me feel obligated to stay with someone." He lifted his chin and met my eyes again. "You weren't the first guy to offer me a solution. You were just the first who wouldn't have gotten something out of it."

"This isn't for me."

"I know. I figured that out when you went to leave without saying anything about getting back together." He moistened his lips. "I appreciate it. I really do. You have access to things I don't, and you used them to help me. That's . . . I couldn't ask for anything more, you know?" His gaze turned distant. "I just can't believe there's finally a way out."

"There should have been a long time ago."

"I know." He exhaled. "Man, it's going to be weird not being scared all the time."

I smiled, caressing his arm.

"Maybe once I've got a better job," he said, "I can go visit my family more."

"Visit?" I trailed the backs of my fingers along his forearm. "Or go home to stay?"

Diego sighed, cuddling closer to me. "I don't know. I like it here. Might like it more once I'm not scared of getting deported." He closed his eyes and let out a long breath. "And there's other people like me, you know? Veterans who got fucked out of citizenship. There's some groups and charities, and there's that place in Tijuana that helps deported vets get their VA benefits, so maybe . . ." He met my gaze. "Maybe if I stay here, I can do something for them."

"Maybe we both can."

He lifted his head. "Yeah?"

"Sure." I trailed my fingertips down his cheek. "I'd follow your lead. Just tell me if there's something I can do—or I can get the Navy to do—and I'll help."

He smiled. "Thank you."

"You're welcome." I moistened my lips. "You know, everything you've told me about vets getting deported—I honestly had no idea it was a problem until I met you. But now that I do, whatever I can do to help . . ." I paused. "Actually, maybe there's something you can do to help me."

Diego raised his eyebrows.

"I put out a memo a couple of weeks ago for the immigrants under my command," I said. "Telling them to come to me if they're interested in pursuing citizenship."

"Any bites?"

"I've had some emails. I've, uh, been cultivating a bit of a reputation for being a hard-ass, though, so I think some of them are afraid to approach me directly."

Diego smiled playfully. "You're *that* XO, huh?"

"Yeah, I am." I chuckled, then turned serious. "I was thinking maybe I could coordinate with the training department on-shore. Have some kind of class or whatever's needed for people who need to know what to do and what channels to go through." I ran a hand through his hair. "If I can get something like this off the ground, we'll need an instructor."

His eyes widened slowly. "Really?"

"You've been there, done that. You're not some white guy who learned the ropes off a PowerPoint."

Diego gave a soft laugh, but it only lasted for a second. "So, like a civilian contractor position? To help other immigrants?" He shook himself. "Is there even enough demand for something like that?"

"Maybe not at Anchor Point specifically, but in the region? I would imagine there is."

"The *region*?" he sputtered. "You're talking about a *regional* position?"

I nodded. "If you want it. I'd still need to coordinate and call in some favors, but . . . yeah, if you want it, I'll make it happen."

He stared at me for a moment, and then a smile slowly formed. "Yeah, I want it. I love the idea. Fuck, I would have sold my soul for a class like that while I was still in."

"I'll see what I can do, then." I smoothed his hair. "I mean, assuming you decide to stay in Anchor Point. Which you don't have to—"

He cut me off with a soft kiss and met my eyes. "I have to say, you're kind of a perk if I stick around."

I laughed. "As long as I'm not the only reason."

Diego shook his head. "No. You're not. And if this job works out . . ." He blew out a breath. "Fuck, that would be amazing."

I just smiled.

He chewed his lip and, after a moment, met my eyes. "Maybe when I go visit my family, you could come with me."

I straightened. "Seriously?"

"Sure." He smiled shyly. "My mom will love you. My abuela might feed you until you can't move, though. She thinks everyone is too thin unless she's personally witnessed them eating five or six piles of food."

"Oh my God. So let's maybe schedule that for after PRT. Or at least weigh-ins."

Diego laughed, and my heart went crazy. We hadn't been apart all that long, but it was long enough for me to miss the way his face lit up when he laughed.

I am so glad I didn't fuck this up.

We lay there in silence for a little while, occasionally kissing but mostly just being together.

"You okay?" I finally asked.

"Yeah." He smiled, though his eyes were suddenly uneasy. "Just thinking about everything. The papers you gave me and ... everything."

"Yeah?"

He nodded, pursing his lips. He searched my eyes, then slid a little closer. "Listen, um, going forward . . . just . . . fair warning, I guess." His brow pinched. "It might take a while for me to get a therapist. And it might take a while for it to help. So all this?" He tapped his temple. "It's not going away overnight. It's . . . probably never going away completely."

I cupped his cheek and kissed him softly. "I know. It's PTSD. It's not going anywhere." I took his hand and squeezed it as I met his gaze. "But neither am I. And you'll probably have to be patient with me too. I made a mess of my marriage, and I don't—"

Diego kissed me. He freed his hand from mine and curved it around the back of my neck, and while his grip was firm and unyielding, his lips were soft. When he finally broke the kiss, he said, "Shut up. You don't need to keep warning me." His lips curved into a smile as they brushed against mine. "I know what I'm getting into."

I surrendered to another long kiss and slowly relaxed against his warm, naked body.

"If you fuck up, we'll work it out," Diego said. "Same thing if I fuck up. And then when we're done, we'll have awesome makeup sex."

I laughed, and it was out of relief more than anything. "I like the sound of that."

"Me too."

I trailed the backs of my fingers along his jaw and whispered, "I love you."

"I love you too." He wrapped his arms around me and drew me in for a long kiss.

We held on to each other, letting the kiss linger for a while before he rested his head on my shoulder. Maybe we'd fuck again tonight. Maybe we wouldn't. I didn't care either way—all that mattered was that he'd still be here when the sun came up.

Closing my eyes, I smiled as I stroked his hair. I'd fucked up a lot of things in my life, but I'd gotten *this* right. I had the sweetest, sexiest man beside me in my bed, and even though this was still a young relationship, it was on the right track. It wouldn't be smooth sailing forever, but the possibility of rough seas ahead didn't scare me. If anything, those would just give us a reason to hold on tighter to each other and work harder to stay afloat.

We'd make it. I was sure of it.

And if there came a day when I asked Diego to marry me, or he asked me to marry him?

It wouldn't have a damn thing to do with a green card.

EPILOGUE

DIEGO

October

I t had been six months since I'd laid eyes on the USS *Fort Stevens*, but now, there it was—moored to the pier on which I was standing with what must have been hundreds of people. I'd been to a couple of ship's homecomings before, but never pier-side. I'd always been aboard, waiting for liberty to be called so I could disembark.

Today, I was in the crowd of family members eagerly waiting to see Sailors who hadn't been home since April. My stomach was fluttering and my heart was going a million miles an hour. After six months, Mark would finally be home.

And almost a year after I'd met him, this wasn't just home for him. For the first time in too long, Anchor Point was home for me too. The US was home. The ground under my feet was stable, and even after the last several months, it was still a novelty to not be anxious, not be worried about money, and not be scared at every turn that everything would get yanked out from under me.

Mark had been true to his word about helping me get a job. Though the ship had started workups shortly after that, and he'd been at sea for a few days or weeks at a time, he'd kept tabs on my applications. No one was allowed to drag their feet unless they wanted a personal visit from him. Not long after he'd brought me all that paperwork, he'd gotten me an interview in admin, and though they'd decided to hire someone else, they'd referred me to the head of training. Turned out he wanted to overhaul the entire department and put a civilian contractor in charge to free himself up to run another department that had fallen in his lap. He'd interviewed several people with more experience, but at the urging of the head of admin—and Mark, I guessed—he'd called me in too.

Clint and I had clicked instantly. Half an hour and a handshake later, I had a job. Before I'd realized which way was up, I had a green card, a base ID, and an office with three people working for me. I wasn't at all ashamed to say that the first time I'd opened my pay stub to see how much was being deposited in my account, I'd cried. So had my mom when she'd gotten the five hundred dollars I'd wired her the next day.

I'd started looking for apartments so I could finally have an actual place instead of living out of my landlady's converted basement. That search hadn't lasted long, though.

"Instead of taking on a whole set of rent and bills," Mark had said one night in bed, *"why don't you split mine?"*

I'd blinked in disbelief. *"Are you asking me to move in with you?"*

The smile had answered the question clearly enough. Cupping my face, he'd said, *"We spend almost every night together anyway."*

"So, it's just for practical reasons." I'd been teasing. Sort of.

Mark had laughed as he'd blushed. *"No. It's definitely not just for practical reasons."* Sobering a bit, he'd looked in my eyes. *"Diego, I want to live with you because I love you. We're going to have to spend some time apart soon anyway because of the deployment. Why not spend as much of the time we have together as we can?"*

A month later, I'd moved in.

And now, after spending half a year alone in the house that had become home, I'd have Mark back in our bed.

Maybe even . . .

I closed my eyes and exhaled, trying to keep my heart from beating right out of my chest.

One thing at a time.

Cheers and commotion brought me out of my thoughts, and I turned to see a Sailor in his dress blues coming down the ramp with his seabag on his shoulders. Apparently he'd been the lucky winner of the first kiss, and sure enough, his wife was waiting for him. In front of dozens of cameras and hundreds of cheering people, they threw their arms around each other and shared a long kiss.

Once those two had cleared out, the rest of the crew started pouring off the boat.

I stayed back a bit. Mark wouldn't be one of the first to disembark. The XO and CO never were. As impatient as I was to see my man again, I'd made it six months. I could wait a little longer.

And finally—there he was.

I inched toward the ramp, which was easier to do now that some of the junior Sailors' families had cleared out. Heart thumping, I wondered for the billionth time how much affection was okay between us. We were sometimes affectionate when we went out, but a very public kiss? Here? That was up to him.

As soon as he'd reached the bottom of the ramp, Mark broke into a run, and a second later, he dropped his bag at our feet, wrapped his arms around me, and kissed me. Well, that answered that. Holding him tight, I let the kiss go on. It wasn't a deep one, not one that would get him into trouble, but there was plenty of promise in it. Promise that we'd probably do some damage to that new king-sized bed we'd bought two weeks before he'd deployed.

"I missed you so much," he said, breathing hard.

"Me too." I kissed him lightly again. "Another month and I'd have wound up with tennis elbow or something."

Mark snorted. "You and me both. What do you say we get out of here?"

"Good idea." I paused, and my heart shifted into overdrive. I'd debated doing this here, and as I looked into his eyes . . . Yeah. This was the perfect time and place. "Except I kind of got you a homecoming gift."

His eyebrows shot up. "Oh yeah?"

I nodded, hoping like hell my nerves weren't showing. "After you helped me get that job, I finally don't have to live on tips anymore. For the first time, I don't have to worry about starving or losing everything. You gave me my life back."

"It wasn't mine to give you," he said softly. "You deserved to have it all along."

"I know, but you cared enough to go through all that. And now I'm on my feet. I'm not sweating about money or getting deported. So I . . ." I swallowed as I reached into my pocket. "I figured the best way to spend some of that money was on this."

Mark's breath hitched, and I wondered if he'd already figured it out even before I opened my hand.

If he didn't, I was pretty sure he caught on when I gingerly went to one knee on the concrete pier. "Mark, I love you. And if being away from you for six months told me anything, it's that I don't want to be away from you. So, will you—" I choked on the words.

Mark smiled, and he took my hand. "You better believe I'll marry you."

We locked eyes, and with his help, I stood again. As he pulled me into another embrace—tighter this time—and kissed me, people all around us broke into applause. I hadn't even realized they'd fallen silent until now, probably because my pounding heart had drowned them all out.

The relief was so profound, it almost made me break down just like that first paycheck had. In fact, as I held him close and squeezed my eyes shut, a hot tear slipped free.

As Mark let me go, he cleared his throat and swiped at his own eyes. Then he smiled. "I guess that changes my plans for tonight."

"What do you mean?"

He reached into his pocket, and when he pulled out the gold band, our eyes met again, and we both laughed.

"You were just quicker on the draw, I guess," he said.

"Great minds think alike?"

"Apparently so." He hoisted his bag onto his shoulder, wrapped his arm around my shoulders, and kissed my cheek. As we started walking, he said, "I'm really glad we're on the same wavelength. I've been freaking out about this the last few nights."

"Same here."

"So, when do you want to do this?"

I shrugged. "I don't know. But I don't think we need to make a decision right this second." I snaked my arm around his waist. "I've got the only answer I needed today."

"Yeah. Me too."

We glanced at each other again, grinned, and kept walking.

A year ago, my life had been a mess of uncertainty. So much anxiety. So many questions.

Today, there was only one question. Only one loose end.

And I didn't mind it.

After all, there were worse things to worry about than when Mark and I would tie the knot.

Explore more of the *Anchor Point* series:

www.riptidepublishing.com/titles/series/anchor-point

Dear Reader,

Thank you for reading L.A. Witt's *Once Burned*!

We know your time is precious and you have many, many entertainment options, so it means a lot that you've chosen to spend your time reading. We really hope you enjoyed it.

We'd be honored if you'd consider posting a review—good or bad—on sites like **Amazon, Barnes & Noble, Kobo, Goodreads, Twitter, Facebook, Tumblr,** and your blog or website. We'd also be honored if you told your friends and family about this book. Word of mouth is a book's lifeblood!

For more information on upcoming releases, author interviews, blog tours, contests, giveaways, and more, please sign up for our weekly, spam-free newsletter and visit us around the web:

Newsletter: tinyurl.com/RiptideSignup
Twitter: twitter.com/RiptideBooks
Facebook: facebook.com/RiptidePublishing
Goodreads: tinyurl.com/RiptideOnGoodreads
Tumblr: riptidepublishing.tumblr.com

Thank you so much for Reading the Rainbow!

RiptidePublishing.com

ALSO BY
L.A. WITT

See L.A. Witt's full booklist at: gallagherwitt.com

ABOUT THE AUTHOR

L.A. Witt is an abnormal M/M romance writer who has finally been released from the purgatorial corn maze of Omaha, Nebraska, and now spends her time on the southwestern coast of Spain. In between wondering how she didn't lose her mind in Omaha, she explores the country with her husband, several clairvoyant hamsters, and an ever-growing herd of rabid plot bunnies. She also has substantially more time on her hands these days, as she has recruited a small army of mercenaries to search South America for her nemesis, romance author Lauren Gallagher, but don't tell Lauren. And definitely don't tell Lori A. Witt or Ann Gallagher. Neither of those twits can keep their mouths shut . . .

Website: www.gallagherwitt.com
E-mail: gallagherwitt@gmail.com
Twitter: @GallagherWitt